INSEPARABLE

David Kruh

DX VAROS PUBLISHING

Published by:
D. X. Varos, Ltd
7665 E. Eastman Ave. #B101
Denver, CO 80231

Book cover design and layout by, Ellie Bockert Augsburger of Creative Digital Studios.
www.CreativeDig
italStudios.com
Cover design features: rear view, confident adult male striding away by ASDF; lonely man walking on a beach by Karuka; Alcatraz and the Oakland Bay Bridge through the clouds and fog by Jeremy.
Author head shots by Robert Mattson of Downstage Images. Original music for the podcasts provided by Rob Johnson.

ISBN: 978-1-955065-40-5 (paperback)
ISBN: 978-1-955065-41-2 (ebook)

Mauzy
I'm supposed to be a writer but words fail to express my gratitude for your never-ceasing support and encouragement. This book would simply not exist without you in my life.

Jennifer
I am awed by your success despite a pandemic which put a screeching halt to the world just as you were starting out. You are amazing and I look forward to more great things from you.

Mom
Your perseverance through the past dozen years is inspiring. Dad would be proud, as am I

Table of Contents

June 11, 1962

9:50 pm

San Francisco was the cruelest trick ever played on the prisoners of Alcatraz Island.

The city was less than two miles away, so close if the wind was just right the cons could hear music and voices and laughter emanating from that glittering jewel of a city. On those nights John Anglin, prisoner number AZ1476, lay in his cot and covered his ears with a pillow because he couldn't bear the sound of all those happy, free voices. But tonight, as he stood at the water's edge of Alcatraz Island, he strained into the breeze, wanting to hear all those sounds because soon he, too, would be free.

Free. Yea, sure, he and the other men on the beach were probably crazy to think this plan would work, that they would succeed where dozens of others had failed... and died. Go ahead, call them crazy but, screw it, John couldn't go back to that crummy little cell on this crummy island, not with all that freedom just a couple of miles away.

Standing near John was his brother Clarence. As they rubbed their arms and stamped their feet to keep warm, they watched the third member of their group, Frank Morris, connect a hose to a concertina he had cleverly modified into a pump. At the other end of the hose was what was supposed to be a raft, the result of six months gluing together strips of rubber from dozens of prison-issued raincoats. But right now, all they had was a mass of blue-green rubber lying flat and inert on the ground. It sure as hell didn't look like a raft. John saw his brother's lips moving in silent prayer as Frank slowly pulled on both sides of the concertina, filling the bellows with air.

"Okay, here we go," Frank said as he brought his hands together, compressing the fabric between the handles. Nothing happened. The thing on the ground was still just a useless lump of rubber. Frank grimaced and pulled out on the instrument's handles and then back in again. Clarence saw it first, in the light of the moonlight, bulging out like the neck of the bullfrogs they used to catch back in Georgia, the rippling blue-green fabric getting larger. The raft was slowly inflating. John couldn't help himself from saying out loud what they were all thinking. "Holy shit, this is going to work."

As Frank continued to manipulate the concertina's handles and blow up the raft, Clarence nudged his brother with his elbow. "Hey John."

"What?"

"Look back up there," Clarence said, motioning behind them to the prison complex they had just left. Clarence was almost giddy. "They don't know. No alarms or searchlights or anything. They really fell for those heads we made −"

"It's ready." They turned and in the dim light saw the rare sight of a smile on Frank's face. On the beach it sat, just like a real raft, inflated and ready for action. "Let's get it in the water," they heard Frank say. The three men

2

gently lifted the raft and carefully, as if carrying a newborn, brought it to the edge of the rocky beach.

"Don't stop," Frank said. "We need get in deeper water so the bottom doesn't get cut by the rocks." John nodded, grudgingly. Frank was right. Again. After all the work that went into making the raft it would have been cruel for it to rip open before they even got it into the water. "Come on. And don't splash. We can't afford to make any noise." The three men gingerly crab-walked about ten feet from the shore, where the water was just over their knees.

"Okay, this is good. Grab your paddles and get in," Frank said. This was it. The final test. Clarence Anglin drew in his breath. Slowly, as if lowering himself into a bathtub of hot water, Clarence got into the raft. He looked up at his brother and nodded. It was still afloat. So far, so good. Then John got in, followed by Frank. For a few seconds they said nothing as they bobbed gently in the water. Even Frank – dour, single-minded Frank – seemed to be enjoying the moment.

Then, without saying a word, all three men thrust their paddles into the water and stroked. The raft slowly moved forward.

"Angel Island, here we come," the brothers heard Frank say as the darkness enveloped them.

1960

January 10

Tommy O'Conner had no way of knowing his adventure would begin today.

The sandy-haired youngster sat hunched over a desk in his sixth grade class at Sausalito Elementary School. His chin rested on one hand as he gazed longingly out the window at the crystal blue water of San Francisco Bay.

"Tommy O'Conner, are you still with us?"

All eyes turned as Barbara Wallrapp, their teacher, skillfully lofted a small piece of chalk into the air. It landed on the boy's head, bounced onto his desk, and rolled onto the floor. The boy bolted upright, suddenly aware of the twenty-five pairs of eyes looking in his direction. A few giggles peppered the room. Busted again.

"Sorry, Miss Wallrapp," he said with a practiced look of contrition. (He was really thinking that this is the school's fault. If they wanted me to pay attention they shouldn't have put in a window.)

Windows. The cruelest trick the school played on kids like Tommy O'Conner.

He was grateful for Miss Wallrapp's gentle smile to let him know he would be spared further embarrassment.

Tommy was lucky because Barbara remembered all-too-well how, a dozen years earlier – in this very same classroom – the same view caused her own sixth-grade teacher to issue her more than a few warnings. A teacher, Barbara remembered, who cared little how clumsily she tread on fragile sixth-grade egos.

Wallrapp returned to the grammar lesson, and soon the blackboard was filled with so many nouns, verbs, subjective participles, and predicates Tommy's mind drifted into a cloud of chalk dust and confusion. Out of the corner of his eye was the glint of the sun off the water. He wanted to be out there so badly it hurt. He grudgingly reminded himself of the promise he had made to his mother to try... just a little bit harder to pay attention. (Okay, okay, one last glance before I go back to those stupid predicates. But gosh, it's so clear out there, I can even see a launch heading for Alcatraz Island.)

What he didn't see was another piece of chalk heading his way....

Frank Morris tried to ignore the rattling of the chains shackling him to the deck of the prison launch as it lurched through the choppy water of San Francisco Bay. The pilot didn't seem to be in a hurry to get to their destination, which was fine with him. He wanted to savor the remaining minutes before they docked at the prison everyone called the Rock. Hunched on a bench, his arms resting wearily on his legs, Frank raised his head to see the lonesome outcropping in the middle of San Francisco Bay getting larger by the second.

A massive building, the same dull sandy color as the ledge on which it sat, jutted grimly upward from the center of the island, thick bars across every window leaving no question as to its purpose; a prison, his home for the next fifteen years. Frank fought a moment of self-pity. He had less than ten years to go for that bank job he pulled down South, but when he saw an opportunity to leave the caring embrace of the Louisiana State Penitentiary he took it. The dopes who ran the place never saw the holes in their security that were so obvious, at least to someone as smart as Frank Morris. Maybe they were just angry it had taken a whole year to find him, and only then because of dumb luck. Why, if that store clerk hadn't – ah, what good does it do hashing over the past?

"All right. Stand up, you."

Frank, jolted from his thoughts, looked up to see the launch had reached the dock at Alcatraz. The other guard, not waiting for him to comply with the first guard's order, pulled him to his feet as the other one pulled on the iron chain which clattered noisily through the eyelet. Frank saw one of the guards smirk, and he scowled.

"This way," the guard said, motioning to the gangplank near the front of the launch. Then, as if move had been rehearsed, Frank slid between the two guards who led him, shuffling, to the bow of the launch.

"Step up."

This was it. His next step would take him onto the island of the most feared and loathed prison in the country. A hand on his shoulder pushed him forward.

"Let's go you. Come on."

He squinted into the California sun and then at the narrow road from the dock up to the prison. He had seen pictures of the island in magazines but the path looked a lot steeper now that he had to walk it in chains. He began to shuffle forward when, to his surprise, one of the guards knelt down and unlocked his shackles.

"Hey, what are you doing?" the other guard said.

The guard who had unlocked the shackles stood up and faced Frank with a smirk. "Don't worry, he's not going anywhere, now," he said. Then, softly, so only Frank could hear, "Don't believe what you've heard about those escapes, Morris. I'm gonna tell you what the warden won't. There's only one way you leave the Rock – on that launch. It's your choice whether it's standing up or laying down in a box."

The three men walked up the path and an hour later Frank Morris became prisoner AZ1441. Ten hours later he was laying on his cot in cell 138 along B Block trying, without much success, to get to sleep. He was used to rooms with bars in place of a wall but he always had trouble the first night. Well-traveled cons like him knew how different each jail could be. Like this place, with an always-present saltwater smell so strong he could almost taste it. He wished he could hear waves to help him fall asleep, then angrily corrected himself – Alcatraz was in a bay, not on the ocean, you idiot.

So he lay there, thinking. Despite his resolution years ago not to dwell on the past, it often bullied its way into his thoughts. What were his parents thinking and what were they feeling the day they abandoned their only child on the doorstep of a church? The Diocese found a nice couple to take in the underfed eleven -year-old and there was hope the boy might have a good life. But the stigma of being unwanted never lifted from his shoulders. Two years later he was arrested and charged with "intent to sell." Frank smiled as he remembered telling the police he didn't see what the big deal was. After all, he told them, he had no "intent to use" the drugs in his possession. He had thought it a clever turn of a phrase but the cops saw only a punk kid being a smart-ass, so they had little reason to cut him a break.

They shipped him to the Lorton Reformatory. Two years serving lunch to prisoners, hearing them lament all the mistakes they made – how they could have, would have, should have gotten away had they done just one... thing... different. Frank listened and knew he would succeed where they had failed. After all, he was smart. Smarter than them all. But after his release from Lorton he botched a gas station robbery which landed him three years at Chillicothe Reform School. More lessons learned by the smartest guy in the pen, who graduated to bank jobs and a fifteen year sentence in the Louisiana State Prison.

Now, Alcatraz. Frank tossed in his cot, sleep still eluding him, the gruesome rewind almost complete. Despite years of trying he had been unable to change the ending of his story. But tonight, as he lay there breathing bay air into his nostrils, something nagged at him... a way, perhaps, to achieve what had eluded him for thirty-four years... a new and better ending. He took in a deep breath of salty air as sleep finally found him.

October 14

"All right you, I see you!"

John Anglin's head popped up from under a pile of dirty prison linen. He squinted into the beam of the guard's flashlight and heard him yell "I got him, I found him, he's here in the laundry basket."

The next thing he knew a meaty hand was reaching down and grabbing him by the wrist, pulling him up and out of his all-too-temporary hiding place in the laundry room of the Atlanta Federal Penitentiary.

"Okay boy, where's the other one?"

Silence.

"Ya'll know he'll get no further than you did, boy."

John winced slightly. Boy. The guards would do that, call you as if you were Negro. It was their way of making you feel like one of them, someone not worth respecting.

"It will go harder on the both of you iffen you don't tell us," he heard another guard say.

John clamped his lips together. He wasn't about to squeal. Not just because it was his brother but, if word leaked out – and the guards would be sure of it – if word got around he had ratted on a fellow prisoner well, his already tough life in the joint would get even harder. His silence only angered the guards even more. John could see one nodding to the other just before they began to close in on him. He closed his eyes and braced himself when a voice pierced the darkness.

"Don't! I'm here." The flashlight beam swung around to reveal the other prisoner, his hands in the air, clumsily trying to extricate himself from a tangle of power cords and hoses behind the row of washing machines.

John exhaled. "Aw, Clarence..."

His brother, now clear of the machines, shook his head resignedly and said, "It's okay, John."

The guards grabbed them both by the arms and clumsily dragged them out of the laundry room. One of them sneered, "Let's go, boys, you know the routine."

The "routine" consisted of small, dank rooms with menacingly heavy metal doors. Once closed, all light and sound disappeared as if they were rumors, leaving too much time to worry what the warden would do to them after this, their third attempt at escape.

John and Clarence were alike in so many ways but differed in how they responded to solitary.

Clarence didn't mind the dark. What bothered him was the absence of sound. In a prison, even after "lights out," there were still lot of noises; the contact made by the hard soles of the guards' shoes on the concrete floor, the

10

soft jangle of keys bouncing in rhythm to their slow patrol up and down the corridor, mixed with the occasional cough from a nearby cell. But here, in "the Hole," there was no sound, except for your own breathing. Clarence got by only by focusing on that sound. It told him at least he was still alive.

John, on the other hand, didn't mind the lack of sound. It was the dark which bothered him. Ironically, to get through this time he would close his eyes (yea, why bother closing them when it was already dark) and conjure a picture he had taped to a wall in his cell. It was a black and white photo of two sandy-haired boys on the cusp of becoming teenagers, their freshly-washed blonde hair slicked and parted. Wearing shirts clean and white and ironed to crisp perfection they both straddle bicycles and smile the undeniable smile of boys without a care in the world. Look at them, the other pickers in the groves used to say... Inseparable, just like Huck and Tom. Why those two –"

"Anglin!"

He raised his hands defensively over his eyes as a searing blast of a light hit him in face.

"Warden. Now."

John sighed. Time for another reckoning. "Clarence, too?"

"Just you, this time. On your feet, let's go, boy. Don't want to keep the man waiting."

John Anglin struggled as he stood, trying to hide his wobbly legs. The last thing he wanted to do was give the bulls any satisfaction. John knew the bulls were pissed. He and his brother had only gotten as far as the laundry room but getting even that short a distance was a black mark on the guards. But John wasn't just putting on a show just for the them. The walk to the warden's office would take him right down Main Street, a double-decked

11

hallway lined with cells. Nothing raised the spirits of the other prisoners like an escape attempt – even a failed one. John and his brother had already delivered a couple of opportunities for celebration, and he planned to enjoy this walk.

He had barely stepped onto Main Street when he was overcome with a queer feeling. Where were the proud smiles and approving nods from his fellow cons? Today he saw only glum expressions as each man, clearly unable to look him in the eye, retreated into his cell as John passed. What the hell was going on?

His escorts smirked. They knew... as did every con. Steel bars and concrete walls were effective in separating the men but, save for those in solitary, no prison had yet been built to prevent news – especially news like this – from spreading. For the moment, only John Anglin (and his brother Clarence, still in solitary) were the only two men at the Atlanta Federal Penitentiary who did not know why the warden wanted to see him.

John and the two guards reached the steel door at the end of Main Street. One of his escorts nodded to a guard on the other side of a small, barred window. A loud creak echoed down Main Street as the heavy door opened. Grim faces now squeezed back through the bars of their cells to watch. John could feel their eyes on him, and he turned to look back for what he instinctively knew would be a last look. An impatient hand landed on his shoulder and pushed him forward and up a set of steel stairs to the one room – other than solitary – where an inmate does not want to go any time before his release.

Warden Hanberry sat behind his large desk, hands clasped together in front of his mouth as if in prayer. John Anglin stood silently on the other side of his desk. After a few minutes (just long enough to make the inmate feel extra uncomfortable) Hanberry picked up a folder from a pile and dropped it dramatically on his desk. He looked up, annoyed. "Anglin, we're going to give you your wish. You want out of Atlanta so bad, we're going to send you on a trip."

John opened his mouth but before he could say anything the warden held up his hand. "I didn't give you permission to speak, Anglin," he said watching the prisoner helplessly close his mouth and bow his head. "Your unsupervised trip to the..." he paused to open the file in front of him and read the top page. He cleared his throat. "...laundromat, yes, well, this latest escape attempt has earned you a trip." The warden pressed a button on the intercom sitting on his desk. "Send them in." Two men in dark suits entered the warden's office and stood silently by the door.

"These men are here to escort you... to Alcatraz." At the sound of the prison's name John felt his legs buckle. "John, what is it with you Anglins? We've got three of you in prison for robbing that bank in..." he paused again to look at the file, "...Columbia. For Christ's sake you boys didn't even use real guns. The police report says you were carrying toy guns. What the hell were you thinking robbing a bank with toy guns?"

"Well, sir, we didn't want to hurt anyone, we just wanted the money."

He dropped his head and shook it as he sighed. Then, to the two men standing by the door, "He just wanted the money." He laughed, albeit ironically. "John, if it were up to me, I'd keep you here," he said, looking up at the prisoner. But this is a Federal prison and the rules say three escape attempts get you sent to the Rock. I'm sorry, but that's the way it is."

"What about Clarence?"

"He isn't on the record for the first one, so he stays."

"Alfred?"

13

"Your other brother wasn't part of your last escape, so he stays, too." John looked crestfallen. The warden surprised himself with a sudden wave of sympathy for the prisoner standing in front of him. Then softly, he said "Behave yourself, John... tell your brother Clarence and Alfred to do the same, and you'll see them after you've served your time."

"But —"

The warden's hard stare cut him off. (He could only afford so much sympathy.) "That is all, Mr. Anglin. Your cell has been cleaned out for you and your things will travel with you on the train for San Francisco, which leaves this afternoon. These officers are federal men. They'll escort you all the way to the dock in San Francisco." Then, still soft but stern, "I honestly wish you the best, son. Do your time, and you'll see your family soon enough."

The warden motioned to the two men, one of whom grabbed John by the arm. They walked him swiftly downstairs, out of the building and into the back the seat of a long, black car. The engine thrummed to life and moved slowly through the prison gate. John looked mournfully back at the prison as the car accelerated for the trip to the train station which would take him to a place known for all the worst reasons as The Rock.

October 31

Tommy sat on the deck of his houseboat with a cowboy, a pirate, and Willie Mays. Across from them sat an Alcatraz prisoner.

"No question about it. This is one of four best days of the year," the pirate said.

Willie Mays turned to the pirate. "What do you think

the other three are?"

"Oh, that's easy," the cowboy said. "Christmas has gotta be number one," an answer which was met by a round of approvals. "Today is definitely number two."

"Ha, you said number two," the astronaut said, as everyone laughed.

"So what's number three?" Willie Mays asked.

"It's a toss-up between your birthday and the last day of school," the pirate replied.

Willie Mays pursed his lips in thought, then he said, "I'd say the last day of school because... well, because it means no school for the summer."

"Yea, summer is the best," agreed the pirate.

"But you get presents on your birthday," the Alcatraz prisoner said, breaking his silence.

The astronaut, the pirate, the cowboy, and Willie Mays all nodded their approval. With the great question of the day having been settled, they all now made plans for what had been decided was the second-best day of the year; Hallowe'en. And, here in Sausalito, this great day always began with a parade downtown, with prizes given out for the best costumes.

Tommy's mom, Molly, emerged from the hold of the houseboat. "Well, look what we have here. Let me see... a pirate, a cowboy, a baseball player, a prisoner and... why it looks like my own little astronaut."

"Mom, please," Tommy whined, unable to hide his embarrassment. His friends grinned, They loved seeing one of their own squirm.

"Well, I'm sorry but I think you all look great. Any one of you could win tonight."

"Are you coming to the parade, Mrs. O'Conner?"

"I wouldn't miss it, Billy... I mean Mr. Pirate."

"I'm Long John Silver," Billy said, removing his curved cardboard cutlass from his belt and waving it

15

grandly around his head.

"Of course, from Treasure Island, I should have recognized you," Molly said as Billy's jaw dropped. "What? You thought girls just read Little Women? You didn't think we also read Robert Louis Stevenson?"

"Who am I, Mrs. O'Conner?" Freddie Green asked.

"Well, judging from your uniform I'd have to say... you're a football player. Are you Y.A. Tittle?"

"No, Mrs. O'Conner, I'm not a football player, I'm a baseball player."

"Oh, so you must be the Giant who hit 29 home runs this past season and drove in almost 200 runs. Now, what was his name..."

The pirate spoke up. "Oh, you're just kidding us, aren't you Mrs. O'Conner?"

Tommy rolled his eyes. "Aw, come on guys, of course she is. She knows darn well Freddie is Willie Mays."

"Spoil sport," Molly said, smiling. Tommy just rolled his eyes again.

The sound of car tires crunching on gravel turned everyone's attention to the parking lot. Tommy scowled when he saw it was a police car being driven by Tony Marianetti, the police chief. He got up and distracted himself on the starboard side of the houseboat as the officer stepped out of his car and dramatically put on his Stetson. The policeman looked at the costumed boys and hoisted his gun belt authoritatively. Tommy rolled his eyes. He hated that move of his.

"Hey, doesn't anyone dress up as a policeman anymore?" Tony said, a grin spreading across his face.

Billy, Raymond, Johnny, and Freddie laughed while Tommy continued to find more important things on the side of the boat.

"Tommy," Molly said, "did you say hello to Officer Marianetti?

16

"'Lo."

Molly sighed. "Astronauts are very serious people, Officer Marianetti, especially just before blasting into orbit."

Tony brightened. "Hey, that's right, we have a Hallowe'en parade in about an hour, don't we?" The cowboy, pirate, prisoner, and Willie Mays cheered. The astronaut remained aloof. "Hey, I've got to get downtown to check on the parade route," Tony said cheerfully. "Who wants to ride with me in the police car?"

"Hurray." said the Pirate. "Cool," said Willie Mays. "I do, I do," the cowboy and prisoner said as they all raised and waved their hands. They looked at the astronaut hopefully.

"Didn't we all agree we were gonna walk there in our costumes? You know, check out the competition and –"

"Yea, Tommy, but come on, a chance to ride in a cop car..."

The astronaut glared at his traitorous friends. Tony winked at Molly, then leaned down and put his hands on his knees. "Tell you what, guys, we can even run the siren."

In unison the boys turned and looked hopefully at Tommy. "Yea, sure, I guess that would be cool," he said with a forced smile. The boys all cheered as they piled into the back seat of the cruiser.

As they drove away Molly sighed. Would she ever get Tommy to understand...?

November 24

Warden Blackwell scowled. He was walking through a dark, dank tunnel under Alcatraz prison, making one of

17

his regular inspections of the prison's infrastructure when he heard a crunching sound under his foot.

"Barone," he said to the guard standing stiffly next to him.

"Yes, Warden?"

"Look at this," he said, pointing to a flaking, rusty pipe.

The guard whistled in astonishment. Embarrassed, he looked apologetically at the warden. "Sorry, sir."

Blackwell smiled. "It's okay, son. I sometimes wonder myself how it all just doesn't fall into the bay. Make a note. Rusting of sewer outfall pipe number 2."

"Yes sir." The guard studiously made a note on his clipboard, then mused, "I guess this place needs a bit more than a coat of paint."

The warden grunted. "A few million dollars more, at least." Blackwell dropped his cigarette on the floor and stubbed it out, the crunching of the fallen rust under his shoe echoing in the tunnel...

December 12

Molly sat pensively on a wooden stool in her studio, her eyes blinded by the thick colored glass of a welding helmet. Behind her sat a large metal box which housed a powerful electric generator. A thick power cord ran from the generator to an electric outlet. In her heavily-gloved hand was the artists' brush for her medium, a metal rod – the electrode – connected to the generator by a second cable. The whole setup looked like sometime out of

Frankenstein's lab.

In a well-practiced move she reached back with her free hand and flipped a large red switch. The room filled with the throaty hum of electricity, corralled and anxious for escape. Now Molly, with only instinct to guide her, slowly lowered the electrode to a piece of steel, her hand tensing with expectation. Just an inch or two above the steel a bolt of lightning shot out from the electrode. But, unlike lightning, this bolt didn't disappear after a few seconds, it remained an unceasing stream from electrode to the steel, fully illuminating the workshop. Were her eyes not behind the dark protective glass in her helmet she would have been blinded.

Then came the familiar smell. Oh, God, she knew it so well. It had filled the air during many Kansas summer afternoons when the air was so heavy with moisture from an impending storm one could almost drink it. It came soon after the sky above was so dark with thick clouds it was as if the sun had been kidnapped and night had taken control of the world. An unseen hand then squeezed the water from the clouds and water fell so hard from above it could knock even the strongest Kansan to the ground. This rain was quickly followed by thick bolts of light splitting the air with such terrifying, unrelenting ferocity that many of the God-fearing people of the plains would tremble in awe.

But not Molly.

While others cowered and averted their eyes, as if shielding their souls from something biblical and awful, she would stand, just barely under the edge of her porch roof, watching chunks of electricity cleave the sky – so close to the apocalyptic spectacle she could feel the heat on her face. Then Molly would inhale, deeply, and greedily taste the electricity lightning had left behind.

Later, at the wartime shipyard where they taught her

how to weld, she learned the taste had a name – ozone. There was something thrilling about the smell of life-giving oxygen mutated by nature's fury. Now, with welding, there was a way to conjure it at will.

When the shipyard closed down after the war many of her fellow welders went back to their lives as farmer's daughters and, inevitably, farmer's wives. But Molly stayed in Sausalito. With no parents or siblings or prospects there was nothing in Kansas for Molly to go back to, anyway. Sausalito, on the other hand, offered plenty of work as well as space in a now-abandoned shipyard building. There, Molly honed her talent for welding inanimate pieces of scrap metal into animals and people and even abstract art. Sausalito also had Connor, a boy whose smile filled her with explosive optimism for the future. They married. Connor had taken over his father's fishing boat and while he fished Molly sculpted. Tommy arrived two years later all pink and pudgy and life could not have been better.

Then, Korea. And Connor was gone.

Jolted from her reverie she opened her eyes and returned to a pitch-black 1960. The bright arc of light and the smell of ozone were both gone. In their place was the unrelenting sound of the generator straining from the electric short caused by the electrode touching the steel. Molly sighed and shut off the generator, which slowly whirred to a stop. She flipped up the lid of her helmet and studied the sculpture for any damage. Molly exhaled relief. It was not damaged. She cursed herself for letting her mind wander. With a quick nod of her head the helmet dropped back in front of her eyes as she flipped Frankenstein's switch and began, again, to weld her latest creation.

1961

January 10

John Anglin hadn't been this happy in a long time. Hell, he hadn't really felt much of anything since arriving at this God-forsaken island. God-forsaken. John heard the expression many times growing up but didn't even know what the word forsaken meant until he asked his convict friend Frank, whom everyone (even the guards) said was the smartest guy on the Rock. Frank told him the word meant to abandon, to make someone feel helpless. Yea, that was it. God has left us helpless on this rock. Helpless to have any say over what and how we eat, shower, shave... even shit.

But, today John Anglin had a reason to feel... happy? Okay, let's not get crazy. It wasn't happiness... what was the opposite of helpless, the opposite of feeling abandoned? Was it hope? He didn't know. Maybe Frank did. All John knew was the three months since he had been transferred to The Rock were the longest he'd ever been away from his brother and today they would be reunited. He couldn't wait to hear what stunt Clarence had tried in his escape attempt from Atlanta, although a part of him felt guilty for being glad it didn't work, because John had another reason for wanting his brother with him. He and Frank had been talking about ways to get off this damn rock. They didn't have an actual plan, yet, but whatever they decided to do they would need help. Who better than his own brother?

The brothers had their reunion on the line for lunch. John couldn't stop smiling as they carried their trays into the mess hall. He saw Frank Morris sitting with another con he knew, a guy named Allen West.

"Hey Frank," John said, beaming.

Frank looked up from his meal and smiled back. "This must be Clarence."

"I told ya he was smart," John said to Clarence.

"Wasn't that hard to figure out, you've been doing nothing but talking about him coming here for the past week. Well, come on boys, have a seat. Clarence, say hi to Allen West. He's in 140 on B-Block with us."

"Yea, I know West," Clarence said. "John and me was in Atlanta with him."

"So John says they caught you two going for the laundry truck," West said with a smirk. John and Clarence lowered their heads like two little boys caught with their hands in a cookie jar. "Ah, buck up, boys, there's no shame in trying." West pointed his fork at himself. "Me? Tried to bust out of Florida State so they sent me here four... no, wait, five... no four years ago."

Frank laughed.

"What's so damn funny?" Allen said, looking combative.

Frank quickly held up his hands, surrender style.

22

"Hey, I'm just thinking how easy it is to lose track of time." The other men nodded. "My first stretch I remember first losing track of hours. Couldn't remember what time of the day it was. Then I started losing track of what day of the week it was. Then months... then years. Imagine the poor bastards who are here so long they can't remember how many decades have passed."

"Jesus, Frank." Allen said with a smirk. "Nice way to welcome the new guy."

May 3

Molly rolled over in bed and her eyes caught sight of the calendar taped to her vanity mirror. Ugh. Today was the third of May, which should have been her fifteenth wedding anniversary.

Her thoughts drifted (damn, she was doing that a lot lately) to the day fifteen years ago when she woke to a cloudless sky and cool temperatures. She remembered thinking how it was going to be the perfect day for her wedding. And it was – until the sound of gunfire and grenades from the middle of the bay punctuated their vows. The day before there had been an escape attempt at Alcatraz and things had gone so horribly wrong that now – the day of her wedding – there were dead guards and a hostage situation. The authorities were sending in the Marines. Which was why, as guests drank champagne and munched on hors d'oeuvres on the deck of the restaurant, their attention, which should have been on the bride, was instead on the sounds of gunfire and grenades coming from the middle of the bay.

"Well, you kids are sure starting off your marriage with a bang," Connor's father had joked.

As Molly drifted back into the present, she sighed. Grabbing her coffee cup she walked onto the deck of the houseboat and looked out to the island prison, gunfire and popping champagne corks from fifteen years ago still echoing in her ears.

"Happy Anniversary, Connor."

October 2

It could have been just another lunch on the Rock with his brother John, Allen West, and Frank Morris. But, today, Clarence would blurt out a simple, innocuous sentence which would change their lives.

"This place smells different."

John and Allen laughed, but Frank (desperate, as usual, for something different to talk about) leaned forward and asked, "what do you mean?"

"I mean, you know how every joint has pretty much the same smell. Sweat. Lots of it. Disinfectant. God, they must buy tankers of the stuff for every joint. And does every guard at every joint wear the same aftershave?"

"Old Spice," they said in unison, and laughed. A nearby guard glared at them and held up his hand signaling for them to "keep it down."

Clarence continued. "But this place, I've been here ten months and I swear everything has the smell of salt water." He pointed to his plate. "I feel like I don't got to salt my food, it's everywhere, you know?"

"Yea, I know whatcha mean" Allen said, nodding his head in agreement. "What do you think, Frank?"

Frank Morris didn't answer. Something in what Clarence just said... had burrowed its way into his head and he couldn't pry it loose. Allen West smirked as he looked at Frank with his furrowed brow and pursed lips. "There he goes again, off in his own world. Hey Frank, whatcha thinking about now?" Even if Frank had heard Allen, he had to no time to answer. The bell in the mess hall rang, signaling lunch was over. It was back to their cells for another afternoon counting seconds, minutes, and hours until dinner.

Frank lay on his back in his cot, staring up at the peeling paint on the ceiling, thinking about what Clarence said at lunch. Salt water. He was right. It didn't just surround the island, it was in the very air they breathed and in the food they ate and... Frank bolted upright with a thought. He got up and reached for one of the few possessions cons were allowed in their cells, a small nail clipper (not considered much of a threat, even to unarmed guards.) Frank walked to his cell door and looked out at the walkway to be sure the guards were patrolling a different part of B-Block. He lay back down on his cot and slid the built-in nail file away from the clippers. Holding it close to his body to reduce the chance a passing guard would see what he was doing, Frank scratched the wall next to his cot, dislodging a small piece of concrete. It fell noiselessly to the ground.

He smiled.

November 17

Few sights bring more joy to a schoolchild than a film projector in the classroom.

It doesn't matter how much a kid likes his teacher (and Tommy really liked his seventh grade teacher Mrs. McCann) but a break from predicates and carrying twos is always welcome. But it wasn't the film projector generating an honest-to-goodness buzz from the children. It was the man in uniform standing next to the projector.

Most of the kids had fathers who had served in World War Two or Korea and had seen them squeezing into old uniforms for parades and reunions. The jokes their mothers made at their father's expense (mommy, what's a gut?) made for great recess chatter. But the man standing in front of the class had wings on his sleeves. Wings! None of the kids had a father whose uniform had wings. Then there was the man himself. Young and handsome with wavy hair and broad shoulders stirring something undefinable in the girls and, in the boys... sheer envy.

"Class, we have a very special guest with us today," Mrs. McCann said. "This is Master Sergeant Gus Winters from the Nike missile base at Angel Island."

The missile base. Wow.

"I want you all to say good morning to Sergeant Winters."

"Good morning, Sergeant Winters," their awed voices filling the room.

"Sergeant Winters is here to talk about a very serious topic so I want you all to pay close attention to what he has to say."

The man in the crisp blue uniform with the wings on his shoulders stood in front of the class with a warm and friendly smile. Then he began to talk, but what he said was anything but warm and friendly. It was downright terrifying... about Russian missiles armed with atomic bombs raining down on their country... on Sausalito... onto their homes, for gosh sake. But, he said hopefully, there was a way for them to survive an atomic attack. Just watch and listen, he said as he started the projector. On the screen a cartoon turtle confidently told the class what to do whenever they heard the town's air raid siren or saw the flash of an atomic blast. Just "duck and cover," the turtle said. Jump under your desks or, if you are outside, next to a building.

After the film Mrs. McCann thanked the good-looking man in the crisp blue uniform with wings on the shoulders. He exited the classroom smiling and waving as if he had just told them the circus was coming to town and they were all getting free tickets. After he left their wonderful, sweet teacher had the students practice putting their interlaced fingers over their necks so, as she explained, when the atomic blast hit "shards of flying glass don't cut your jugular vein."

Swell, Tommy thought. I'm gonna sleep great tonight.

December 15

"I have a plan."

Lots of cons say the same thing. Few ideas get beyond the mess hall. But today it was Frank Morris who said it. John Anglin heard a lot about Frank since he arrived at Alcatraz. "Smart" was the word he heard most often – although not always as a compliment. Many of the cons felt he was "stuck up" and "aloof" which, to John, just meant they were jealous. This guy actually made it out of that joint in Louisiana for a whole year. John wanted to hear more.

"What do you mean, Frank?"

"This place is falling apart."

Allen West rolled his eyes. "Shit Frank, I been here since '57. I coulda told you that. Everyone here knows that."

"So what is everyone they doing about it? I'll tell you what – nothing. They're just sitting around waiting... waiting for either parole or death," Frank said, leaning back with his trademark scowl.

"Jesus Frank, what's your point?" John Anglin asked.

He leaned in again and looked around the table at each man. "Do you know how many escape attempts have been made since they opened this dump in '34?" He was met with blank stares. "Over a dozen. A guy in the prison library has a list. I studied it."

"What the hell for?"

"To learn what didn't work so I could figure out what would."

The three other men nodded, and Frank continued. "Now some guys, like Floyd Wilson, tried to go it alone."

"I heard about him," Allen West said. "That was just a few years ago, right? He made it down to the shore but didn't get off the island before they nabbed him."

"Right. Most solo artists didn't make it, although a guy named Giles got onto the Angel Island ferry in '45."

"No shit."

"Yea, no shit. You gotta give him credit. It was a pretty good idea. You see, during the war they used to have cons do the army's laundry. Giles stole pieces of army clothing and made himself a sergeant's uniform. Then he just walked onto the ferry to Angel Island."

"That's genius," John said, smiling.

Frank shook his head. "Not so genius. This is why they do a count every half hour here. They counted and found they were one short and figured out the only place he could be was on the ferry."

"Yea, those damn counts, it's almost like they don't trust us." West said with a smile. Clarence and John laughed.

28

Ignoring them with another scowl, Frank continued. "Now the second type of escape is when cons band together. One bunch was gonna build a raft from driftwood they saw lying on the beach. They got to the beach all right, but the dopes went during the day so by the time they had collected enough wood a guard in one of the towers saw them."

Now, Frank got very somber. "The last type of escape is when cons decide to use force. Three guys killed a guard with a claw hammer in '38. A stupid thing to do. Killing a guard just gives the bulls an excuse. All three were shot and killed. Then, of course, there was the Battle of Alcatraz in '46."

"They sent the fucking Marines in for that one," West said.

Frank nodded. "Four cons died. Two more got the chair for killing a couple of guards." He stopped to let that sink in. "So, what do almost all those escape attempts have in common?" he asked, scanning the somber faces across the table for an answer.

"Other than they didn't make it?" Allen again with another smirk.

"Every attempt was made during the day."

"Well, shit, Frank, of course they were. That's the only time we get let out of our cells is during the day," Allen West said. "How can we escape if..." His voice trailed off as he saw the smile growing slowly on Frank's face. "How?" was all he could croak.

"We're going to leave at night, right after the last count."

Clarence shook his head. "But how can we leave if we're stuck in our cells?"

Keeping one eye on the guards slowly circulating around the mess hall, Frank reached into his pocket and brought a balled-up fist over the table. He motioned with his other hand for the three men to get as close as possible. He opened his fist. Inside was a handful of small concrete pieces. "They'll only think we're in our cells. Like I said... this place is falling apart."

Now it was Allen West's turn to scowl. "Okay, Frank, so we can get out of our cells, but there's still a count every thirty minutes."

"Which is why we're all going to enroll in the warden's art program."

Now it was John's turn to scowl. "Why?"

"Because we're going to make fake heads. Whenever we leave our cells to work on the raft we just leave them on our pillows and –"

"Wait a second. Did you say raft?"

"Yes. We're going to make a raft," Frank said matter-of-factually.

"A raft? Where the hell are we going to get the wood for a raft?" Clarence asked.

Frank smirked. "We're not going to make it out of wood, Clarence. We're going to use raincoats."

Allen West almost fell backwards from his seat. "Fucking raincoats? You want to make a raft out of fucking raincoats?"

"Keep it down, West. Look, you're welcome to swim for Angel island. But you won't make it. That water is too cold. You'd be dead in no time."

"But a raft made of raincoats?"

Frank stealthily looked around to make sure no guards were close by, then opened the top two buttons on his shirt to reveal a Popular Mechanics magazine. John saw the banner on the top of the front cover and read it out loud. "'All the '61 cars in color.' Shit, Frank, you planning on us driving out of here?"

Clarence laughed. Allen West sneered. Frank ignored them both. "Any of you birds know what

30

vulcanization is?" He was met with blank stares and smiled. "It's all explained in an article here," he said, indicating the magazine with a tip of his head. "We cut the raincoats into strips and buff the edges then glue 'em together. The glue kinda melts the rubber pieces together and makes a watertight seal. Clarence, you work in the glove shop, right?" Clarence nodded. "The glue they use for leather is just what we need. You'll lift us a bottle." He looked around the table. "As soon as you've got your fake heads ready and the vent holes in your cells are big enough to get through you'll come up to the workshop I set up."

Clarence's jaw actually dropped. "Wait... what? A workshop?"

"In a space I found right above B-block." A rare smile crept onto his face. "Can you believe it? Right above our cell block."

The other men looked at each other, silently, first in disbelief. Slowly, grudgingly, they began nodding their heads. They were in. Frank smiled. Of course they were in. He was Frank Morris, the smartest guy in the joint. And soon the whole world would know how smart he is.

1962

January 15

Only the government would take escape artists from prisons all over the country and put them in one place. What could possibly go wrong?

Frank Morris, Allen West, and the Anglin brothers were going to show them.

"Is everybody ready for tonight?" Frank asked.

"Yea, yea, you've asked us already."

Frank scowled at Allen West. "Hey, you're the asshole who's been mixing his cement wrong."

"That was that one time, why don't you lay off?"

"Keep yer voice down," Frank said casting a furtive look around the room. "It was more than once. Just remember it has to be strong enough to keep the vent in place when you're not in the cell –"

"– but loose enough to remove it every night. Yea, yea, I know."

Frank growled. This is the sorta guy who can screw it up for everyone. But they were stuck with him now that two other cons he had recruited had given up trying to loosen their vents. They claimed they couldn't chisel out the cement but Frank knew it was bullshit. He figured they looked at the odds of pulling this off and chickened out. Fuck 'em. Didn't matter. It was the four of them, now, and that was enough.

"Have you all got your heads ready?" Frank asked.

A strange sentence to hear anywhere... even stranger in a maximum security prison. But the fake heads were key for the plan to work. The guards had to believe all four men were in their cots after lights out. That would give them the whole night in the workshop. All had dutifully followed Frank's recipe (toilet paper, toothpaste, soap, concrete dust) to make their ersatz papier mache heads. A coat of paint (thank you Warden Blackwell for the arts program) topped with hair from the prison barbershop and, hey, they looked pretty convincing tucked underneath a blanket.

Tonight they would see if they were good enough fool the guards.

The clip-clop of Paul Barone's hard soled shoes hitting the floor echoed down B-Block. He was performing what he always felt was the most menial of jobs, checking on sleeping inmates. Paul derisively called it "snore patrol." But it was part of the job so there he was, around eleven o'clock, clip-clopping his way from one cell after another when, subconsciously, he stopped in front of cell 135. Frank Morris' cell. Which smelled of... was that paint? Barone reached for the flashlight in his belt and directed its beam onto the sleeping inmate's head (waking a con was not very high on his list of concerns.) He saw a tuft of hair sticking out from under the blanket and... there it was... the smell of fresh paint. Something didn't look or, rather, smell right.

"Hey, Barone."

Paul whirled around to see Bill Coreno, a new guard

34

from McNeil Island, standing just a few inches away. "Jesus, Bill. What are you doing here? I thought you had C-Block tonight?"

"I did, was just taking the long way around getting a cup of coffee. What's going on?"

"You smell that?" Barone asked.

Coreno shrugged his shoulders. "Smell what?"

"Paint. Fresh paint. This cell stinks of it. Now that I think about it, I was smelling it in a few other cells, too."

Coreno took out his flashlight and moved its beam around the cell until it found a small canvas leaning on an easel. "Barone, look."

It was a painting of a vase of flowers. A painter's palate, covered in globs of different colored paints, lay nearby on top of the toilet. Barone chuckled. Not just at his paranoia about the smell but at the painting. "What piece of crap," he scoffed. "My four year-old daughter Katherine can paint better than that."

"Yea, but it gives 'em something do, right?" Coreno responded as he looked at his watch. "Jeez, I gotta get back and I still need that coffee. See you around, Barone."

"Yea, sure," Paul said as he holstered his flashlight. Just as he was about to turn away and restart his patrol, he looked one more time at the tuft of hair poking out from the blanket.

"Boy, that Morris is a sound sleeper."

February 19

John Glenn almost ruined everything.

Prison makes men slaves to a never-changing routine. Wake, wash, shit, shave, eat and then... wait for the next break, however mundane, to distract them from

35

the mind-numbing emptiness of another day. Maybe an hour in the yard where you can toss a ball or just feel the warmth of the sun on your face and pretend you are free. Or, if you've earned the privilege, a morning in the wood shop or tending to the prison garden. Distractions which always ended too quickly and then it's back to your five by nine cell. A prisoner calls his sentence a "stretch" because, with no breaks from this rigidly enforced routine, time itself stretches to impossibly, sometimes intolerable lengths.

But Frank Morris, Allen West and the Anglin brothers had found a way to use that same routine against the prison. Each night, after lights out at 9:30 they would place their fake heads on their pillows and tuck them under a blanket, squeeze through the carved-out vent holes in back of their cells and enter the service corridor. After pulling the vent cover back over the hole they would shimmy up a pipe into their ersatz workshop. Passing guards on "snore patrol" would see a sleeping prisoner in an unremarkable cell. Long before the morning bell rang at 7:00 the four would have returned to their cells and swapped places with their doppelgangers. It was beautiful.

Until the Space Race came to Alcatraz.

"Tomorrow morning," the warden said the guards at the end of their daily staff meeting one day, "NASA is going to send this fellow John Glenn into orbit. I think it will be good for the inmates to feel a part of something happening on the outside. Let's bring them into the mess hall early – with the time difference 5:30 sounds about right – so they can listen to the launch on the radio. Might inspire them to do better on the outside."

A nice thing for the warden to do, sure. But warn a guy, could ya? Besides, none of the four men up in the workshop needed John Glenn for inspiration. Escaping

36

their island prison was inspiration enough. What they needed was for a way to make the work to go faster, because problems were mounting up. The knives they lifted from the mess hall were dull and sometimes tore the rubber. Every time that happened they'd have to start all over again on a new strip of rubber. A pair of sharp scissors would help. Then there was the glue they were using to create a waterproof seal between the strips of rubber. It took a long time to dry and sometimes the seal leaked and they had to start over. But they could hardly expect the warden to bring them sharp scissors or a better brand of glue.

February 20

"Rub-a-dub-dub, four men in a... raft."

John laughed as his brother Clarence sang the old nursery rhyme with two small changes; it wasn't three men in a tub, it would be four in a raft... made of raincoats.

Tonight they were in the shop later than usual. Frank was on his knees battling and cursing his knife as he tried to cut strips of rubber from a raincoat. John and Allen were having a time of it, too, waiting for the prison-issued glue between strips of raincoat to dry. Clarence was off in a corner trying, without hammer or nails, to assemble a paddle.

A frantic tapping on a pipe froze everyone in place. A voice echoed from the corridor below.

"Hey! They're rousting the whole block. You guys gotta get down here, fast."

Frank jumped up. "Shit. Drop whatever you're doing and get back to your cells."

"Jesus, Frank, do you think they know?" Allen West

wailed.

"How the fuck should I know. Just get down there, now."

John was at the pipe first, with Allen West right behind him. He looked behind them and saw his brother was still on the other side of the shop.

"Let's go, Anglin," Allen West said as he pushed John's shoulder.

"Just wait a second." Then, to his brother, "come on, Clarence, we gotta go."

"I'm coming, John, gimme a second, I just have to–"

"Did you guys hear me? The bulls are coming," came the increasingly urgent voice from below.

"Would you birds get moving?" Frank said as he muscled himself between John and Allen.

"Not without Clarence," John said, shaking his head.

"Fine with me," Allen said as he squeezed past John and slid down the pipe.

"Morris, you too, go around me," John said.

Frank grabbed the pipe. "John, if one gets caught we all get–"

"Yea, yea, I know."

Another scowl from Frank and he was down the pipe, just as Clarence finally crossed the workshop and reached his brother. "Go," John commanded, as he pushed his brother in front of him. He watched Clarence disappear down the pipe to the corridor below. John followed quickly and was right behind him as they raced for their cells.

As they passed Frank's cell they saw him putting his vent back into place. He heard their footsteps. "You guys aren't in yet?" they from inside his cell. "Get the hell back into your cells already."

"We're almost in," John said as he watched Clarence's feet disappear into his cell. The clip-clop of a guard's hard-soled shoes got louder as John frantically squeezed into his cell. He had just enough time to push the vent into place and race to his cot. With no time left to hide the fake head he shoved it under his blanket. Then he raced to the cell door and stood at attention just as a guard walked by.

"Coreno, what's going on?" he called out. "Why so early today?"

"Special treat for you birds," the guard replied. "The warden will tell you when you get... hey are you okay? Are you feeling sick?"

"No, I feel fine. Why?"

"You're sweating."

John ran his hand over his forehead and felt moisture. With a chagrined look at the guard he said "Oh, yea, well... I was dreaming about a blonde."

Bill Coreno smiled. "Yea? Next time ask her if she has a friend for me."

John exhaled relief as the guard walked away with a smirk. He wiped away the rest of the sweat on his forehead with his sleeve.

Within half an hour all the inmates were in the mess hall listening to the radio coverage of John Glenn's orbital flight around the planet. It was exciting, sure, but John couldn't help thinking how Glenn had the whole U.S. government working to make his mission a success... the same government fighting him and the others from completing theirs.

March 14

Each man had their assignment. Allen West searched the machine shop for parts they could use to make a drill. John scoured the barbershop for their never-ending need for sharp knives and scissors. Clarence took on the role of raincoat supply man.

Clarence's job was easier than all the others. Word had spread among the inmates of their need for prison-issued raincoats and they all wanted to help.

Up in his perch above the recreation area, Paul Barone scowled. "Hey, Bill," he said to another guard. "Didn't that prisoner —"

"— Which one?"

"That one there. Dussi."

"Joe Dussi, the safe cracker?"

"Yea."

"What about him?"

"Didn't he have a raincoat on when he came into the yard?"

"Beats the shit outta me. Don't we have enough things to be looking out for? What do you care if he was wearing a raincoat?"

"Because he's not wearing one now."

"So?"

"So it's not raining today."

April 6

"What do you mean we're not ready yet? I thought we was leaving next week?"

Allen West glared at Frank Morris, who calmly continued cutting another strip of rubber from a raincoat. "I said we would leave when we were ready."

"So why ain't we ready?"

Frank looked up from his work. "Because we have to make life preservers."

Allen West grunted. "Life preservers? What the hell

for? We got a raft."

Frank looked back, blankly. "A raft made of raincoats."

"Which was your idea."

"Look, I'm not saying the raft won't work. But what if something goes wrong? What if a seam pops or there's a puncture? It's two and a half miles to Angel. Life vests can keep us afloat... give us a fighting chance."

"So why all of a sudden do we need life vests?"

"It was in this article I read last night," Frank said, pulling a page torn from a magazine out of his pocket.

Allen West rolled his eyes. Frank was always reading something.

"It says 'if you don't need them they're useless but if you do, they're priceless.' Look, none of you birds wants to get out of here more than I do, but by spending a few more weeks we improve our odds we make all the way to Angel. And by waiting a couple of months the water will be a bit warmer, too."

The other men looked at each other and grudgingly nodded their heads in agreement. Frank smiled. He was, after all, still the smartest guy in the joint...

June 8

Even before he stepped inside the old brick school building Tommy O'Conner was counting down the hours until the final bell. Today was the last day of school. At three o'clock... summer. Sweet, glorious summer. Oh, sure, you could swim and bike and boat and do all that stuff any time of the year, but not having school hanging over your head, well... there was nothing better. As the hours whittled down to minutes his anticipation grew.

41

This was gonna be a great summer.

Just over a mile away, on Alcatraz Island, four men were thinking the same thing...

June 11, 1962

9:30 pm

You can set your watch by prison's ruthless routine. Tonight, Frank Morris, Allen West, Clarence Anglin and John Anglin would bet their lives on it.

It was 9:30 pm. The lights in their cells had been doused after the guards had finished their rounds making sure all the prisoners were in their cots. The bulls would not be back for another 30 minutes. More than enough time...

With the dim light of an incandescent bulb in the walkway casting gloomy shadows of prison bars across the floor, Frank got to work. As he had every night for the past six months he removed the vent in the back of his cell, reached into the corridor and brought in his fake head. Frank crouched and duck-walked to the bars of his cell to make sure a guard wasn't taking an extra lap around the block. Nope, not a guard in sight. Grateful for the prison's reliable routine Frank turned and placed his doppelganger on the pillow, then rolled up a couple of blankets to simulate his body. He lay a third blanket over the cot and stepped back to admire his work.

He wasn't much for sentiment, and there was a schedule to keep, but Frank could help but take one last look around the cell which had been his home for two and half years. He scowled. Home? What a stupid word for a prison cell. Okay, Frank, he said to himself. Enough of this shit. He dropped to his knees and squeezed into the service corridor, then reached back into his cell and pulled the vent towards him. A few pieces of concrete flaked off but it lodged into place nicely.

He stopped first at Clarence's and then John Anglin's cells. As arranged, both had already removed their vents so Frank could hand them their fake heads through the holes. A quick thumbs up from both brothers and Frank loped sideways in the narrow corridor to deliver Allen West's doppelganger. Frank arrived at cell 140 and was annoyed to see the vent still in place. He knelt down to look through the vent and was surprised to see a pair of eyes meet his from the other side of the latticework.

"West, what the hell?" he whispered.

From the other side of the vent he heard West's plaintive voice. "Shit, Frank, the vent is stuck. I can't get it loose."

"All right. Give me a minute to think." A minute? They didn't have a minute to spare. The key to the plan was getting off the island quickly to give them as much of a head start as possible. Now this asshole had – no, this wasn't the time. He had to make a decision. "West, I have to get everything set up in the workshop. I'll have the Anglins come by and help you out."

Silence.

"West? Did you hear me?"

"You're not gonna leave me, are you?"

"For Christ's sake, no. But we have to stick to the plan. I have to go."

Another moment of silence and then, softly. "Okay."

Frank shimmied down the corridor, all-to-aware of the crunching of flaked-off bits of rust and concrete under his shoes. He reached the Anglins and motioned for them to move closer. He whispered, "West is having trouble with his vent. I need one of you with me up in the workshop. Which one of you wants to help West to –"

"I will," Clarence said.

John put his hands on Clarence's shoulders and looked into his eyes. "Are you sure?" In the dim light John saw Clarence nod. John returned with a nod of his own, and a smile. "Okay. See what you can do. But one minute. No more. We got places to be." He turned and nodded to Frank. "Okay, let's go." They moved quickly to the pipe. As they shimmied their way up, John could see Clarence kneeling outside Allen West's cell.

"West," Clarence said, softly. "What's the hold up?"

"God-damned vent won't come loose," he heard from inside the cell. "Maybe you can kick it from out there?"

Clarence hesitated. Shit. How much noise would that make? He glanced towards the water pipe. Frank and John had disappeared up into the workshop and by now had probably opened the access to the roof. Time was running out. But he knew he couldn't just walk away without trying something. He looked behind him. The corridor was pretty narrow, just small enough for him to lean with his back up against the far wall and push the vent with his feet. Yea... that might work.

"West, step back, I'm gonna try and loosen the vent from out here," he said through the latticework. He got up, turned around and pushed his feet against the vent.

It didn't budge.

Shit. He pushed harder and, for a second, thought he was making progress but quickly realized it was the center of the vent bending inwards. This thing wasn't budging.

He swung around and whispered through the vent.

"West," he said, somewhat harshly. Then, softer, "Allen... it's no good." He could hear disappointed breathing from inside the cell. "Look... I gotta get up there with the others. Don't give up... keep trying, maybe chip around the vent some more. There's still time. We gotta get down to the water and... look, you know where to meet us."

"Yea," was all he heard from behind the vent.

Clarence Anglin stood up and sighed. Poor bastard. At least he could say he tried. He reluctantly walked to the pipe and shimmied up to the workshop. Laid out on the floor were the results of months of work. The raft... the paddles... the life preservers... and the modified concertina which would inflate the raft.

He was sorry about Allen West, sure, but even sorrier he wouldn't see the dumb looks on the dumb faces of the guards tomorrow morning.

Even the normally blasé bartender did a double-take when the couple entered the Valhalla, Sally Stanford's popular Sausalito restaurant.

Calling them 'May-December' would have been charitable. She was more on the cusp of March and he looked to be sometime the following year. With his bald head and walrus mustache he could have modeled for the character on the Monopoly game cards. The woman (blonde, of course) embodied the essence of a description the bartender heard on a TV show of being made of 'loose hips, a tight skirt, and wet lips.'

Bartenders at Sally's were trained to be neutral observers of the clientele, but how could he not smile as the woman's eyes swept around the restaurant, first to the magnificent Tiffany lamps on tables swathed by

46

emphatically embroidered red tablecloths, then to the deep red velvet curtains draped luxuriously in front of stained glass windows. The whole place seemed to be riding on a sea of plush, deep-red carpeting.

"Harold, sweetie," the blonde said to the Monopoly man (in a voice loud enough to be heard across the bay in Tiburon) "are you sure she's not running a brothel anymore?"

An older woman seated nearby in a big red barber's chair burst out laughing.

The Monopoly man turned and smiled. "Hello, Sally." With a gentle touch at his wife's elbow, he walked the blonde over the big red barber's chair.

"Hello, Harold," the woman said as a parrot, perched on her shoulder, emphatically bobbed its head.

"Sally, this is my wife, Marlene."

"Number three?" Sally replied with a smirk.

Monopoly man coughed. "Um, four, actually."

Sally extended her hand to the woman. "Nice to meet you, honey. What do you think of the decor?"

The blonde smiled as she shook Sally's hand. "It's very red."

"How's the used car business, Harold?" Sally asked as the brightly feathered bird on her shoulder emitted a squawk.

"Not as good as the restaurant business," he replied as he looked around the crowded room. "A Tuesday night and you're full up. Not bad."

"You know, Harry, it's funny. Some people come here for the food. Others come here for the view of San Francisco from the deck. And still others come here to see me, wondering if the stories are true." She leaned forward to the couple, as if imparting a great secret. "The bottom line is, whatever the reason, when they come here they eat and they drink –"

47

"And they pay," Harold said.

Sally smiled. "Come on, kids, I have a special table for you out on the deck." She got out of her chair and as she stood, raised a finger to the parrot, who eagerly hopped on. "That's a good boy," she said as she extended a finger and transferred the bird to a perch hanging near the bar. She turned back to the couple, gently taking one hand of each into hers and guided them towards the deck. "You're going to love it. It's a beautiful night, we have a great view of the city and Wes Montgomery is playing tonight."

10:00 pm

They were gone. Even as he climbed down the rocky path to the beach Allen West knew it as fact. After Clarence Anglin had failed to dislodge the vent with kicks from the service hallway Allen had continued to chip away at the concrete until, finally, it came loose. He had squeezed through the hole and scrambled up to the workshop, empty now except for the discarded tools used over the past few months to construct the raft, life vests, and paddles. From the workbench he had hoisted himself onto the roof and headed for the beach.

Now he stood, shivering at the water's edge, scouring vainly in the dark for the raft on which Frank Morris, John Anglin and Clarence Anglin were now paddling to freedom. From the west a breeze stroked his cheek and carried with it the sounds of – could it be? No, not men on a raft but... was that a guitar? It was. And laughter? Yes. A woman's laugh? Oh, yea, there was no mistaking the sound, it was like nothing else in the world. She was blonde, for sure. Allen West sighed and thought a

48

ridiculous thought. Maybe if he breathed in deep enough he could smell her perfume.

San Francisco Bay was cruel like that.

"Good luck, boys," he said, glumly, to the dark. Then he turned and headed back to the prison and to his cell.

Tomorrow was not going to be a good day.

11:50 pm

It had been two hours since the three men launched their raincoat raft into the bay. John Anglin's arms ached from rowing, but the last thing he was going to do was let his brother or Frank know how much. As he rowed through his pain John grinned at the thought of the bulls making their rounds, making their bed checks every thirty minutes and being completely fooled by the fake heads poking out from underneath their blankets. Every few minutes John would treat himself to a look over his shoulder at Alcatraz, quiet and dark for now, but hiding an explosive secret.

The currents were stronger than expected and energy was needed for rowing, which kept things quiet. John saw his brother Clarence also looking back toward the prison several times, after which he would angrily stabbed the water with his paddle. "Clarence," John said between heavy gulps of air, "There was nothing else you coulda done." His brother's only reply was to ferociously jab the water.

"Your brother is right," Frank said without turning around. "Let's just be thankful he didn't get us caught."

Clarence grunted. "It t'ain't fair. He did as much as any of us to make this happen."

"And come tomorrow morning if we're all drowned

49

will it be fair then? He'll be sitting in his cell – alive – saying 'thank God I was too stupid to mix concrete the right way'."

"Jesus, Frank," John said.

"Yea, well, all I know is we could use the extra pair of arms for rowing. Maybe if he were here we would have made it to Angel Island by now."

They continued to row in silence. John turned again for a reassuring look back at the prison. Then he looked to the right, then forward. An uneasy feeling began to creep over him. "Hey Frank," he said, hesitation in his voice.

"What?" Frank replied, annoyed, in between breaths.

John stopped rowing. "Those lights over there," he said, pointing in front of the raft. "Is that Angel Island?"

Frank kept rowing. "No, Angel Island doesn't have a lot of lights. That's one of the reasons we're –"

"Yea, but where we heading does," John interrupted.

Frank stopped rowing and looked ahead, then to his right. Clarence, roused from his rhythmic task, stopped as well. In the dark, the brothers heard only one word.

"Shit."

"Frank, what is it?" Clarence asked.

"We should be going in that direction," he said, pointing to the right.

"I thought we were heading north," John said.

"We were, but the current..." his voice trailing off. In the light of the half-moon John and Clarence saw confusion on Frank's face. "Shit," he repeated. Then, as if possessed, he stuck his paddle on the opposite side of the raft and began to furiously paddle, as he yelled, "We're off course, God damn it! We have to turn right."

"Frank, what the hell?"

Wheezing from the sudden exertion, Frank stopped rowing and turned to the Anglins. In between gulps of air he said, "It's West."

50

"What are you talking about? West never made it out of the prison."

"That's the problem. There were supposed to be four of us in the raft, two on each side."

"I don't understand," Clarence said, "what are you–"

"Stupid, instead of going straight we've been going in a curve."

"That's enough of that, Frank." John said. "There's no reason to jump all over Clarence. Let's not panic. We still got the raft and we can see land just ahead. We'll just head there."

Frank shook his head. "No. We turn north and head to Angel, just as we planned."

"Look, Frank," John argued, "I'm no sailor but it's obvious we're much closer to the lights in front of us. Why don't we –"

"Lights mean people, you idiot."

"I told you enough of that shit. You're so damn smart, you were supposed to know which way the damn island was," John said as Frank angrily thrust his paddle back into the water.

"The current... it's stronger than we thought..." Frank wheezed as he stroked, trying turn the raft north.

"You mean it's stronger than you thought," John said, his eyes narrowing.

"Then help me, God damn it."

"My brother is right," Clarence said. "We're much closer to those lights than we are to Angel Island."

Frank angrily pulled his paddle out of the water. "You're both idiots. That's Sausalito. It's a town. There are thousands of people there. Angel Island –"

"– is too far, Frank," John replied. Pointing north John said "It's a military base, right? Which means they have guns. I never really liked the idea, anyway." Then John pointed west. "Look to that area to the left of the town. It's dark. No people. And if we go there we'll be on the mainland instead of another island."

In the moonlight the brothers saw Frank's jaw clench as he gripped his paddle menacingly.

"Take it easy, Frank." John said.

The raft wobbled. Water sloshed over the edge.

"Don't tell me to take it easy," Frank said, waving his paddle at the brothers as more water began to splash over the side of the raft. "We should have been on Angel island by now."

"But we're not, Frank. Look, we're still floating. The raft is holding, just like you said it would. And look back at Alcatraz – no search lights. They still don't know we're gone. Breakfast won't be for hours. We can still do this, Frank, but we have to face facts. The original plan is fucked."

As raft bounced softly in the water, John and Clarence could only wait and watch Frank's face for a sign he was ready to accept their situation. But... just in case, John sent a silent signal to his brother. It was a well-practiced look from years of getting into – and out of – scrapes, something only Clarence (and their other brother, Alfred) could pick up; a slightly raised eyebrow and a subtle curve of the upper lip. In unison, the brothers slowly gripped their paddles. It was all up to Frank how this was going to play out.

Funny, the places one goes when faced with utter exhaustion and uncertainty. John found himself thinking about a day many years ago when his parents, flush with some extra cash given them by a grateful farmer whose harvest had been especially good, took them to a movie. John still remembered the feel of the nickel, heavy and cool in his hand as he and his siblings lined up outside the theater. He couldn't remember the town, but he remembered the movie.

Mutiny on the Bounty.

Now, as he sat in a raft floating in San Francisco Bay, John remembered Clark Gable as Fletcher Christian and his revolt against Captain Bligh. Their raft was no Bounty, and Frank Morris was no Bligh, he was just another con who had made a mistake. Now they waited for him to realize the only answer to their survival was –"

"You're right." Frank's voice cut through the air like a knife. "We'll head for that place south of Sausalito, that area without any lights. We can boost a car and head north."

Was Frank really ready to change his plan? John and Clarence looked warily at each other. They had been double-crossed before. With subtle nods of their heads they wordlessly agreed to accept Frank was telling the truth. For now.

Frank had been watching them warily. As they slowly lowered their paddles into the water, his followed. "All right, let's get moving." On cue, all three began to paddle towards their new destination. With each stroke of their paddles the shore got closer and an unspoken confidence began to build. The crisis was over, and this impossible thing no one had ever done, escaping from the island prison of Alcatraz, was within sight.

What could possibly stop them now?

June 12, 1962

Midnight

Sausalito police chief Tony Marianetti sat quietly in his patrol car, watching traffic along Bridgeway, the main road through Sausalito. It was an open secret in town this was his favorite spot for catching speeders. Every now and then a local would honk their horn as they drove by, some waving and a few laughing as they passed. He often waved back. He wasn't interested in hassling locals. But out-of-towners who treated Bridgeway as a drag strip? A different story.

Tony liked this spot for a lot of reasons, starting with the great view it provided of the bay. On nights like tonight when the humidity was low and the air was clear he would get out of his patrol car with his binoculars, cross the street, stand at the water's edge, and survey the sights around the bay. He started to the south... San Francisco. He sometimes felt like a traitor to Sausalito for loving the city so much, but it was so beautiful this time of night, like a soft blanket of lights had been draped over its hills. He then swept his gaze east to the Bay Bridge... the air so cool and crisp Tony could actually make out individual cars gliding between its towers.

Now to Alcatraz Island, jutting grimly out of the water. The sight of "The Rock" always brought a jumble of feelings to the 38-year-old police veteran. There were training sessions by the Feds for law enforcement departments whose jurisdictions were near maximum security facilities. Tony could never rid himself of the nagging feeling from the fellows at places like Ossining and Leavenworth that they thought Alcatraz being in a bay made his job easier than theirs. After all, an escapee from Sing Sing was already on dry land, while here they had to first swim miles to reach land. On the outside, Tony took the not-so-subtle jabs with good humor. On the inside... not so much.

He lowered his binoculars and filled his lungs with cool bay air, then looked at his watch. Almost midnight. His shift would be over soon. From the Valhalla restaurant, a few blocks away, he heard laughter mixing with the clinking of glasses, the strumming of a jazz guitar, and the rattling of dishes. Maybe it was time to try again to get Molly to go out with him. Sally would make sure they had a good meal. He smirked. Former madams knew how to please their customers, even if now it was with just food, drink, and music.

The roar of a speeding coupe's engine broke Tony's reverie. He eyed the car and considered giving chase but looked at his watch. His shift was over. He'd get them next time. At the risk of losing himself again, he took one last, long look across the bay, with nothing but a gentle lapping of water on the rocks below to break the still of the night. As he turned to go back across the street to his patrol car he thought about how nice it would be to be out there on the bay tonight...

1:13 am

The mood on the Bounty was turning foul.

"Frank."

"What?"

"How far out do you think we are?" Clarence asked.

"I don't know," Frank replied between heavy breaths. "Closer than we were the last time someone asked." Then, after a few more strokes of his paddle, he pointed ahead of them to the right. "Look, you can just about make out some buildings over there."

John pulled his paddle out of the water and motioned for his brother to do the same. "Frank, let's take a break."

"Why the hell for? Look how close we are."

"Yea, well, it's obvious we don't know how close, so we don't know how much longer we need to row. Maybe let's rest up for a final push, okay?"

Frank glared at the brothers but, rather than argue, petulantly pulled his paddle into the raft. He didn't want to admit it, but he was glad for the break. His arms were tired, too and – "What's that?"

"What's what?"

"Shhh, quiet. Listen."

The brothers froze in place as they watched Frank lean forward and peer into the dark night in front of the them.

"You hear that?"

Clarence looked over at his brother and in the light of the half-moon saw his eyes widen.

"Shit."

"John, what?"

"A motorboat."

Frank turned to the brothers, his eyes narrowing.

"God damn it, this is why I wanted to go to Angel Island."

John held up his free hand. "Take it easy, Frank."

"Don't tell me to take it easy, what if he sees us?"

"I don't know but you keep yelling like that he's bound to hear you."

The three men bobbed silently, listening to the whine of the motorboat.

"Wait. I think he's going away," John said quietly.

Heads turned in all directions. John was right, the motorboat was heading away from them. Clarence heaved a sigh of relief. Frank nodded and started to bring his paddle around to put back into the water when he froze. "What's that sound?"

"What? Another boat?"

"No, something else, it sounds like –"

"Shit. Oh, shit. It's the raft. Frank, behind you, I can hear it, the fucking raft is leaking."

In as much time as it took John to say those words pressure from inside the raft tore through a tiny break in the seam and burst open. There was no time to say anything else. Within seconds the side of the raft where Frank was sitting deflated and collapsed into the water, sending him flailing backwards into the bay. John saw Clarence reach helplessly for Frank's leg just as their side of the raft deflated and they, too, tumbled into the water.

To his horror John felt his life preserver pop off his neck and he sunk into the water. He kicked back against the water's grasp and felt cool air against his wet face. He gasped for air and kicked to keep his head above water.

"Help!"

It was Frank, who was thrashing about trying to free his legs, which had gotten tangled in the deflated raft. John yelled to him. "Hang on, Frank, I'm coming over to help." He began to swim towards him when he had a horrible thought. Where was Clarence? John swung his

58

head around, hoping he would see Clarence floating nearby. But his brother wasn't there.

"Clarence!" he called out, but there was no reply, only the sound of splashing as Frank fought the raft. John could only help one of them. Frank still had his life preserver. His brother was under water. It was an easy decision.

What John hadn't seen was, seconds earlier, Clarence saw Frank begin his frightful tumble backwards. The younger Anglin had instinctively launched himself across the raft to help. But, as Frank hit the water, his left foot had flown upwards and struck Clarence in the head, snapping it backwards. As the last air from the raft escaped into the night, Clarence sank below the surface.

"Last one to the raft is a rotten egg," Clarence yelled as he dove into the chilly Lake Michigan water.

The Anglin family had a rare day off from cherry picking, so George and Rachel packed lunches and took their kids to the shore. The screams of laughter from her children made Rachel smile. The future looked bright as George had been in touch with some farmers down in Florida who were offering year-round employment. Their days of vagabonding between Michigan and Florida were over.

For a kid who didn't get into the water very often, Clarence Anglin was a pretty good swimmer, and he easily kept ahead of his brothers Alfred and John, who were chasing him. Michigan was hot in September, hotter still in the middle of the expansive cherry orchards where they had been working this month. Clarence stopped in mid-stroke, about halfway to the dock moored off shore, enjoying the sensation of being nice and cool without a care in the world. Maybe they would just let him float here for the rest of the day. Maybe, when his family stopped chasing harvests and settled down in Florida, he could swim every day.

"Clarence!"

What did his stupid brother want? Couldn't he feel how great the water was?

"Clarence! It's John, wake up."

Now what's he doing? Let go of my arm... ma said we could swim all day –

"Clarence!"

What the hell is he doing now? Why is he slapping me?

Clarence's eye popped open.

What the hell? Where had the sun gone? And what was this stabbing pain in his chest?

"I got you, brother, I got you. You just gotta breathe now. Come on, you're okay, just breathe for me."

Clarence opened his mouth to speak but nothing came out. The pain in his chest was getting worse. He was confused as hell. A moment ago it was sunny and warm, now it was dark and cold. The pain in his chest, why won't it go away? And why was someone hitting him on the back now?

"Clarence, come on, buddy, I know you're alive, just breathe."

Wait... it was John. John was pounding on his back and screaming at him to –

There is no word to describe the sound which emanated from Clarence as his lungs suddenly, greedily sucked in all the air they could hold. The pain in his chest... it was still there but was easing. Slowly, his breathing, although heavy, became regular. He tried to speak, but only a rasp came out.

60

"It's okay, Clarence, you're gonna be okay now."

Clarence tried to speak, but his lungs still ached, demanding as much air as he could take in. He managed a grateful smile before gulping in more air.

"Clarence, we're in trouble. The raft..."

Still gasping and unable to speak, Clarence weakly nodded. He knew. With a determined look, he managed to mouth one word to his brother. "Frank..."

John shook his head. Clarence nodded. They floated together for a few more minutes. There was no need to speak. Both knew. No raft. No life vests. No Frank. And no idea how far it was to land.

"Ready?" John asked. Clarence nodded and the two men began to swim toward the lights which now seemed so much further away. They swam for a while, in silence.

"Hey, John?" Clarence's voice was still raspy but getting stronger.

"Yea?"

"This ain't that cold."

"No?"

"Michigan. That water was cold. Remember? You, me, Alfred..."

"Yea. Alfred."

"If we make it, we gotta let him know."

"Save your energy. Let's make it, first."

They swam for a while longer. John sure he could see the lights ahead getting bigger and brighter. He allowed himself the wild thought they might actually make it. But... best not jinx it. Just focus on getting to shore as quickly as possible.

"Damn shame about Frank," Clarence said.

"Yea, damn shame," said John, trying not to think about poor Frank floating out there, dead.

But they were wrong. Frank was alive. And he was pissed.

2:30 am

"Clarence."

"Yea?"

"You... okay?" John asked, each syllable punctuated by the splash of his arms through the cold water.

"Yea," replied his brother. "You?"

"I was thinking."

"About what?"

"This picture I saw in LIFE magazine. Or LOOK. I can't remember which one."

"What about it?"

"These people in Boston who jump into the water on New Year's Day. Call themselves Polar Bears."

"They sound like idiots."

"Yea, that's what I thought, too," John said as he momentarily stopped swimming. Clarence gratefully stopped, as well. The two of them dog-paddled for a while, both sucking in as much air as their lungs could hold. "How's your head?"

"Hurts. Frank got me good."

"As long as you're awake, brother. We'll see how bad it is after we get to shore. You ready?"

Clarence, still catching his breath and shivering noticeably, nodded. In unison the brothers kicked and pushed their bodies towards the shore. John looked to his left as he stroked into the water. The Golden Gate Bridge. It was definitely getting bigger. Boy, what would the people driving across it think if they could see him and his brother out here? Couple of crazies, they'd say. Like them Polar Bears up in Boston.

"John?"

"Yea?"

"I don't know how much longer I can go on."

"I know."

"I'm so cold, John."

"I know. Me too, but you gotta keep going."

"I'm trying."

"Do you want to stop again? Rest?"

"No, I just want to be out of the water already."

"You will be soon," John said as he looked at his brother with concern. "I think we're almost there."

"Yea. Please, John don't –"

"No, I mean it. I can make out a cliff or something ahead of us. And I think the water's getting warmer."

"Warmer? Yea, right."

"I'm not lying to ya," he said in between gulps of air. "Like when we'd go swimming in Lake Michigan in the summer, remember?"

"I remember," Clarence replied. He didn't know how to tell John he had just been in the lake a short while ago.

"The water got warmer closer to shore. I remember it..." John said, his voice trailing off.

"John, what is it?"

"I think we're almost there. Can you see it? It's a beach."

"Are you sure? 'Cause I'm not sure how much longer I can keep going."

"Damn it, Clarence, you'll keep going as long as you have to."

"I'm so cold, John," Clarence said again, his voice trailing off. "So cold..."

John put his arm around Clarence. He could feel his brother's body shaking. "Clarence, look... look ahead. Can't you see it? That little beach? We are soooo close, brother. So close."

"I'm tired John. So tired and cold," Clarence said as

63

he flipped onto his back and floated. "Oh, man, look at the stars, John. So many stars up there, just like we used to see at night in the fields, remember?"

"I remember."

"What happened, John?"

"What do you mean?"

"How'd we end up here? Were things that tough? Or are we just... bad?"

"No. Don't ever say that. We're not bad. Things just... happened. We didn't plan it. They just... happened."

Still on his back, looking up into the night sky, Clarence's voice seemed to be getting weaker with each word. "I'm so tired. You go ahead, John. You got a better chance if you –"

"Hey, stop that shit now. No one is leaving anyone behind," John said as he began kicking and using his free arm for stroking forward. Every few minutes John, near the point of exhaustion, would stop and let his legs dangle beneath them while he slowly dog-paddled. He didn't want Clarence to know the cold was starting to get to him, too. It felt like his mind was drifting away from his body, from Clarence. He looked at his brother and saw his eyes were closed.

"Clarence," he said loudly.

"I'm here," his brother replied, softly, without opening his eyes.

The sight of his brother looking so helpless – perhaps near death – filled John with regretful rage. This is my fault. I prayed for Clarence to be sent to Alcatraz so we could escape together and now... no, damn it, not now. John took a big gulp of air and began kicking and stroking with a vengeance. But after only a few strokes his body fought back, forcing him to stop and lower his legs again. He began a slow dog paddle when he felt one of his feet hit something.

64

"Clarence. Clarence."

"I'm here, you don't have to yell."

"I think I touched bottom."

Clarence's eyes opened slightly. "Don't lie to me."

John looked and saw the shore was now so close he could make out details of a bluff in front of them. "Hang on Clarence, just hang on. I swear to you we are almost there." With more difficultly than he would admit, John brought his legs up and began kicking again. All he needed was to get a few more feet closer and... he slowed and brought his legs down to...

"Clarence, I can stand."

"What?"

"My feet... they're touching the ground," John said as he placed his arms around his brother and began trudging through the water moving Clarence, still on his back, closer to shore. The water was soon only waist-high and John felt a surge of exhilaration as he saw how close they were to the beach. "Clarence, I'm going to get you as close as I can but you're gonna have to help me when we get there, okay?" His brother nodded faintly as John pushed him forward toward the beach, which he could now see was a very small triangular-shaped spit of sand in front of a steep bluff.

John hoped he had enough energy to get Clarence out onto the beach. He grabbed his brother's shoulders. "Okay, I'm going to pull you onto the beach here, okay? But I need you to bend your leg and push, okay?"

Clarence nodded and did as his brother commanded. He bent his leg and felt his foot touch solid ground. He smiled and nodded to John.

"Good, good," John said. "Okay, now push." Clarence grunted softly as he stretched out his leg and pushed as John pulled him forward. The water was now several inches below John's knee, and he could feel the cool air against his wet pants. "Again," John commanded. They repeated the same moves; bend, stretch and push once more... then a third time... and finally a fourth time. To John's great relief Clarence was finally on the beach. He looked ahead towards the bluff and saw about eight feet of sand separated them from the shelter of a large rock.

"Clarence, we're going to move up on the beach now, okay? I need you to push once or twice more," John said, gripping his brother's shoulder's firmly. "Come on, lift your leg... that's it... now push against the sand... good, good. Now give me one more. Use the other leg now, you got it, now push." John pulled extra hard this time and Clarence slid a few feet up the beach next to the rock. John fell to the ground and fell backwards onto the sand, gasping.

"Holy shit. We made it."

In the moonlight John could see a smile creep across Clarence's face. Dry clothes, food, water... those were things to worry about tomorrow. For now, all John wanted was sleep.

2:34 am

I'm dead.

Frank Morris opened his eyes to see, looming high above, a tower bathed in glorious light. He stared in wonder at the beautiful apparition and was filled with gratitude. He had made it. He was in Heaven.

Wait a second. Heaven? How the hell did I qualify?

His question was met by a jolt of cold so overwhelming and painful his body seized up, his back arched and he screamed. Shit, this ain't Heaven, he realized. This must be the other place. This was where everyone said he would end up if he didn't – wait... Hell was supposed to be hot, so why was he shivering from the cold?

Through the darkness, confusion and wracking pain Frank slowly became aware of a distant, as yet unrecognizable sound, like that of a giant machine. A memory forced its way through the cold... of falling asleep to the steady hum of a power plant. His temples throbbed as he tried to remember where that was – a prison! Yes, he was living in a prison. But which one? He had been in so many and they all sounded and smelled the same. No, wait, that wasn't true. There was one place with a unique smell. Of salt water... crumbling concrete... rusting rebar.

Alcatraz.

That was it. He had been at Alcatraz. Now he was... not. He was here. But where was here? Here with an unforgiving cold drawing him towards the calm nothingness of oblivion. Maybe, he thought through chattering teeth, he should submit, if only to stop the endless cycle of crime, conviction, imprisonment, and escape. Escape. That was it! He had escaped. Then almost drowned... but didn't.

Now it all came back in a rush, the realization striking him with such force the cold was momentarily forgotten. He was Frank Morris and he had escaped from Alcatraz with two other men in raft. It had sprung a leak. And they had swum away, leaving him to drown. Those rat bastards, they left him to die. Why, without the plan – his plan, damn it – they'd never have made it more than a hundred yards off the island and... well, they were probably dead, anyway. Serves them right. And if they're not dead, they'd better hope the feds found them before he did.

The anger drove Frank into full consciousness. He sat up and saw he had landed on a jetty, his feet mere inches from the water. It frightened him to realize he couldn't remember climbing up the rocks. Frank took another deep breath, trying to clear his head as he slowly, gingerly pulled his feet away from the water and checked for broken bones or bruises. He seemed to be in one piece, thank God.

He looked to his right and got another surprise. No more than twenty feet away was a huge concrete block sitting directly under what he now sheepishly realized wasn't a heavenly gate, but a tower of the Golden Gate Bridge.

Okay, so he knew where he was. The numbing cold told him what he had to do next – find a place to get warm... find dry clothes... and food. But where? Certainly not under the bridge. Nothing there but that big block of concrete. Frank looked in the other direction and saw, on a rocky spur of land sticking out into the bay, a haphazard jumble of buildings. From where he lay Frank couldn't see any lights. A good sign. Hopefully, they were empty of people. Only one way to find out.

Steadying himself with his arms he rose and, after a brief wobble, carefully clambered up the rocks, spider-like, to the shore road above. Once there he stood up and turned to look back at the rock-strewn pile where, just a few minutes earlier, he had woken. Frank shuddered at the sight of the jagged rocks and wondered how his body had not been smashed to bits. Shaking off the somber feeling of death eluded, he slowly limped to a set of concrete stairs which lead up to the landing. He gingerly climbed the stairs, crouching every few steps to make sure he hadn't been seen. So far, so good. At the top of the stairs he ran (well, more like a fast limp) behind a shed and peered cautiously around the corner at the largest building on the landing.

He eyed the darkened building enviously as a jolt of

agonizing cold twisted his body, a cruel reminder of his desperate condition. Inhabited or not... stocked with supplies or not... he had to get inside so at least he could get warm. Frank stepped out from behind the shed and, after another furtive glance to make sure no one was around, hurriedly limped through the moonlight to the door. Hanging next to it was a sign:

LIME POINT LIGHTHOUSE
U.S. COAST GUARD
FIRST OPENED 1883

Coast Guard? Was anyone inside? Were they armed? Frank grimaced. He was too wet and cold and desperate to care. Under the doorknob he saw a simple Yale lock. It would have been a piece of cake to jimmy open – if he had his tools. He could smash a window with a rock, but that would wake anyone inside – the last thing he wanted to do. Frank stared in chilly frustration at the doorknob and had a wild thought. He reached for the knob and turned it. Son of a bitch, it was unlocked. The door swung open and, after a furtive look inside, Frank entered the building.

2:45 am

Seaman Recruit Hector Gonzales lay on his bunk at Coast Guard Station Golden Gate, looking through heavy, barely open eyelids at the pillow his mother had embroidered with the Coast Guard's motto. It always bothered him how everyone seemed to know the Marines were *Semper Fi...* *Always Faithful*, yet few knew the Coast Guard was *Semper Paratus... Always Ready*. Hector liked to joke the

69

motto should be changed to "always exhausted." But tonight, he couldn't blame his exhaustion on the Coast Guard's rigorous training.

A few hours ago, after a long day on the water he and his fellow cadets had been in their bunks, grateful to be off their feet and on dry land, when a Lieutenant had entered the barracks and announced the commander was so pleased with their performance he was granting passes into town for the whole class.

Eight bodies had leaped in unison out of eight beds. Of course they were going out. When you are 20 years old and away from home for the first time who has time to be tired? Besides, tomorrow he and his buddy Ian were assigned to drive down to the Lime Point to calibrate the lighthouse's new, automated system. Easy duty.

Hector closed his eyes and smiled. Yea, tomorrow was gonna be a nice.... easy...

Sleep.

3:20 am

The unlocked door felt like a trap. Frank had heard inmates back at Lorton cursing traps like open doors and windows which landed them in the reformatory. But he was simply too cold and tired now to care. He opened it, anyway, and stepped inside. It was dark and – save for his own, labored breathing – quiet. But it was warm, and just being inside made him feel better. With no voice in the dark challenging his presence, he decided it was worth the risk to turn on the lights. He felt around the wall and found a switch, tensing as he flipped it upwards. Light filled the room. Frank stood motionless at the door, prepared for an encounter, but none came. He was alone.

Before him was a small, dull gray room with three bunk beds lining a far wall. They had been made with military precision, although none looked like they had ever been slept in. Across from the bunks was a small kitchen area where he saw a refrigerator, a stove, and a sink. On the wall between the bunks and kitchen was a row of metal lockers. None had locks, which made him smile.

Fighting back another tremor-inducing shiver Frank stumbled to the first locker and opened it. It was empty and he cursed. He stepped left to the next locker and repeated his action (including the curse) when he saw it, too, was empty. Frank took an anxious breath as he stepped to the next locker and opened it. Jackpot. Inside hung a few denim shirts and trousers of different sizes. At the bottom of the locker were a couple of pairs of heavy work boots and an empty duffel bag.

Now to find some shorts and socks. He saw a trunk at the foot of one of the bunk beds and staggered over to it as jolts of cold stabbed deep into the marrow of his bones. Despite the agony he still smirked when he saw it had no lock, either. Didn't the Coast Guard care about its property? No matter. He flung the lid open and saw his prize; two neat piles of clean socks and shorts and... what was this... a pile of fresh towels, too? He grabbed what he needed and stuffed them into the duffel bag. With a burst of renewed strength he stood up and looked around for... yes, there it was, a door marked HEAD. Clutching his booty Frank stumbled across the room and entered the bathroom.

He dropped the dry clothes, shoes, and towel onto the closed lid of the toilet, then reached into the shower stall and turned on the water, cranking the spigot as far to the "hot" side as it would go. He could feel the water getting hot almost immediately. Frank peeled off his wet

71

clothes as fast as he could and stepped into the shower. He almost screamed with joy as the hot water began to exorcise the cold from his bones. The relief was exquisite - almost too much at once – and he felt his legs start to buckle. He leaned against the back wall of the stall as the hot water poured over his body.

He laughed at an irony only other Alcatraz cons would appreciate. Back at the Rock the showers were always hot. The prisoners couldn't adjust the temperature any lower because the warden didn't want them to get acclimated to the cold temperatures of the bay. Frank could attest how well the warden's scheme worked, as his time in the water was sheer agony. But now he could stand as much hot water as he needed to get his body temperature back to normal. Thank you, Warden Blackwell.

Frank felt as if he could spend the whole night in the shower but reminded himself he didn't know when (assuming when, not if) the inhabitants might return. Reluctantly, he turned off the water and stepped out of the shower, dried himself off and got dressed. The shirt and pants were a little baggy and the shoes a bit loose but, hell, at least they were dry.

He looked on the floor at his wet prison uniform and grunted. The shirt and pants had his prisoner number on them. Christ, those were the last things the authorities should find if they were to think he drowned. He couldn't carry them with him – they were sopping wet and too heavy – so he picked up the wet pile of clothes and shoes and carried them outside. He looked around the jumble of shacks and sheds looking for something he was sure he had seen before – ah, there it was! A large metal dumpster. Peering over the edge Frank saw it was filled with debris from a construction job. This was perfect. He hoisted himself up into the dumpster and laid some wood

72

and plasterboard over his prison uniform. Would this be enough to cover up his visit? It would have to be because the clock was ticking. In a few hours Alcatraz would be waking up.

He went back inside the barrack. Now that he was warm and dry it was time to find some food. Frank crossed to the kitchen area, opened a cabinet door, and felt his heart sink. There sat a neat stack of small, gray cardboard boxes on which the words 'MEAL, COMBAT, INDIVIDUAL' were written in block letters. C-Rations. Just like he heard from guys who had served in Korea. Which meant this so-called food was at least ten years old. Then he had an even gloomier thought. What if these weren't from Korea but World War Two? That would make them twice as old.

Frank was struck by another irony. Alcatraz may have been the most strictly run prison in the country, but it had the best food in Federal Penitentiary System. The food was so good even the warden ate it. Frank was no connoisseur but had gotten used to eating well during his two and half years on the Rock. Now, the same con who just risked his life to get out of prison was wishing he were back there for a good meal. But the rumble in his stomach reminded him beggars – and escaped convicts – couldn't be choosers. He stuffed several boxes of rations into the duffel bag.

He then grabbed a canteen hanging in one of the lockers, filled it with tap water and slung it over his shoulder. Frank looked around and took stock of his situation – he had gotten a shower, clean clothes and enough food and water to last him over a week. Too bad there weren't any weapons (a gun would be a good thing to have.) But no complaints, he had done okay here. He smiled. Everyone knew Frank Morris was the smartest con in the joint. Now he felt like the luckiest one, too.

Except... he was supposed to land at Angel Island, not the Golden Gate bridge. Frank instinctively knew he should head west but had no idea how far it was to a town where he could boost a car and – wait... this was too good to be true – pinned to a cork board outside the bathroom, was a map. Someone had even put an "X" on the lighthouse's location. With his finger he followed a path which ran from the lighthouse and under the bridge to the west, where he saw markings for a series of forts. He smiled when he saw the word ABANDONED above them. Perfect. They're empty and far from everything.

Frank was always happier when he had a plan. It wasn't the original plan... but this one might be even better. He'd follow the path under the bridge to the first abandoned fort. He would hide out there during the day and get some desperately needed sleep. Then, at night, he could head west, hopping from fort to fort until he reached a town where he could boost that car and... well, the rest would work itself out. This map had to come with him.

He anxiously grabbed the bottom of the map and pulled, cursing when it ripped in half along a fold. He stared for a moment at the upper half, still hanging on the wall, then shrugged. He only needed the part in his hand which showed the locations of the forts, anyway. Frank shoved the map into his shirt pocket and walked to the door, turning for one last look around the barracks. The place was a mess. Open lockers... clothes and boxes of food strewn on the floor. He smirked. Somebody was gonna get in trouble for leaving the door unlocked. "Look at what some vagrant did here," he said out loud, in mock indignation.

Frank turned off the lights, stepped outside and shut the door behind him. He took a deep breath of cool bay air. Things were gonna be okay. At the bottom of the concrete stairs he turned right onto the narrow road along the shore and began walking north, away from the bridge and lighthouse. Looking to his right he saw, in the distance, Alcatraz Island. Still no searchlights, no alarms, no nothing. First whistle isn't until seven and according to the clock in the lighthouse, it was now about four in the morning. He had three hours until the bulls would discover they were short three prisoners. Then, all hell will break loose. He quickened his pace.

4:00 am

Exhausted beyond comprehension John Anglin lay on the tiny spit of sand on which he and his brother had miraculously landed a few hours ago. Every muscle in his body ached and his brain screamed for sleep, but John refused to succumb. All he wanted to do was cradle his injured brother in his arms and keep him as warm as possible. Protecting Clarence was his job. Had been ever since his younger brother was born.

The family never believed John when he said he could remember the day his mother delivered Clarence. "You was only a year old," one of his older sisters later taunted, "you can't possibly remember."

But John did remember, not just the sound of the wailing newborn but of the palpable fear in the room something might be wrong with the newest Anglin child. His mother would later tell John how he began to bawl, in unison, with Clarence. His sister Evelyn said them crying together meant they would be the closest of all of the Anglin children. "Thick as thieves," she would later say without a trace of irony, long after they, along with their older brother Alfred, began committing petty burglaries around town.

Now, on the tiny beach south of Sausalito, hard as he tried to stay awake, John Anglin had succumbed to sleep. Only the stars and the moon saw him wince.

4:30 am

There was a battle raging inside Frank Morris as he trudged up the path to Fort Spencer.

It had been ten grueling hours since escaping Alcatraz and the adrenaline had long worn off. His body screamed for him to stop and rest. His brain hollered back that the sun will be up in less than two hours and there's no time to stop until we reach the fort. Frank's muscles responded with spasms of pain to his legs. He staggered and fell to one knee, gasping for air as if he had been gut-punched. The duffel bag fell helplessly off his shoulder onto the ground. His other knee buckled and he was now on the ground.

No, damn it. It's not going to end here. It can't.

Frank looked ahead and, in the dim light, swore he could see something... a small structure... and instinctively knew it was the fort. What else could it be? Ignoring the searing pain in his legs, he wobbled to his feet and gingerly slung the duffel bag over his shoulder. He took a deep breath and staggered up the hill.

He was not prepared for what he saw when he reached the top.

Frank flashed to a television show he had seen after his escape from the Louisiana State Penitentiary back in fifty-nine. He had met a woman at a bar and one thing led to another and there he was, enjoying fresh sheets and a real bed for the first time in years. She wasn't so good-looking but she had a television set so there was something else to look at. One night they were watching this show about a guy who woke up alone in a town without any people, just buildings and cars and even an ice cream parlor. Twilight Zone, that was the name, yeah, and in the end it turned out the guy was an astronaut, training for space in an isolation chamber and he was imagining everything. As Frank stepped into the abandoned fort he understood how that guy felt.

Lining both sides of the path were squat, single-story concrete buildings. There were openings for doors... but no doors. There were cutouts for windows... but no windows (the glass was long gone.) He guessed these were once barracks or offices and, for a moment, he imagined he could see the bustle of soldiers flitting in and out of the shadows. Then he blinked, and they were gone.

Frank walked slowly to an opening meant for a window and peered inside, but it was too dark to see anything. (He cursed himself for not taking flashlight from the light house.) "Hello?" he said softly, so as not to wake the ghosts. There was no reply, save for a brief, halfhearted echo. He was then aware of the all-too-familiar smell of concrete fighting a losing battle with salt water and time. It made him depressed; for all his efforts over the past eight months he was back in a cell, alone.

He had been in solitary many times yet never felt more alone than he did right now. "Damn you," he admonished himself. "When did you turn into such a pussy? Sleep. That's what I need. Sleep. And stop feeling sorry for yourself. This place is only until the heat is off and I can head north, boost a car and head up to Oregon, maybe. Or Washington or Idaho. Get a job at a place where they don't ask a lot of questions and pay in cash. Then buy a gun and start making some real money." He took a deep breath, hoping to stave off the musty smell of

77

despair, and stepped into the room.

The sun, just beginning to rise, filled the room with hopeful yellow beams of light. But Frank didn't feel any hope – the light just confirmed how dismal this place was. Almost all the paint had peeled away from the walls and the floor was littered with dull gray chips which crunched loudly under his feet. He walked to the center of the room and dropped his duffel bag on the floor. Frank laid down with another annoying crunch, rested his head on the duffel bag, and closed his eyes.

Frank's last waking thought was how badly he wished the Anglins were alive... so he could kill them for leaving him out in the bay to drown. How surprised he would have been to know they were only half a mile away on that beach at Yellow Bluff.

5:00 am

Even now, lost in the deepest sleep of his life, John instinctively cradled his younger brother, as if to let go of Clarence would permit him slip away forever. John wouldn't let that happen, not after almost losing him when their raft burst apart. As John slept, he dreamed he could reach across the country and tell his mother they were okay and not to worry. "I know you will take care of your brother," Rachel would say.

"I will, Ma," John replied as he gazed lovingly at her in his mind.

He saw her face, awash in sad regret. "Your pa and I... after all those years of migrating we thought Ruskin would be the answer."

"It wasn't your fault, ma. You and pa... you did good. You got us a home to live in just like other families."

"It was a nice place wasn't it?'

"Yea, ma, it was. You fixed it up real home-like."

"But it wasn't enough, was it?"

"You didn't do nothing wrong, ma, we just..."

"Everyone said 'that's just boys being boys' but we thought with regular schooling and not moving around maybe you and Clarence and Alfred... that you'd... oh, I don't know... grow out of all that trouble-making, somehow."

"Aw, Ma, being honest we wasn't just a getting into a little 'trouble-making.'"

"I know, I know." Rachel closed her eyes and nodded, smiling a mother's sad smile.

On the beach John, still asleep, winced with regret. He and Clarence and Alfred... they didn't 'grow out of it' and the trouble-making became petty crimes which got bigger as did the prisons to which they were sentenced. Now he and Clarence were free, sure, but his brother lay desperately close to death on this tiny beach with no food, no water, and no plan. John clutched him even tighter. "I'm sorry, ma," he said into the ether as a single tear trickled down his cheek and dropped mournfully on the sand.

7:00 am

As he did every day he was assigned to the first shift, Guard Paul Barone woke up around five. He was married and shared an apartment on Alcatraz Island with his wife, Sharon, and their two daughters. Taking a job at the country's most notorious prison was not an easy decision for the young couple. They had been comfortable in Virginia, where Paul was a senior guard at the Petersburg penitentiary. He saw the invitation to work at Alcatraz as an opportunity to move up in the ranks of the Federal Penal system. Sharon did not see it that way. Paul remembered the conversation.

"Five thousand a year is pretty good," he had said to his wife when the job offer came in the mail.

"Yes, five thousand a year is pretty good," Sharon said, not looking convinced.

"And the free apartment, don't forget the free apartment."

"Of course, yes, that's fine, too but – "

"And it wouldn't hurt to get the experience, maybe get bumped to Lieutenant. That's a few hundred more a month we'd have for the girls."

"But living so close to those men. Look at this magazine. The article says, 'Death is better than Alcatraz."

"Let me see that."

Sharon handed him a LOOK magazine, folded to the article. He unfolded it and saw at the date on the cover. "I thought this looked old. This is from October of 1939. That was almost twenty-five years ago. Before the war, even. Of course they made it sound as bad as possible. You know, scare kids from thinking about a life of crime."

"I spent three years worrying about you getting killed in Europe. If Japan didn't surrender you were going to be sent there, next. Every day you go off to that horrible place in Petersburg I hold my breath. Now you want to go to a place that's worse?"

Paul cupped his wife's face in his hands and said, softly, "you're forgetting the big difference between Alcatraz and the war. At Alcatraz, the enemy doesn't have guns."

It had now been a year since they made the move and Sharon had to agree life on the Rock wasn't as bad as she feared. The girls had several friends their own age and she had become close to some of the other guard's wives. In fact, today Sharon and her friends were going to join their children on the boat for school in San Francisco, so they could have a day shopping downtown. As Paul dressed for work he could hear his wife singing to herself as she cooked breakfast.

"Daddy, daddy," his oldest, Stephanie, screamed as she burst into his bedroom, followed right behind by Katherine. "Guess what today is?"

"Is it Christmas already? Did Santa come and leave me presents?"

Stephanie giggled. "No, silly, today is the day Mommy is coming on the boat with us."

"Really? Wow, that sounds like fun."

"Can you come, too?" the younger Katherine pleaded.

"I wish I could honey but daddy has to work today."

Paul loved the first shift for these moments with his children. "Okay, girls, come on let's see what mommy has made for breakfast."

"Hurray," they squealed, in unison, as he took their hands in each of his and walked them to the kitchen where his wife had eggs and bacon waiting for them.

"Who has the best mommy?" Paul shouted.

"We do," the girls responded.

"You bet we do," as he winked at his wife.

Getting to work on time was not just a matter of pride for Paul Barone, but a mandate from the warden. He felt discipline from both inmates and guards was essential for maintaining order in the limited space of the island. Today the assignment board noted there were 264 men currently sleeping in the three cell blocks inside the prison. The first task today was the same as it was every day – wake the prisoners and get them to the mess hall for breakfast. To combat the monotony, as well as to keep guards and inmates from getting too chummy, the guards' assignments were rotated. Paul checked the duty log and saw he was assigned to B block today.

Then it was on to the daily meeting, when the deputy warden advised the guards of any releases or arrivals. There would be none today. After dismissal the guards, almost all ex-GI, saluted and walked to their assigned cell blocks. Then, as it had every day for almost thirty years, a loud whistle blew inside the prison. From all three levels of cells along A, B, and C block prisoners could be heard stirring. Once out of their cots they were to wash, dress, make their beds, clean their sinks and toilets, and then sweep out their cells. Then the cons were to stand behind their cell doors and wait for a guard to check they were standing at attention. Once all the prisoners were accounted for, a second whistle let everyone know the cell doors were about to open. The cons would then be allowed to step out of their cells onto the walkway. A guard would blow his whistle, the men would turn and march in line to the mess hall.

If it sounds tedious that's because it was. Deliberately so. Just like the army. Mind-numbing routine to keep order and compliance. Following the script, Paul Barone slowly marched past the cells of B block, remembering how, during training, a grizzled veteran guard admonished his students to remain vigilant and to look every con in the eyes. "Don't ever let your guard down," the old man had said. Paul honestly thought he was making a joke (a guard letting his guard down, get it?) and had laughed. That's when holy hell rained down on him.

"Do you think this is funny?" the guard yelled, veins bulging from his neck. "Maybe you think this is funny, too," at which point he pulled open his shirt to expose two bullet-sized scars on his gray-haired chest. Above the scars was a tattoo; "The Battle of Alcatraz, 1946." After

82

class Paul looked it up and read about the escape attempt that killed three inmates and two guards. Fourteen guards were also injured during a three-day battle which began when the guards made the mistake of... he had to say it (but now, without laughing) letting his guard down. It was one of many stories he had never told Sharon and hoped she would never hear.

But the sight of those bullet scars made an impact. From his first day on the job up until this very moment – even when performing the most mundane task – Barone always remembered the lesson of never letting his guard down. So, as he walked methodically down B-block, making eye-contact with every prisoner, he kept one hand on his billy-club. Cell 130... Cell 131... and onward his gaze meeting, more often than not, eyes emptied of hope from Alcatraz's endless routine. Cell 137... Cell 138...

Wait. Cell 138. Where were the pair of eyes meeting his from inside? This was Frank Morris' cell and Barone saw he was still in bed, fast asleep. Morris was smart, sure, but also a bit aloof. Barone didn't much care for him. Smart cons often thought the rules didn't apply to them. Rules like standing at attention on time for breakfast. Paul's training kicked in as he tightly gripped his baton and called over to Bill Coreno, who today had been assigned to the cell door control panel. "Open 138." With a metallic thunk, the lock on the steel door released and Barone stepped into the cell. He saw the covers pulled so far up Morris' body only the hairs on his head were exposed.

"Morris. Wake up." The figure in the bed did not move. "Let's go Morris, it's time to get up."

Paul was struck by an odd thought. It's one thing to be sleeping soundly, but shouldn't the blanket be rising and falling with Morris' breathing? Crap. Was he dead? Paul leaned slightly forward and gently nudged the body with his club. Barone almost fell forward onto the cot. There was no body under the blanket, just more blankets. What the hell? With one hand still firmly on his club, Paul grabbed the blanket near Frank's neck and whipped it off the bed. No amount of training, not even his months of brutal front line combat in Europe could have prepared Paul Baron for what heppened next.

Frank Morris' head rolled onto the floor.

"Jesus!" Paul staggered backwards from the gruesome sight of... wait a minute... where was the blood, it should everywhere... buckets of it on the sheets and the walls and on the floor. Catching his breath Paul leaned forward trying to grasp the meaning of the bloodless scene before him when he was suddenly frozen by another, even more confusing question: why was Frank's head hollow?

Funny how fast the mind can work. This whole scene, from when Paul pulled back the blanket to the moment he realized Frank Morris had escaped, took less than half a second. Barone grabbed his whistle and was about to blow it when he heard a shrill whistle coming from a nearby cell. He stepped out of Frank's cell and saw another guard whose expression of disbelief matched Paul's. "You won't believe it," the guard said.

"Fake head?" The other guard, his look of shock matching Paul's, nodded back.

"Barone, what the hell's going on?" It was the Lieutenant. Routine had been disrupted. He was not happy.

Paul pointed to the fake head on the floor of Frank Morris' cell.

"Shit." The lieutenant whirled around and yelled to Bill Coreno, still at his post at the control panel. "Sound the alarm. We have an escape of..." he looked to Paul for the bad news.

"I got one and Jimmy at 150 says he's missing

another –"

"So two?"

"Three," came a third guard's voice from outside another cell further down the walkway.

"Fake head?" Paul asked. The guard nodded.

Lieutenant Mitchell took a deep breath then, loudly as a siren's wail began to fill the prison, "All right. This is what we train for. I want a check of every goddamn cell in this place. I want to know exactly how many are gone."

"Yes, sir," came the reply from the guards as they dispersed and went to their assigned places for a prison-wide count. He grabbed Paul's arm and said, quietly, "Blackwell is on his fishing vacation. Until we can get him back we do everything by the book, understand?" Paul nodded. "I'm going up to the office and alert the Bureau, the Coast Guard, and the locals." He turned and strode quickly towards the warden's office, the echo of his hard-soled shoes on the concrete floor mixing rhythmically with the rise and fell of the siren.

As the Lieutenant passed his cell, Joe Dussi, the safe cracker in B-107, couldn't resist. "Hey, Lieutenant... what's for breakfast?"

As laughter from other cells filled B-block, Paul Barone answered, silently to himself, "Crow."

7:50 am

There was a bass nearby – a big one, too, he could feel it in his bones. An ever-present cigarette dangling from his lips, the man cradled the handle of the fiberglass rod on which was attached a brand new Penn 700 spinning reel. Fifty weeks a year he was Olin Blackwell, the warden of Alcatraz. This week, he was just another fisherman trying to hook a big one. Out here on Lake Berryessa there were no budgets to approve, no disciple to mete out and, best of all, no having to answer questions from the guards about whether Alcatraz was going to be shut down.

Blackwell closed his eyes and enjoyed the gentle rocking of the boat as he listened to the sounds of the lake. Of course lakes have sounds – especially ones with big bass – every fisherman knows that. There's the lapping of the water on the hull of your boat... the wind rustling through nearby trees... and the sound of someone calling his name. Wait. What the hell? He opened one eye and looked toward the shore and, son-of-a-bitch, there was some clown waving his arms and yelling in his direction. Olin Blackwell sighed and pulled his fishing rod into the boat. "I'll be back for you tomorrow," he said to the bass that he just knew was tantalizingly close by. He took a last drag from his cigarette and flicked it into the water as he wrapped the starter rope around the outboard engine and pulled. The engine roared to life and he steered himself towards the shore, skillfully cutting the engine so the boat gently skidded to a stop on the beach. A young man in a park ranger outfit ran up to him.

"Olin Blackwell?" asked the young man.

"Yes," he replied as he grabbed the pack of cigarettes from his shirt pocket and pulled one out with his lips. As he lit it he said, "but I assume you wouldn't have made all this fuss if you weren't sure."

"Sir, you have an urgent message from Alcatraz. I'm instructed to tell you there's been an escape."

Blackwell took an extra long drag on his cigarette. "Okay, son, let's get me to the nearest telephone."

He sighed and looked wistfully out at the lake. The bass were going to have to wait.

86

7:55 am

Rookie deputy Roger McGloin sat behind his desk at the Sausalito Police Station and tried, unsuccessfully, to stifle a yawn. He considered having another cup of coffee but a glance at the clock on the wall showed it was close to 8 o'clock. Almost time to go home. No, no coffee, he decided. The day shift would be here soon enough. He stretched and thought about calling his wife, Sandy, to see how things went last night with James, their new baby. They often joked how Roger probably got more sleep working graveyard than Sandy did with a fussy newborn.

It had been an uneventful shift. Roger had made his usual rounds of Sausalito in the patrol car, making sure the front doors of businesses were locked, answering a prowler call (which turned out to be a stray cat overturning a trash can) and a "disturbing the peace" call at Juanita's Galley. All in all, it had been a routine weekday night in Sausalito. Just enough excitement – but not too much – for a rookie cop. In just three months on the job Roger figured he had just about every challenge a small town like Sausalito could deliver.

He was about to be proven wrong.

The clanging of bells jolted Roger from thoughts of his wife and baby. Instinctively he grabbed the heavy handset of the phone and brought it to his ear. "Sausalito Police Department..." he began, stopping when he realized he was speaking to a dial tone. Confused, he placed the handset back on its cradle. The clanging bells resumed, noisily filling the room. Chagrined, Roger realized it was the teletype machine announcing an alert. Grateful no one was around to see his confusion (wouldn't they have a field day with the rookie) Roger bolted to see the machine's keys rapidly swinging up and down, smashing out a message on a roll of paper:

ALERT

(JUNE 12 7:56 AM PST)
FROM: FEDERAL BUREAU OF PRISONS
RE: ESCAPE OF PRISONERS FROM ALCATRAZ
AT 7:00 am AT LEAST THREE PRISONERS ARE
MISSING FROM THEIR CELLS AND
PRESUMED TO BE OFF ALCATRAZ ISLAND,
POSSIBLY SINCE LAST NIGHT.
A CONFERENCE CALL WITH ALCATRAZ
WARDEN TO BE HELD THIS MORNING.
DETAILS TO FOLLOW.

30

Roger took a deep breath and reached for the phone to call the police chief. Out loud, to the empty station, he said "I guess I better have that cup of coffee now."

8:00 am

The blast of an air horn shattered the early morning calm of the barracks at Golden Gate Coast Guard Station. Ian Jacoby bolted upright in his bunk, his head narrowly missing the springs of the upper berth.

"Now hear this... now hear this..." came a voice from the large speaker mounted on the wall. "This is not a drill. All personnel to assemble in the mess hall in ten minutes. I repeat, all personnel – including recruits and

88

apprentices – to report to the mess hall in ten minutes."

Shaking off the still-present effects of the drinks he had just a few hours earlier, Ian began the arduous task of getting out of his bunk. It wasn't fast enough for the Petty Officer in the next bunk who was already on his feet.

"Apprentice Jacoby, you plan on joining us?"

Ian jumped out of his bunk and stood at attention. "Yes, Petty Officer Oveson." He breathed a small sigh of relief when, after an officious nod, Oveson strode away. Ian then turned around to see Hector, still prone in the upper bunk. Furtively looking around to be sure no other ranking seamen were nearby. He leaned over the bed. "Hector, hey," he said in a stage whisper. "Come on, man, before someone sees you."

"Ian, I swear I have never fired a gun in anger, but if you don't let me sleep –"

"How did the air horn not wake you up? Jeez, you must really be in rough shape."

"I'd have to work my way up to rough."

"Hec, you can sleep later. Didn't you hear? They've called an 'all hands.' That means us, too. Come on."

Groaning, Hector slowly raised himself to a seated position. He looked dourly at Ian. "Asshole, you had as much to drink as I did last night. How the hell are you so chipper?"

Ian smiled bravely through his own hangover. "Clean living, my friend... clean living. Now come on, let's get to the mess hall and find out what this is all about."

Within minutes they had staggered (well, Hector staggered... Ian's gait was defiantly jaunty) to the mess hall. They jumped to attention when the station Commander, followed by his Lieutenant, entered the room.

"At ease, men. This won't take long." He pulled a piece of paper from his breast pocket and held it up. "At oh-seven-thirty this station received a telex from Alcatraz Federal prison informing us at least three prisoners were missing from their cells at the morning count today. At this time it is assumed all made it off the island and are somewhere in the bay."

The buzz of excited chatter spread across the room like a grass fire. The commander turned to his Lieutenant who yelled "That's enough, men. At ease doesn't mean talking." The grass fire quickly died.

"This is an 'all hands' which means even boots will man some of the boats," the commander said.

"Hear that? Boots, that means us," Ian whispered to Hector, who nodded grimly.

"Boats from Golden Gate, Fort Point, Point Reyes, and all other stations around the bay are being scrambled to assist the Federal Bureau of Prisons..." he paused to look down at the paper... "to search San Francisco Bay for the prisoners and, if found, to return them to Alcatraz Island." He stopped again to look up at the assembled seamen. "Officially this is a search and rescue mission. But if those men were foolish enough to swim it's more than likely they suffered hypothermia and drowned. I'm told – unofficially – we should be prepared that they might have arranged for a boat to pick them up off the island. If that's true we should also assume they have firearms. Therefore all of you you will all wear your sidearms."

The Commander took a moment to let his last order sink in. This time, it was quiet. Almost somber. Good. He only wanted to see serious faces. "Your boat assignments will be posted on the board shortly. Get some breakfast in you. It's going to be a long day." His tone then shifted quickly from official, to fatherly. "This is what you've trained for. We wouldn't send any of you out there, especially you boots, if we didn't think you were ready.

90

You've had the best training in the world. So do your job, but do it safely, and always remember, one hand for the ship..." He paused, waiting for the trained reply from the assembled seamen.

"One hand for you," the all said in practiced unison.

"Dismissed."

8:03 am

Jim Albright was pissed.

The count, so far, was three. Three prisoners missing from the country's most "escape-proof" prison. Which meant instead of an easy morning's duty in one of the island's towers the veteran Alcatraz guard was tediously taking attendance like he was a damn kindergarten teacher. Albright walked slowly and purposely, making sure to make eye contact with each con. None made the effort to hide their smirks. Albright returned each smirk with a practiced scowl. He'd love to take his baton and wipe those smirks from their –

Wait a second. The guy in front of this cell wasn't smirking. His eyes... had he been... crying? Albright checked his clipboard. Prisoner AZ1335. Allen West. Right where he was supposed to be.

"What's the matter, West? Bad news from home?"

The prisoner on the other side of the bars said nothing. Albright could swear he saw another tear beginning to form in the con's eyes. Wait... what's that just over West's shoulder? Holy... he had been so focused on West's tears he hadn't seen the vent cover, laying on the floor. Albright could see directly into the service corridor behind the cell. He turned to the guard down the block. "Barone."

91

"What? I'm busy."

"Get unbusy. Now. Come here."

Paul Barone sighed and walked over. "Yea?"

With a tilt of his head Jim Albright motioned for him to look inside Allen West's cell.

Paul's eyes widened. "Oh, shit."

Both guards looked incredulously at the inmate as another tear slowly rolled down the his face.

Molly rarely had trouble falling asleep even after the most hectic nights at Juanita's. But earlier this morning, after she had gratefully slid her tired body into bed, sleep had eluded her. She had tried meditating to the rhythmic lapping of water against the hull of the houseboat, yet was unable to excise a strange feeling in the pit of her stomach. When Connor was alive and she'd get these feelings, her husband would say they were premonitions – a gift she should cultivate. But she always cynically dismissed her so-called premonitions as a trick the mind played after an event had happened. Yet tonight, unable to sleep, she again felt the feeling of something... she didn't know what... being amiss.

Connor. She missed being in his arms so much it hurt. If he were here he would hold her and tell her everything was going to be okay, and she would believe him. Connor. No one else in the world could convince her the light at the end of the tunnel wasn't a train heading in her direction. Connor. Only a boy when he had gone to Korea saying, "it's my turn to serve," just as his best friend Tony had done in World War Two. "I'll come back," she remembered him saying with a sweet smile. "Tony survived the Pacific and he'll get us both through Korea."

Molly had been below deck a year later playing with two year-old Tommy when the same grim premonition had gripped her. She could never explain how, though she hadn't yet seen the two somber men standing on the dock, ramrod straight in their dress blue uniforms, she had felt their presence. In something akin to a trance she put down the toy blocks she was holding, stand up, and walk up to the stern of the boat to hear the men speak of a place in Korea called the Punchbowl and of a brave young Marine who died saving other Marines.

That was eleven years ago.

Now, this morning, as Molly lay inert in her bed, she wondered what those young men must have thought of her. They delivered the worst possible news to a soldier's wife yet... she displayed no emotion. How could she explain to them her premonition, how she already knew about Connor and, within the short walk to the deck of her boat, already accepted her husband of only five years was gone... forever.

Molly opened her eyes to 1962, and was suddenly possessed by a need to see Tommy. She swung her legs over the side of the bed and walked through the galley to her son's bedroom. Pulling open the accordion door a few inches she peered inside and saw the blanket covering her son gently rise and fall with his breathing. She smiled with relief. He was fine. So... why today was she enveloped by the same feeling as that awful day eleven years ago? This June morning was so perfect with a cool breeze and soft waves and her son sleeping so peacefully. She started to feel foolish to be in such a dark place. Life is good, Molly, why do you do this to yourself?

I don't know, she answered back. But I do know it's time to get some sleep.

8:43 am

"Son-of-a-bitch! That cheap son-of-a-bitch!"

Ron Lowendowski had been hunched over the typewriter in the KRAN newsroom, preparing for his next newscast, when he heard the cascade of expletives emanating from the neighboring studio. "So much for sound-proof walls," he said to himself with a wry smile. Through the large pane of glass separating his newsroom from the main on-air studio, Ron saw Nick Sullivan, the station's morning disc-jockey, furiously hurl a cartridge tape across the room.

Leaving the script for his newscast on the table, Ron opened the heavy door separating the not-so-soundproof rooms and laughed. Sullivan was standing with his hands on his knees, trying to catch his breath.

"Jesus, Nick, if throwing a cart gets you winded maybe it's time to quit the habit."

Sullivan, hunched and breathing hard, didn't bother to look up. "Well, he did it again. That cheap son-of-a-bitch did it again and I'm left holding the bag."

Ron placed his hands on his own knees, mimicking the disc-jockey's stance, so they were face-level. "You know," Ron said in a drawl exposing his southern roots, "it was tough enough to get the old man to put a crowbar in his wallet and buy those cart machines. And you can be sure he's keeping track of each and every cart. Come on, this bending is no good for my back," he said as he helped the disc-jockey stand up. He looked at the mangled pile of springs, plastic and recording tape. "You know those sum-bitches are expensive."

Nick chuckled as he stood up and said "Yea? He can take it out of my pay."

"Don't think he won't."

"How's he going to know it was me? Unless you rat me out," Nick said with narrowed, accusatory eyes.

"I think you got more important problems, my friend."

"Yea? Like what?"

Ron smirked. "Like your record is ending."

Nick's head whipped around and saw the needle on the spinning record perilously close to the center of the turntable. "Shit."

Ron watched as Nick leaped across the studio (no small feat for a big guy like Nick) and turn on his microphone just as the last notes of the song faded into scratches of empty vinyl. The disc-jockey had already begun his patter as he clumsily grabbed for his headphones. "Fifteen Ten K-R-A-N with today's sound for today's San Francisco. That was Gene Pitney number five on the R-A-N hit list with "The Man Who Shot Liberty Valance..."

A quick glance to Nick's left revealed an empty turntable. A glance to his right and he saw the cart machines were empty, too. It was the classic disc-jockey nightmare; nothing to play and dead air looming. Ah, but not so fast. Without missing a syllable Nick continued his patter. "K-R-A-N morning drive time is eight forty-five and we've got a sunny start to this June twelfth, San Francisco..." As he spoke he grabbed a record from the top of a stack and, with a flick of his wrist, flipped the vinyl out its protective sleeve and dropped it precisely in the middle of the turntable.

Ron grinned. He loved watching Nick in action, especially when he had to scramble like this. He watched as the disc-jockey spoke to his audience with bookie-confidence about the Giants' chances in today's game against the Cincinnati Reds, as he simultaneously lifted the tonearm, set it gently on the outer edge of the record, then push the button which started the turntable spinning. Through the Nick's blaring headset (how he wasn't deaf was a mystery) Ron heard the first notes of a song as Nick shouted, "and now boys and girls let's all go across this great country to New Jersey with Freddie Boom-Boom Cannon and Palisades Park." Just as Nick stopped talking Cannon started singing "Last night I took a walk after dark..."

The disc-jockey turned off his microphone, threw off his headphones and slumped in his chair.

"Nice. Very nice," Ron said, applauding.

"Ah, shit, if you can't hit the post you don't belong on the radio," Nick said as he picked a new record off the stack and laid it on the other turntable.

"So why so pissed?"

"Oh yea, so get this," Nick said as he took out a pack of cigarettes from his shirt pocket and pulled one out with his lips. "Last Friday the Colonel –"

"– Oh, man, I hate when you call him that. He was a supply sergeant during the war."

Nick smiled. He loved getting Lowendowski's "Irish" up. Even if the newsman's family was from Poland. "I know, I know. And he was stateside the whole time, too."

Ron scowled. "Yea, well, just because some veteran's group decided to hand out an honorary title to a rich kid whose daddy bought him a radio station..." He stopped and exhaled, shaking his head. "Sorry man."

"No, I'm sorry, I know it gets your goat."

"Anyway, finish your story."

The disc-jockey brightened. "Yea, right, so the Colonel – sorry, Mac Bailey – he comes in here last Friday and hands me a piece of paper and says, 'announce this every hour.' So I ask, 'what is it' and he says 'I heard another station is giving away a pony. We're gonna give one away, too.' So, you know me, Ron, I'm a team player

96

_"

"Oh, yea, you're a regular Willie Mays."

Ignoring him, Nick lit his cigarette and, in between puffs, continued. "So I start saying every hour 'hey kids K-R-A-N is giving away a pony to some lucky listener.'" He stopped and took a drag from his cigarette.

"So?"

"So? So? So there's no fucking pony that's what's so. Bailey calls on the hotline this morning and says to announce a contest for Giants tickets. I ask him 'what about the pony?' and he says... now get this... he says 'oh, we're not gonna do that anymore.' Now I gotta answer calls from listeners who want to know 'where's the fucking pony?'"

Nick knew it was the situation at which Ron was now laughing, but he couldn't resist a return zing. "So what about you, Cronkite?" he said as he took another drag on his cigarette while he loaded a commercial into a cart machine. "Still dreaming about that TV gig?"

"Now why would I want to leave all this?" Ron said as he waved his arms around the studio.

"Oh yea, we're living the dream," Nick replied, rolling his eyes. "At least the checks don't bounce."

"As long as you're one of the first to cash them on Friday."

The two men laughed at the sad truth, for there were Fridays when the slowest employees had handed a bank teller their check only to be told funds were not in the account to cover it.

Ron looked down at the ground and sighed. "I just need a break, you know? A story that's all mine. A big story, you know, one where I'm not picking up the crumbs from the Chronicle or KCBS." Nick smiled. He'd seen the desperate, hungry look in his friend dozens of times. He had also heard the newsman's rant enough times to know what was coming next. "Ah, but who am I kidding?" Ron said. "They all have vans with remote transmitters. I have to drive my own car and all we have is an old reel-to-reel tape machine."

"Look at this way," the disc-jockey said before taking a drag from his cigarette.

"Yeah?" Ron said, impatiently.

"With your radio face you're better off not being on camera, anyway," Nick said, smirking. Before Ron could reply, the disc-jockey put on his headphones and held up his hand, indicating he was about to turn on his microphone.

Ron stood there watching as Nick flawlessly read another commercial with such sincerity even Ron believed he bought floor tile from Murray the Bay Area Tile Guy. Meanwhile, at the same time, he picked up another record and placed it gently on a turntable while, with the other hand, gymnastically flipped off the newsman. Who says you don't develop skills in radio? Ron chuckled to himself. He might have stayed in the studio but, through the station's "sound-proof" walls he heard a series of bells coming from the newsroom.

A bulletin was coming across the teletype machine.

Tony Marianetti had lived in Sausalito his whole life and knew it was impossible to keep a lid on the biggest news since the Golden Gate Bridge opened. He was right. The alert from Alcatraz had come into the station barely over an hour ago but the phone was already ringing off the hook from callers who claimed to see the escapees simultaneously at a dozen different locations around town. It would be funny were it not so serious.

He had called an "all hands" meeting for nine and now Tony stood, hands on hips, thumbs firmly tucked in his belt, patiently waiting for his three deputies, dispatcher and secretary to settle into their seats.

"All right, let's get started," he said as the last rumble of chatter died off. Tony paused, employing a little trick he learned from one of his sergeants in the Marines. Taking that extra moment ensured all eyes and ears were fully focused on him. He cleared his throat. "You all know that three men escaped from Alcatraz last night. The likelihood any survived in the water long enough to make it to land is very low. But it's still a possibility, so I want you to pay special attention to any reports of thefts. Clothing... food... cars. Especially cars. If any of these boys did make landfall they're going to want to take it on the lam... fast and far." He scanned the room, making a point of looking everyone directly in the eyes (another lesson from his old sergeant) and was glad for the serious expressions on everyone's faces. Now it was time to soften his tone. "Finally, let's remember there are citizens out there who are scared. We want them to know that we have their safety in mind at all times and this department is taking every report seriously."

"Even Ethel Mackenzie?" came a voice from the back of the room. Laughter and a few groans filled the station. Ethel Mackenzie. Every jurisdiction has at least one Ethel, a person for whom every barking dog, snapping tree branch or back-firing car was a reason to call the National Guard.

Tony held up his hands and acknowledged their derision with a small smile. "Yes, even our Miss Mackenzie. I know, she can be trigger-happy but she's been around this town a long time."

"I heard she was here to greet the Indians," said another voice in the back.

Tony smiled – just enough for the sake of camaraderie – as the group laughed. Then he held up his hands and got serious again. "You all have your assignments. Stay focused. Make me proud. Dismissed." He watched, with satisfaction, as they dispersed. Tony was sure they were up to the challenge of keeping the town calm over the next few days. He was also sure the Coast Guard would find their bodies floating in the bay. There was no way those men made it more than a few hundred yards from the prison before the cold water pulled them down to their deaths.

Don't throw up.

Hector Gonzales had been repeating it to himself ever since the Coast Guard boat lurched from its mooring at Golden Gate Station, swung passed Port Cavallo and accelerated north. Between the nervous beating of his heart, the rhythmic pounding of the boat attacking the water and the throbbing of his hangover, keeping everything down was a challenge. His only comfort came from the refreshing spray on his face as the boat bounced emphatically through the wake of a large cutter which was leading the flotilla. Occasionally Hector would look across deck at Ian. He didn't seem to be suffering any ill-effects from their night at Juanita's. In fact... he seemed to be having the time of his life. Asshole.

"We're going to start our run," the captain of the TRS (one of the many sturdy 36 foot wooden boats in the Coast Guard's fleet) shouted through a megaphone. "You boots remember to keep one hand on the railing at all times. I don't want to have to turn around to fish you out of the water." Hector looked around deck and saw everyone at their assigned positions. Despite the hangover's relentless reminder of last night's bad decisions he was excited to be a part of this mission. No doubt everyone in the fleet was wondering the same thing – could three men who entered

100

the water at Alcatraz Island last night still be alive? And what if they somehow procured weapons? Tangling with armed escapees was not something Hector wanted to do on his first real assignment on the water. His hope was, as the commander said during the briefing, the bay had claimed three more lives and theirs was just a mission to locate the dead bodies.

Hector gripped the port railing and scanned the water between their small wooden motor launch and the line of sheer cliffs south of Sausalito, bathed in yellow from the rising sun. The boat was now passing a large rock – as tall as the cliff itself – which jutted into the water. Wedged between the rock and the cliff was a tiny notch of sand. As the boat plowed forward something on the sand caught his attention... a fleeting glimpse of... was that a man... or just a shadow? Hector fumbled to bring his binoculars to his eyes but by the time he found the notch of sand and adjusted the focus... his ghost was gone. Hector looked hopefully at the two other crewmen stationed on his side of the boat, but saw their binoculars were still hung around their necks. He shook his head (a move his hangover caused him to regret) and pursed his lips. A shadow caused by the rising sun? A leftover from last night's revelry? He didn't actually see a body. And shadows are not something a brand new Coast Guardsman on his very first mission should be reporting.

Hector watched the tiny beach and the large rock disappear from view as the boat continued north.

Tommy O'Conner's eyes popped open. The sun was already up and the prism hanging in front of his only window was splitting its light into a beautiful rainbow. He liked to lay on his bed and study the colors as they slowly spread across his ceiling. The world had decreed there were only seven; Red Orange Yellow Green Blue Indigo and Violet (good old ROY G. BIV) but Tommy knew the answer was more complex. In between those seven colors were hundreds more, making it impossible to tell exactly where red turned to orange or green turned to blue. It got even harder because in between those hundreds of colors were hundreds more colors in between them... a thousand shades of red and orange and yellow. The supposedly simple rainbow of seven colors? It was more complex than that, and Tommy liked this feeling of knowing something everyone else did not.

Holy cow, he almost forgot! Tommy threw back the covers and jumped out of bed. Today was the day he and Billy were going to work on Billy's new boat. Tommy liked hanging around with Billy, even though his family was rich. Okay, maybe not rich like mansion rich but Billy wasn't living on a houseboat. His home was up in the Marin Hills. Yet, for all his family's money, Billy hadn't yet gotten a boat of his own which was kind of funny to Tommy, who years ago had gotten an old skiff and fixed it up real nice with the help of some of his mom's friends. Billy's boat was a new aluminum job... real sweet. It wasn't tied up here at one of the old gates in Sausalito, either, it was down in Horseshoe Bay at the Presidio Yacht Club. The Yacht Club!

Having a mom who worked nights had its advantages if you were a kid, for sure. Tommy wasn't subjected to a lot of "where are you going?" and "what time will you be back?" Of course Molly cared about Tommy but raising him by herself meant he had to grow up a bit faster than other boys. Which is why the chalk board was introduced into the houseboat. Molly was always pretty proud of herself for coming up with the idea. There were always a few "tut tuts" from some of the other parents who questioned how any child could develop without constant supervision and monitoring. Tommy proved them wrong, although Molly would never hear anyone admit it.

In the kitchen/common area Molly had attached a small chalk board to the refrigerator and tied a piece of chalk and an eraser on strings so they could leave each other messages.

TOMMY
BROUGHT HOME LEFTOVERS FOR YOUR
LUNCH. HAVE FUN WITH BILLY! IT'S
CHILLY! WEAR YOUR WINDBREAKER!

Another advantage of having a mom who worked at a restaurant was the food Juanita let her take home at the end of her shift. Tommy opened the refrigerator door and saw the brown paper bag his mother left for him. The bag opened with a crinkle and he inhaled. Oh boy, lunch was gonna be good! Tommy placed the bag on the small table and reached back inside for a bottle of milk for his cereal. The morning was chilly enough for some hot oatmeal, but he was too excited and anxious to bother. Tony the Tiger would suffice this morning.

Cereal consumed and the bowl (kinda sorta) cleaned, Tommy ran back to his room to grab the windbreaker from his closet and then ran back to the kitchen. He was just about to step up onto the deck when he remembered the chalk board. He grabbed the eraser and wiped off his mother's message, picked up the chalk and wrote:

GOING TO BILLY'S
THANKS FOR THE LUNCH
TOMMY

Why Tommy always signed his message he couldn't say, but he had been doing it since they started using the

103

blackboard and it became both a habit and kind of a joke between them. He stepped up onto the deck and felt a cool breeze coming off the bay and decided his mother was right about the windbreaker. Chilly as it was, he was still looking forward to the ride down to Horseshoe Bay on his bike. It was gonna be a good day.

Then he heard the crunch of tires on gravel and saw Tony Marianetti exiting his police cruiser.

Ugh.

"Good morning, Tommy," the policeman said as he walked up the gangplank.

Tommy had been reminded too many times to always be polite. "Morning... sir," he coughed out as he walked off the deck.

"Where are you heading?"

Tommy wanted to ask him what business it was of his, instead he mumbled, "Horseshoe Bay."

"Well, just be careful and keep an eye out for anything unusual, okay?"

Unusual? What the hell was he talking about? Tommy said to himself. He wondered if he was doing a good job hiding his annoyance at the interruption.

"You didn't hear about the escape?"

Tommy shook his head.

"Cons broke out of Alcatraz last night."

Wait a second. What? This was big. His eyes widened with the exciting news. "No kidding?"

Tony grinned. The kid was putty in his hands, now. "Yep, every police force around the bay is on alert. Coast Guard and Army have been mobilized, too. Look," he said, pointing out to the bay. "You hear all the boats out there this morning? Helicopters, too, see?"

Tommy turned. Gosh, he had been so excited about working on Billy's boat he hadn't noticed all the commotion out on the bay. Tony was right. Lots of boats

104

and Tommy could even hear the thumping of helicopters off in the distance. What a cool way to start the summer. He couldn't wait to tell Billy and the rest of the guys.

"Not that anyone thinks they could have survived, anyway," Tony said as he patted his belt authoritatively. Tommy's eyes rolled. "But if they did and they show up in my jurisdiction we'll be ready."

Tommy hated how he emphasized the word *my*. "Yea, well, thanks for letting us know, Chief."

"Make sure you tell your mom I was here, okay? And tell her not to worry, I've got everything under control."

"Well, she's asleep but I'll leave her a note."

"And remember to tell her I was here."

Tommy nodded grudgingly and walked back down the steps into the kitchen. Over at the chalkboard, under his original note, he added:

LISTEN TO THE RADIO
FINALLY SOME EXCITEMENT
AROUND HERE!

Should he mention the escape? Nah, no sense is making his mother worried. Besides, she was going to be asleep until the middle of the day and by then they'll either have captured the men or found their bodies.

Tommy hated that Tony actually seemed to want them to show up in Sausalito. Maybe if he spent more time out in the bay he'd know how ridiculous it was to think those men could have survived, anyway. He peered topside to make sure the policeman was gone. One conversation a day with Tony was enough. Tommy reached into the fridge and grabbed his Boy Scout canteen which he had filled the night before. Then he went topside to his most treasured possession, his bicycle.

Raised on TV westerns Tommy and his friends felt

105

their bicycles were just like cowboys and their horses. His friends liked Wyatt Earp and Laramie but Tommy's favorite was Sugarfoot, a show about a cowboy who was studying to be a lawyer. Sugarfoot was different from all the other television cowboys, even if none of the other guys thought he was as tough. Tommy thought it was neat that the hero carried around a law book.

One thing about Westerns all the guys could agree on was the horses. They were the real stars. Some horses were even smarter than the people who rode them. How many times did the wounded hero instruct his horse to "head back to town and tell the sheriff I need help." Tommy and his friends all wished they had horses. Instead, they had bicycles, which couldn't go back to town and get help by themselves.

Okay, so bicycles were not as smart as horses, but Tommy liked to pretend he was on one as he raced down Bridgeway along the waterfront, passing City Hall and the Library and the toy store, slowing down only once... as he passed the bakery to take a deep breath and smell. On the way back, he promised himself, I'll pick up something for mom. His trusty horse now carried him past Hurricane Gulch and, after a few twists and turns, onto East Road which ran along the bay. Tommy looked at his watch and, seeing how early he was, decided to pull over to the side of the road near Yellow Bluff.

All the locals knew Yellow Bluff. It was a huge rock jutting out into the bay used by boaters as a landmark for navigation. It wasn't useful for much else, you couldn't anchor and picnic there because of the small boulders and even smaller rocks piled below the bluff at water's edge. The only reason to even think about anchoring below Yellow Bluff was a small, triangular patch of rocky sand on its south side. Boaters generally stayed away. No one was keen to have their hulls breached – they are expensive to repair and, worse, it was embarrassing to be known as the boater who did something so stupid. Tommy had heard rumors of one couple, seeking privacy, taking the risk. They had rented a motorboat and tried to picnic on the beach and do something adults would only smirk about. The couple needed to be rescued when their boat sank right in front of them.

Tommy lay his bike on the ground and walked along a dirt path to the edge of the bluff and smiled the kind of smile a boy of thirteen makes when he has a bunch of good friends and a whole summer ahead of him with no school. The view from here was pretty cool. Off in the distance, across the bay, he could see the sun rising over the four towers of the San Francisco-Oakland Bay Bridge. To his right was the more famous bridge, the Golden Gate, so close it seemed he could almost touch its distinctive red towers. He took a big, happy gulp of fresh, free air and his smile got even bigger.

He looked down the bluff to where the little patch of sand met the water and – what is that on the sand? Tommy blinked, thinking that the sun had blurred his vision. He looked again. Blinking had not erased the image of something... an object of some kind on the sand. Tommy looked at his watch. Well, he was early anyway. Plenty of time to investigate.

To reach the beach below he would have to climb backwards down a steep, narrow path, like a mountaineer. Turning his back to the water he felt around with his foot until it rested on the path and then, step by tentative step, he slowly crawled his way down. When Tommy felt the crunch of sand under his feet, he knew he had made it to the bottom. He turned around and realized what he had seen from the top of bluff.

There were two bodies.

And they were moving.

Tommy inched closer and saw there were two men. They were alive and breathing, although it seemed just barely. He moved closer for a better look. His foot landed on a twig which made a decisive snap, jolting one of the men, who looked up. He stared disbelievingly into Tommy's eyes and mouthed something which the boy couldn't make out. He stepped closer.

"Water. Do you have any... water."

Tommy dumbly nodded. He motioned to the top of the bluff, and the man acknowledged with a blink of his eyelids. Tommy nodded, turned, and crawled back up the path, his mind still not comprehending what he had seen. Once at the top of the bluff he ran to his bicycle and slung the canteen over his shoulder. He was about to head back when he saw the brown bag lunch his mother had left for him. They were probably hungry, too. He tucked the top of the bag into his belt so his hands would be free for the trip back down the bluff. Tommy repeated his backward crawl and, once on the small beach, took two short steps to the men.

He handed his canteen to the one who had called out so desperately for water. But, instead of drinking, Tommy watched him reached under the shoulders of the other man in his arms and try to sit him up. It was obvious he didn't have the necessary strength. He looked at Tommy who instinctively ran over, reached under the second man to help bring him to a sitting position. Tommy looked at the second man's legs. One of them didn't look right. Kind of twisted. He watched as the canteen was raised to his lips.

"Clarence. It's John," the first man said. "We made it, brother. We made it. I got water. Come on. Drink."

Now Tommy knew both their names. And he knew they were brothers. He watched as John poured a small amount of water over Clarence's lips which parted, his tongue reaching out for the liquid. "That's it, Clarence, good," he said as his brother pursed his lips and took a swallow of water from the canteen. John smiled gratefully at Tommy, who saw how parched John's own lips were. He must have been equally as thirsty but was intent on serving his brother first. Clarence took a couple of small swallows of water and then weakly pushed the canteen back to John.

"Are you sure?" John asked. His brother nodded and John gratefully took a few swallows. Then he looked up at Tommy and in a hoarse voice asked, "Where?"

It took Tommy a few seconds to realize what he was being asked. He sputtered out "Sausalito. South of town, really, about a mile. We call it Yellow Bluff."

Tommy couldn't be sure, but he thought he heard Clarence – the one still sitting on the ground – ask his brother something like "what now?" He got no response. John was busy looking around, first at the steep path to the top of the bluff, then around the small beach and then back at his brother. It must have been the first time he realized there was something wrong with his brother's leg. Tommy heard Clarence say something – he wasn't sure what – then heard John say, "it's too steep."

They were all quiet for a while as John and Clarence took turns with the canteen. The sun, moving slowly up into the sky, reflected off the bluff behind them, warming the beach. The only noise was of seagulls noisily circling overhead, waiting for returning fishing boats.

John looked up at the birds, and then at Tommy. It was clear speaking was difficult, but he managed to croak out a question. "What's your name, kid?"

"Tommy."

John took another small swig from the canteen. "I'm John," he said with continuing difficulty. "This is my brother Clarence. We... we were on a ship last night and

109

fell overboard. Well, Clarence here did and I went in after him. Couldn't do nothing, right? The next thing we knew the ship was gone and we had only one chance, to make it to shore."

Like most kids, Tommy knew adults have a certain way of talking when they're full of shit. Like the time one of Tommy's classmates died from polio (his parents wouldn't let him get vaccinated) and all the adults said things like "he's with God, now" as if he and the other kids didn't know what death is. Parents say kids are terrible liars but what do kids have to lie about? Stealing a cookie from the cookie jar? Breaking a window playing ball? Parents are the ones lying about death and divorce and really big things...

Like escaping from prison.

Tommy looked at the two bedraggled men on the ground and got angry they thought he was so stupid to believe their story about falling off a ship. They were lying. Just like every adult. If their story were true wouldn't they have begged him to "get the police" or "call our shipping company"?

If the brothers were aware Tommy knew who they really were, they didn't show it. John and Clarence had been in enough scrapes together and were well-practiced in displaying innocent demeanors.

His first thought was to return the lie and tell them he would go back up the bluff to get more water. He would, instead, bike to a telephone and tell the police what he had discovered. Tommy would be a hero for turning in two escaped convicts. Boy, wouldn't that be something? Then, this fall, when the teacher asked, "what did you do on your summer vacation?" he could reply "I found the men who escaped from Alcatraz." He thought about how proud his mother would be to see his picture on the front page of the newspaper. Then, as the image coalesced in his mind, another figure appeared in the picture.

Tony.

Damn it. Yellow Bluff was in Sausalito. If he called the cops it would be Tony who showed up. Tommy could just see him taking all the credit as he patted his gun belt and loudly told his mother how he had rescued her son from two escaped felons. The thought made him sick. He knew who Tony really was. Despite what his mother said, he knew what happened in Korea. Tony was no hero.

Tommy looked carefully at the brothers. John could barely sit up and something was seriously wrong with Clarence's leg. These men weren't dangerous. In fact, Tommy thought, they were actually kind of pathetic. There was something else about them. It was the way John, thirsty as he must have been, made sure his brother Clarence got water before he did. To have a brother who would do that... well, all his life Tommy had wondered what it would have been like to have a brother, how different life would be if Tony had done what he promised and kept his father safe. So yeah, it would go against all logic for a thirteen year old boy to help two escaped convicts from getting caught. But it also went against logic he should go through life without a father.

Tommy then remembered a poem the teacher had once read in class. There was this one line she had made a big deal about, of two roads diverging and what it meant to take the one less traveled. Tommy was only ten at the time but the idea of being at a place in life at which one could make a decision affecting the whole rest of it... well, it really stuck with him. Mostly because he couldn't see how a boy living on a houseboat in Sausalito whose every move was dictated by mom and by school could ever get the chance to make such a decision. But here he was, only three years later and Tommy could see the two roads diverging.

111

The decision to travel down the road less traveled? It was not as hard as he imagined it would be. Clouded as it might be by anger at the world at least it would be he making the decision, not his mother or God or the Bomb making it for him. But Tommy first had to make clear to the men shivering before him they were not to treat him as a child. He took a deep breath. "I'll help you," he said to the two men.

"Thank you," John said. "We'll need –"

"Wait," Tommy interrupted. "First, you have to tell me the truth. I gotta know I can trust you. You didn't fall off any ship, did you?"

John looked at Clarence, who returned with a nod which began a conversation with their eyes. Tommy watched, a bit jealously, as they silently communicated. John sighed and nodded again before looking up.

Sometimes the hardest thing to say is the secret everybody knows, because saying the secret out loud gives it substance and weight and makes it real. "All right, Tommy," he began, "You're a smart kid. You're right. We didn't fall off any ship." John took a breath and said the words. "We escaped from Alcatraz last night."

There it was. And now, Tommy knew, he had taken the first step down the road not taken, one from which there was no turning back. He listened to the distant whine of motorboats crisscrossing the bay. Growing up on a houseboat Tommy had heard the sound hundreds of times from hundreds of boats, and it had always soothed him... made him feel a part of the bay. Now, the sound made him nervous. Nervous? No, that wasn't it... it was some other feeling. Nervous is what you got before a test. Those motorboats and ships and helicopters were hunting the two men laying on the beach before him. Now that he had agreed to help them, they would be hunting him, too. It should have scared the hell out of him. But it didn't.

"Thank you for telling me," he said to the brothers.

"You still gonna help us?"

Tommy nodded.

"Thank you," John said.

"Yeah, thank you," Clarence croaked.

"Okay, first things first," Tommy began, surprised by the confidence in his voice. He decided right away he liked that sound. "You need dry clothes. More water. Food. I can get that stuff from home now. Then, tonight, when my ma goes to work –"

"Tonight? Geez, kid, we're sitting ducks out here."

"Actually this is the best place you could have landed. Almost no one ever comes here. The beach is too small and no one wants to risk ripping their boat open on those rocks," he said, pointing to an outcropping near the shore. "Just stay in the shadow by this bluff and you should be okay. I'll come back tonight with my skiff –"

"Your what?"

"Skiff, it's like a small boat. It has a flat bottom so I can bring it right onto the beach and take you someplace on the mainland."

"But where? My brother's leg... I don't think he can walk much."

John was right. Clarence didn't look very good. Tommy paused and pictured a map of the coastline in his head, crossing off potential landing spots as either too busy or too steep for Clarence to climb. Then he brightened. He remembered the perfect spot.

"You got a place," John said, smiling.

Tommy nodded. "Yea, I do. Okay, I'm gonna go now but I'll be back as soon as I can." He was about to turn away when he realized he still had the brown bag of food tucked into his belt. "I totally forgot," he said holding out the bag to John, "This was gonna be my lunch."

John took the bag. It opened with a satisfying

crinkle. The young boy watched as John pulled out a hamburger, wrapped in wax paper. It was obvious to Tommy how hungry he was but John first tore off a piece and placed in his brother's mouth. Clarence chewed slowly, with his eyes closed. John looked gratefully at Tommy. "Thank you," he said, before taking some for himself.

Tommy nodded, watching for a few more seconds as the brothers ate before turning and climbing back up to the top of the bluff. From there, he would continue his trip on the road less traveled.

Warden Olin Blackwell scanned the sky and then looked impatiently at his watch. When one's job is watching over hundreds of men serving prison sentences – men who have nothing but time on their hands – patience is not just a virtue but a necessity. But Olin Blackwell couldn't stop thinking how, sixty miles away, somewhere in or near San Francisco Bay there were at least three men who had escaped from his prison. And this made him very impatient.

The game warden had brought him to the Seaplane base on Lake Berryessa so Blackwell could phone the assistant warden, Art Dollison, for an update. Blackwell knew Art was a good man who had been at The Rock since '54, twice as long as he and so knew the island like the back of his hand.

"Art, can you hear me okay?"

"I can hear you just fine, Olin."

"Give me the bad news first. What's the count?" Blackwell asked as he pulled another cigarette from the pack with his lips.

"Three."

"Jesus."

114

"Yea."

"Do we know when?"

"That's the next bit of bad news, Blackie. They left after lights out last night and we didn't know they were gone –"

"– until this morning," Blackwell interrupted, looking at his watch. "Yea, I guessed as much. So they've had at least a ten hour head start."

"Yes, sir."

Shit. Ten critical hours... lost.

Dollison could feel the warden's frustration over the phone. "On the plus side I've had the island searched by the guards. They've checked every corner, including the launch at the dock."

Blackwell nodded with satisfaction, taking another puff from his cigarette. "Good. I wasn't expecting you'd find them on the island, but it was a good use of the time in case they planned this as diversion."

"I'm glad you agree."

"What's the status of the search off island?"

"Well, to start, the army is sending a squad to Angel Island."

Blackwell allowed himself a chuckle. "Heh, I almost want those prisoners to have gone to Angel so they can face a squad of armed soldiers."

"Well, that's where the Coast Guard says last night's currents were most likely to bring them."

"Okay, what else?"

"We sent a telex to the state police and they relayed it to all the local police and sheriff departments. Let them know to keep an eye out and to call us if they get any solid sightings."

Blackwell smiled. He could just imagine the excitement the escape was providing some of those small towns. "Did you reach Washington?"

"Fred Wilkinson's coming on the next flight out."

"Fred's a good man."

"Yes, sir. How soon until you get here?"

"I'm waiting for a seaplane that makes a regular run up here. The bureau asked they take me directly to the island. They'll radio when we're close. When I get there have everyone meet me in the conference room. I'll want a full report. Hey, I think I hear a plane. Yea, the ranger's nodding it's the seaplane. I'll see you shortly."

"Yes, sir," the assistant warden said. There was silence on the phone, but something told him not to hang up.

"Damn shame," he heard Blackwell abruptly blurt.

"We'll find them, Warden," Dollison said.

"No, I meant the fish. They were really biting today."

Pavlov's dogs.

As Ron Lowendowski raced around the corner into the KRAN newsroom he thought about the scientist who trained dogs to salivate at the sound of a bell. Ron liked to joke he was like one of those dogs except the bells clanging from the teletype machine didn't signal food, but a story. The more bells, the bigger the story. The bigger the story, well... the bigger the opportunity to shine and maybe get the attention of a TV station in need of talent. And so, the more he salivated.

Ten bells were reserved for only the biggest stories like the attack on Pearl Harbor or the death of Franklin Roosevelt. Ron experienced ten bells just once, five years ago. He had been hovering over the station's ancient Model 15 teletype machine (think of an over-sized, much noisier typewriter) as its keys flew upwards towards a black ribbon, where they would pound out the latest news on a roll of cheap yellow paper. On this particular

116

afternoon Ron was not waiting for a news story. He had gotten three-to-one odds on the Braves to beat the Yankees in the World Series and those fifty bucks he handed to a bookie gave him more than a rooting interest in what was now a seven-game series. With the seventh game tied in the seventh inning, Ron's head was mere inches from the paper when the machine suddenly clanged like a fire engine, ten bells comically sending him backwards onto his heels. As he rocked forward he saw the bulletin as it was being printed: POPE PIUS VII DEAD. The World Series – and his fifty bucks – would have to wait. Within minutes he was on the phone with the head of the Archdiocese, Bishop Mitty, getting the time-worn "local angle." The result was his usual solid report with a nice "sound bite" of the Bishop expressing sadness for the Pontiff's passing. But it was nothing special. Nothing to separate him from the pack.

As he ran to the newsroom this morning Ron silently counted bells. Four... five... six... then, silence. He slowed his pace to a funereal crawl. It wasn't a president or pope's death. Probably nothing better than a boating accident or a politician announcing a run for higher office. (Yes, 'better' was how he expressed it.) He lumbered disappointingly to the machine and retrieved the paper on which he read the following:

BULLETIN

SAN FRANCISCO JUNE 12 - - - THREE, POSSIBLY MORE, CONVICTS HAVE ESCAPED FROM THE PRISON AT ALCATRAZ ISLAND. MEN ARE NOT BELIEVED TO BE ARMED BUT STILL CONSIDERED DANGEROUS.
COAST GUARD TO JOIN SEARCH OF SAN FRANCISCO BAY. ARMY UNIT BEING SENT

TO ANGEL ISLAND, CLOSEST TO ALCATRAZ.
LOCAL POLICE IN TOWNS SURROUNDING
THE BAY ON HIGH ALERT.

30

Dumb bastards. They'll freeze to death out there, just like all the others. (In the mood he was in there wasn't much room for sympathy.) But a story is a story – even if it was the same one every other station around the bay would report. He sighed as he ripped the paper off the teletype. Ron started walking to the main studio to deliver the bulletin when he was stopped by a thought. Maybe there was something here. A few years ago... Mac had him do a puff piece on the Coast Guard station at Golden Gate. Mac was always pushing for stories about one service or another so Ron had dutifully driven over the bridge and interviewed the station commander and a few of the cadets. Ron scowled, remembering Mac actually stood behind him while he edited the tape to be sure he really pumped up the patriotic angle.

An idea began to foment in the newsman's brain... maybe he could do a story on the search for the escapees... hitch a ride on one of the Coast Guard's boats... get lots of sound of the boat churning through the water... the chatter between the men on deck... there was lots of action there... oh, man, that's the kind of story that would show other stations what he could do.

"Hey, Lowendowski."

"What?" Ron, jolted from his thoughts, said brusquely. It was Nick.

"The Giants are playing the Reds tonight. I can get you some good odds. They've lost six in a row but I figure with Marichal on the mound they got a good chance."

"Uh huh." Ron said, still not looking the disc-jockey

118

in the eyes.

"Hey man, I was thinking I could even get the Colonel to throw down a few bucks. That old Commie-hater would love betting against a team called the Reds, right?"

Silence. Rick took two steps toward the newsman. "I said, the Colonel would love betting against a team called the Reds."

Nothing. The disc-jockey shrugged his shoulders and was about to walk out when Ron suddenly said "Hey, Sullivan."

"Oh, he can talk?" Nick said with a smirk.

"Where's the key to the equipment closet?"

"Um, same place it's always been, on the chief engineer's belt, with all the other keys to this place."

Ron snapped his fingers. "Right, Phil Shea has them," he said as he brushed past the disc-jockey.

"Where are you going?" Rick asked.

"I need a tape recorder," Ron replied as he headed down the hallway.

"What the hell for?"

"My new job on television."

Rick laughed. "Yea. Good luck with that," he said even though Ron was already out of sight. Then he turned and headed back to his studio just as the record he was playing faded to blank vinyl...

10:00 am

Tommy's heart raced a he pumped his bicycle back towards his houseboat. Out in the bay he could hear the whine of motorboats and the occasional huffing of helicopters. What if someone saw John and Clarence?

Would the brothers tell the authorities about how Tommy had just helped them? They'd have to explain how they got the canteen, wouldn't they? The canteen! Tommy froze and the bicycle coasted to a stop as he realized, to his horror, all the kids in his troop had written their names on their canteens. How could he explain why he gave water to the escapees? He'd have to say he didn't know who they were. Could they really expect a thirteen year-old boy to figure out the two men escaped from Alcatraz? Adults thought kids were stupid, anyway, right? Tommy slid his feet back onto the bicycle's pedals and pushed forward.

He had been riding north on Bridgeway for a while and soon saw the sign for Gate Four, where his houseboat was moored. He slowed, stepped off his bicycle and, after looking around to be sure there was no Tony Marianetti – or any other policemen – around, he lay his bike on the ground and walked onto the floating dock next to their home.

As soon as his foot hit the deck, he heard his mother calling from below. "Tommy, is that you?"

"Yes, mom," he replied as he stepped down into the kitchen. His mother must have been up for a while, as she was at the table having her usual breakfast – a cup of coffee and a cigarette. He gave her a kiss on the cheek. "Morning."

"Good morning, sweetie. I thought you were going to the marina to help out Billy this morning."

Ugh. Never mind the police, how was he going to explain things to his mother? "Oh... yea, well, when I got there Billy said his mother had some family thing they needed to do."

"Sorry, honey, I know you were looking forward to it."

Tommy, anxious to change the subject, said "you're

up early today."

"Well, I just couldn't sleep. There's been so much commotion out there today."

"Yea?"

"Yes," his mother said in no-so-subtle way adults have of correcting children's speech. "You left me the note on our message board, remember?" she said, pointing to the blackboard.

Tommy felt the muscles on the back of his neck tense. "Oh, yea, right..."

"Well, you know Mrs. Porter from two slips over? She couldn't wait to come over to tell me the news," Molly said as she took another drag from her cigarette. "That woman knows everything, of course, except that I work nights."

Tommy laughed at the joke, then quickly said "Sorry she woke you."

"That's all right, like I said I had trouble sleeping, anyway. I'll grab a nap later. So, what have you heard?"

"Oh, probably what everyone else has. There was an escape. You know..." her son said, trying to keep from fidgeting.

"Well, those poor men are probably dead from the cold."

"Yea?"

"Yes," Molly said, giving Tommy that parent-as-English-teacher look again as she took a long drag from her cigarette. "They must have been crazy to think they could swim in that water." Then, as if emphasizing her statement Molly jammed the remains of her cigarette into the ashtray. "Damn shame."

What an interesting – and surprising – thing for his mother to say. "What do you mean?" Tommy asked.

Molly picked up the pack of cigarettes and with two fingers deftly pulled one out. She stared at it for a few seconds. "We put them in that place because they did something wrong and they have to be punished. But now we'll never know if those men could have changed."

"Changed?"

"Stop being criminals, dear."

Without knowing, Tommy's mother had given him another reason – on top of all the others he had already constructed – to help John and Clarence. He smiled.

"So what are you going to do today?" his mother asked. Tommy hadn't expected her to be up, so he hadn't prepared a story for why he needed water and food and – toughest of all to explain – some of his father's clothes.

"Oh, you know, hang out with some of the guys, maybe. Nothing special."

"Well, since you're not meeting Billy and you don't seem to have any plans why don't you come with me to the Purity and help me shop?"

Normally this was not an invitation welcomed by a thirteen year-old boy, but Tommy knew he had just been handed an opportunity. "Sure, mom," he said as, in his head, he began making a list of what to bring the Anglins later, when his mother took her nap.

"Wonderful. Give me a few minutes to get dressed."

"K"

"You mean 'yes, mother.'"

"Yes ma'am."

She smiled and went into what passed for, on their small houseboat, for her bedroom. Tommy took the time to peek inside the kitchen cabinets to see what canned and boxed food they had. He pursed his lips and was thinking of a plan to replace what he was going to take with him to Yellow Bluff when his mother slid open her bedroom's accordion door. "Are you ready?" she asked as she adjusted a sweater on her shoulders.

"Huh? Oh, yeah, sure. I'm ready."

"Everything okay?"

"Yea, why?"

"Nothing, just asking." Another mom question, delivered in a tone meant for Tommy to know she had detected something unusual in his behavior.

"No, I'm okay."

Now a classic mom 'I-know-you're-really-not' look as Molly said, "Come on, get the cart and we'll go."

Tommy reached into a thin cabinet next to the refrigerator where they kept what he and his mom called their "Little Old Lady" cart; a wire basket with wheels they used to haul groceries from the supermarket. (When you can't afford a car you improvise.)

It wasn't far to the Purity, but as they made their way along Bridgeway they heard lots of people exchanging excited chatter about the escape.

"No way they could have made it..."

"That place should have been closed years ago..."

"Those poor men..."

"They were criminals who got what they deserved..."

Pronouncements of justice and fate by the citizens of Sausalito mixed with the sounds of motorboats and helicopters searching for what Tommy knew they would not find, the bodies of John and Clarence. He wondered how people could think they knew these men so well to proclaim they 'got what they deserved.'

"Some excitement, huh?" Molly said as they approached the entrance to the market.

"Yea," he said and then, seeing the look from his mother he quickly amended to "I mean, yes." Molly studied her son. Something about the way he was reacting to the escape just didn't seem... like Tommy. Why wasn't he more excited or showing even a little interest in what was, after all, the biggest story to happen around town in a long time. Was he distracted by something? About what, she couldn't guess. Could it be a girl? Why not? He was, after all, now a teenager.

They entered the Purity, the town's only general grocery store, which was located inside a corrugated metal Quonset hut leftover from the war. Since he was a little boy Tommy had always liked the way the place smelled. It was like no other place in town; a unique blend of fresh meats and cheeses from the old-style butcher counter, the tang of the oil used to clean the wooden floors topped off with the sting of hairspray holding up the housewives' bouffant hairdos.

"Well, hello Molly, hello Tommy." It was Dotty, one of the Purity's ever-pleasant and always-talkative clerks. Molly diplomatically called her inquisitive, Tommy knew that just meant nosy. And nosy was something Tommy could without today.

"Nice to see you both here today. Say, did you hear about the excitement? Those three prisoners from Alcatraz?"

Tommy groaned to himself. Definitely much too talkative. Wait a minute. Three men? Come to think of it, Tony hadn't said how many men escaped. And since Tommy only found two men at Yellow Bluff –

"Yes, we were just talking about it," Molly said.

Dotty turned to Tommy. "You were too young to remember the last time. Four years ago, it was, two of them went into the water. One of them drowned," she said with genuine sadness in her eyes. She turned to Molly. "You remember, don't you dear?"

Molly nodded, grimly.

Dotty pressed on. "Well, the radio is now saying the three of them must of swam out last night. They're really just looking for the bodies, now."

From behind the butcher counter, a man's voice interrupted. "Dotty, would help this customer, please?"

"I have to go now. Well, it was good to see you and

Tommy you keep helping your mom, okay?"

"Yes, ma'am."

"That's a good boy. Have a good shop, you two, maybe see you when you check out."

Molly watched as Dotty flitted over to the butcher counter with what she always thought looked like a horse's gallop, except on tip-toes. It was a pretty funny sight, and she turned to Tommy, expecting to share a laugh about it with him, but he wasn't smiling. There was something in her son's face which stopped her in her tracks. "Tommy, what is it?"

What could Tommy say that wouldn't give away everything? Up until a few minutes ago his main concern was how to get some extra food into the cart he could then bring to the two men. Now he was burdened with the burning question of a third man. Where was he? Did he end up somewhere else in Sausalito? Would the police find him and decide John and Clarence were also in the area? Then another, more sinister thought... what if the brothers had done something to the third man? They just didn't seem like the type who would hurt anyone but how could he be sure?

"Tommy," his mother said, with a soft, sympathetic expression. "Is everything all right?"

"Yea. I mean yes. I'm fine, ma, can we just go shopping now?"

Molly sighed, knowing it would do no good to press the matter here in the supermarket. But she also knew eventually one of two things would happen; either he'd solve the problem on his own or come to her for help. She resigned herself to doing the hardest thing a mother can do, which is nothing. It was time to start shopping, anyway. Unbeknownst to Molly, it was not going to be a typical shop. Today, they were shopping for four.

If there had been a camera it would have captured

Molly, followed by Tommy and the cart, walking up and down the narrow aisles of the Purity. Molly would stop to pull a can of something off a shelf, turn around, place it in the cart behind her, then turn forward to the next item on her list. No sooner did Molly face forward when Tommy would reach up and place more items – a couple of cans of beans, a package of crackers, canned peaches – just enough to get the Anglins through the day at Yellow Bluff. The tricky part for Tommy was not adding too many items to raise suspicion. Each time Molly turned back to place an item in the cart Tommy would hold his breath and as they reached the last aisle of the store it looked as if he were home free, when –

Crap.

Billy's mother just entered the Purity. Tommy's heart raced. There was no way they would not see each other in the small store.

"Oh, look, there's Mrs. Winslow," she said. "Cynthia, hi!"

Tommy panicked. His mother was bound to say something about Billy canceling their work on his boat, which wasn't the truth. His heart sank. One lie and already it was over. Then, an idea popped into his head. With no time to decide if it was any good he raced to place himself between his mother and Mrs. Winslow.

"Hey, mom," he began, using his best no-one-is-supposed-to-know-this voice he said "Ummm... uh... the thing that Billy said his family was doing? He wasn't very specific, you know, I think because it's kinda personal... and I don't think he was supposed to tell me anything at all."

Ugh. He hated the taste of the lies coming out of his mouth. But what else could he do? This road diverged was starting to go through a swamp.

"Oh, dear, really?" his mother said as she cast a

126

sympathetic eye towards Mrs. Winslow. "Well, I'm just going to go over to say hi to her and not say anything about this morning..."

"Oh, gee, mom, I don't know if that's a good idea."

"Nonsense, my son and her son are best friends," she said. Seeing Tommy's look of consternation she smiled. "Don't worry dear, I won't say anything about what I'm not supposed to know about." Tommy still shuddered as she gaily called out "Hello, Cynthia, dear."

"Hello Molly. Oh, and hello Tommy. Bet you're excited summer vacation has started."

"Yes, ma'am."

"How nice that your boy comes shopping with you," Mrs. Winslow said to Molly. Then, as if she were revealing a great secret, "I could never get Billy to come with me."

"And how is Billy?"

Tommy winced. The way his mother had asked the question it sounded like she had just heard Billy was in a full body cast after a car accident. Mrs. Winslow seemed a bit taken aback, at first, but quickly recovered and said sweetly "He's just fine dear, thank you for asking." The two women looked awkwardly at each other for a few seconds. Molly was the first to break.

"Well, it was nice seeing you, dear. I'll let you get on with your shopping."

"Yes, I have to get a roast for tonight. Nice seeing you both," Mrs. Winslow said as she made her way to the butcher's counter.

Tommy should have felt guilt for bringing his mother, unknowingly, into the subterfuge. What he felt, instead, was exhilaration and... could it be... pride? He shook his head. This road less traveled sure has some surprises.

As they walked to the front of the store Tommy saw, at the cash register, the annoyingly talkative Dotty. Ugh.

He didn't have time for this. John and Clarence were on that beach wet and cold and hungry. He wanted to get back there as soon as possible. He didn't have time for Dotty and her – uh oh, was it his imagination or was his mother looking suspiciously at the items he was placing onto the counter. Each punch of the cash register's keys clanged loudly, announcing to the whole world every extra can and jar. Tommy needed a diversion. He beamed. Of course. He could use the talkative Dotty.

"So, Dotty," Tommy said (Purity protocol allowed children to address adults by their first names,) "what else have you heard about those three men who escaped from Alcatraz?"

Dotty's face lit up as she eagerly dished out the latest information. "Well, she said with a smile, "the butcher has the radio on and the latest news says they haven't found anything yet. Oh, but they did say the FBI is involved. They want to know how the men got away in the first place."

"Do they think those men could still be alive?" Molly asked.

"Mmmph," Dotty grunted, behaving as if the authorities were personally denying her the answer. "They won't say one way or the other. "But if you ask me..."

As his mother and Dotty dove deeper and deeper into a conversation about the escape, Tommy began to feel another rush of elation from his well-executed diversion. Finally, Dotty's concerto in NCR Minor ended and Tommy watched his mother pull a few bills out of her purse and hand them to the cashier. "What a fine, young gentleman you have," Dotty said to his mother as Tommy hurriedly picked up the bags and place them in their "little old lady" cart for the walk back to their houseboat.

Back home, Tommy pleased his mother again by

volunteering to carry all the bags onto the boat and into the kitchen. His next task was to get her out of the kitchen so she wouldn't see the extra food. This one was almost too easy. "Ma, I'll take care of these, you probably want to get back to sleep."

She smiled, gratefully. "You are so sweet, honey. You know, I was up early today so I think I'll take you up on that offer. Thank you." She cupped his face in her hands, kissed him on his forehead and went into her bedroom. Tommy watched and, when the door was fully closed, exhaled. There was still a lot to do, but he allowed himself a moment to reflect on the battle of emotions raging inside his head; the thrill of successful deceptions versus the pangs of guilt for the ever-lengthening list of those deceptions...

The road less traveled seemed to be getting bumpier and bumpier. No matter, he had work to do.

The view from the front seat of a seaplane landing in the water is not for the faint of heart.

Olin Blackwell was veteran of war and of the federal prison system. He was also used to sitting in the back of a commercial airplane, his only view that of the seat in front of him. Nothing prepared Blackwell for the sight of water rushing up towards the tiny plane as it descended into the bay near Alcatraz Island. He was grateful for the calm voice of the pilot through the headset as he talked his way through his checklist. "Wings level... Gears up, flaps down, water rudders up..."

Blackwell's eyes widened as the pilot throttled up the engine and he felt his body push back in his seat. The pilot smiled. He had seen the same surprised expression on most of his passengers' faces. "We throttle up because we need the power to stay in the air as we lower our rate of descent," he said, reassuringly, over the headset. "And to take off quickly if something gets in our way. Kind of like the way planes land on a carrier. Air traffic control knows we're here but there's lots of action out on the bay today. Nothing to worry about, Warden."

The warden nodded grimly and returned his thoughts to the challenge ahead. He had earlier asked the pilot to fly around the bay so he could get an aerial view of the search effort. The trails left by the Coast Guard boats had reminded him of water bugs skittering across the calm water of Lake Berryessa. After the plane banked over Raccoon strait and the north side of Angel Island, Blackwell saw a squad of soldiers at Ayala Cove assisting residents as they evacuated the island, before performing a building-by-building search – by some wild chance – the escapees had actually made it to Angel.

The pilot's voice broke into his headset and his thoughts. "N1701 at one thousand requesting final clearance to Alcatraz Island."

In his headset, Blackwell heard "Roger N1701 we'll have you do a go-around Treasure Island and vector north for landing east of Alcatraz."

"N1701, roger," he spoke into his radio, Then, to Blackwell, he said "They want to keep us away from other craft so we're going to loop around –"

"– I heard, yes," Blackwell said, instantly regretting the brusque interruption. Damn, he needed a cigarette. "I appreciate you keeping us safe, son."

It seemed to take forever as the plane slowly descended to where it was just above the water, and even longer to drop the last few inches to the surface. Then, just like that, they were no longer a plane, but a boat. He exhaled. Blackwell liked being on the water. The rocking of the plane as they taxied to the Alcatraz dock was soothing after the mild terror of landing.

"Alcatraz Island, this is N1701 requesting docking."

Over the headset, Blackwell heard "Copy N1701. Docking approved. Tell Warden Blackwell the men are waiting for him in the conference room."

Blackwell nodded.

"He heard you Alcatraz, stand by to take in the lines."

Within a few minutes Blackwell was shaking hands with the pilot, exiting the plane, and stepping onto the dock. The first thing he did was take out a cigarette and light it. He took a deep, satisfying and much-needed drag before walking up the path to the administration office.

10:13 am

Ron Lowendowski liked to say being a reporter was a pretty glamorous profession... unless you happened to be a reporter. The job was mostly waiting for something interesting to come across the wire, retype it for a two minute newscast, and then read it on the air. A small station like KRAN, without a mobile studio to do live reports from the field – and only two newsmen and one tape recorder – simply didn't offer much opportunity to do any real reporting. Unless, like Ron, you were hungry. Really hungry. So hungry he was willing to ask the station's owner to spend money.

Going to Mac Bailey's office was like a trip to the principal's office in elementary school, when you were so small standing on tiptoes was the only way to see over a massively huge desk. At KRAN keen eyes had noted the legs on Mac's desk had been extended to add even more height to the already-large edifice. To complete the act of supplication, Mac had a platform for his large leather chair placed behind the desk. There would be no question who was the 800-pound gorilla at KRAN.

Ron used to hate his visits to Xanadu (what some at the station derisively called Mac's office) until he heard the story of a long-suffering disc-jockey who, upon securing a job at another radio station, broke into Xanadu, dropped his pants... and left a "present" on Mac's desk. It tickled Ron even more to hear how much Mac had liked the DJ because "that young man is always smiling when he comes to see me." Ron liked to imagine the moment when "the Colonel" unlocked his office on the fateful morning and saw the disc-jockey's resignation letter.

"So what did you want to talk about?" Mac asked, beaming at Ron.

"Well, sir, you've heard about the escape this morning..."

"I did. Terrible business."

"I agree. So I was thinking, Colonel, with Coast Guard and Army personnel on high alert now is a good time to feature some of our men in uniform in some special reports."

Mac pursed his lips and nodded. "Go on..."

"Thanks to that piece you had me do on the Coast Guard a few months ago I have a relationship with the commander over at Golden Gate and –"

"Say no more. I like your thinking. What do you need?"

"A few things, sir. To start, the Chief Engineer says he can't give me the station tape recorder without your permission."

"Well, I see no reason why you cannot use it, as long as you remember any damage or loss of station equipment comes out of your pocket."

Grimacing inside but still displaying a practiced, gratuitous smile, Ron nodded. "Of course."

132

Mac nodded. "Good man," he said as he picked up some random papers on his desk, a not-so-subtle cue for Ron to know his time in Valhalla was up. But, peering over the papers, he saw the newsman still sitting before him. "Was there anything else, Robins?"

Ron winced hearing the name he had been forced to use on the air because, as Mac had loudly declared during the job interview, "Lowendowski sounds Russian. You need an American name if you're going to work at my station." Ron had just met Mac but instinctively knew it was pointless to explain his family was Polish and they hated the Soviets as much as anyone. So Ron Robins was born.

"Yes, sir, there is one more thing," Ron said. "I've taken the liberty of speaking to the PR man at the Coast Guard station and he said – once I had your permission, of course – that I can ride on one of the boats. There is one more thing..." He paused.

"Yes? Out with it, man."

"The thing is... I'd have to be at the dock no later than six in the morning."

"So...?" Mac responded with an impatient look.

"I need someone to cover my shift... to do the morning newscasts, so I can –"

"– whoa, whoa, hold on there," Mac said waving his arms. "I'm not paying two people to work the same shift."

"But how else can I –"

"It's simple. Come in early and record your newscasts."

Ron let that one sink in for a moment. "You want me to record the news?"

"Sure."

"But what if something happens when I'm not here?"

"Come on, Robins, the news doesn't change in just four hours. We'll be fine. Hell, newspapers are filled with

133

yesterday's news and no one complains that they're out of date, right?" Mac smiled and picked up more random pieces of paper. Without looking up, from behind the papers, he said "that will be all, Robins."

With a smile still firmly plastered on his face Ron stood up and, as he exited Valhalla, seriously questioned his decision not to work in his father's used car lot in San Rafael.

10:26 am

Tony Marianetti liked to say, "there's no town in America like Sausalito." Being a Sausalito lifer he was biased, of course. Except for his tours of duty in the Marines during World War Two and Korea, he had spent every night of his life here. His family had also played a big role in the town's storied history. There were still plenty of natives who remembered Tony's dad from his days piloting the ferry from Sausalito to the Hyde Street terminal in San Francisco. His mother had been a first grade teacher at the elementary school, so it was a sure bet you were either transported across the Bay or taught your ABCs by a Marianetti, and more than likely both. And, now that Tony was Chief of police, the town was being protected by one, too. Which helps explain why he took any threats to Sausalito personally. Those cons, if they somehow did make it across the bay and, by some quirk of fate, landed here, well... they better hope the Feds got to them before he did.

Immediately after his "all hands" meeting at the police station Tony got in his cruiser and made his way down Bridgeway to check in with store owners and residents. He patiently explained to everyone what little chance the escapees had of making it to land, but also told them (in as calm a manner as possible) to – just to be on the safe side, mind you – make sure the doors to their homes and cars were locked. "If you think you see something out of the ordinary, don't do anything except call the station," he told them. "We'll be here in five minutes, tops."

His two favorite patrol stops were at opposite ends of the Bridgeway. On the northern side, near where a wartime shipyard had cranked out Liberty ships and tankers in record numbers, was Juanita's Galley. Juanita Musson, all 220 pounds of her, was a force of nature. In her trademark muumuu she prowled her restaurant, a converted ferry, challenging recalcitrant customers to either "eat it or wear it." (It was not a threat to be taken lightly, as many who wore their dinner home could attest.) She embodied the gritty Sausalito which actor Sterling Hayden once described as "a sailorman's town... on the waterfront lay the rotting hulks of schooners, barks, and brigs."

On the opposite, southern end of Bridgeway, stood the Valhalla restaurant, owned by Sally Stanford. Sally was the Sausalito intent on reinventing itself by casting off overalls stinking from fish guts and welding slag, donning, instead, bow ties and tailored tuxedos. Sally knew all about reinvention. Born Mabel Busby she renamed herself after the university and ran a Nob Hill bordello popular with politicians and power brokers. After a raid by a zealous District Attorney Sally, like so many of the upwardly mobile after the war, crossed the Golden Gate Bridge to Sausalito. This time, her business was straight as an arrow – although the rich, red wallpaper and Victorian settee hinted at the libidinous source of her funding. And you can bet her waiters wore tuxedos.

Tony had made his way down along Bridgeway and was now standing on the deck in back of Sally's restaurant, the two of them silently looking out into the bay, past the docks populated with the sleek sloops which had replaced the "brigs and barges" of old Sausalito. Tony cradled a hot cup of coffee, enjoying a brief respite from an already hectic day.

"Sorry Chief, I just don't see it's possible," Sally said, looking across the water to Alcatraz Island.

"Yea, but I have to assume it is."

"You're not worried about me, are you?"

Tony turned to face her. "I worry about everyone in my town."

"Honey, what these boys want I don't sell anymore," Sally replied, with a wink.

Tony laughed. "I'm pretty sure that's low on their lists of priorities."

"I was in that business long enough to know it's never low on any man's list."

Tony chuckled, then took a sip of coffee. "All kidding aside Sally. If, on the outside chance they really did make it here, what these boys want most are dry clothes, food, and a car. In that order." He paused then, with a smile, "which I say with all due respect to your former business."

Sally nodded and, feeling a chilly breeze from the bay, flung her signature red boa around her neck. "Well, Chief, if there's nothing else..."

"No," he said before chugging the last of his coffee. "Thanks for pick-me-up. I'll bring the cup inside."

"No, that's okay. You go do what you have to do," she said holding out her hand. "I'll keep my ears to the ground and let you know if I hear anything."

"Thanks," he said, handing her the cup before turning and walking off the deck.

"When this is over," she called out to him as he walked away, "I mean... I guess when they find their bodies... come back and I'll have a nice steak dinner waiting for you."

Sally saw Tony give her a "thumbs up" as he got into his cruiser. She turned and looked out at the bay one more time, shaking her head, before walking back into the Valhalla.

10:27 am

As soon Molly closed the door to her bedroom Tommy went to his own room and pulled out his Boy Scout duffel bag from under his bed. He would pack in here, just in case his mother woke up and came into the kitchen. The duffel bag was just the right size for the supplies he promised to bring the Anglins. He would start with some dry clothes.

He quietly entered the kitchen and knelt down in front of one of the many storage areas which had been squeezed into every nook, cranny, and corner of the houseboat. Tommy trembled slightly. In here were worn and tattered shirts, pants and pea coat his father wore when fishing. He was only three when his father died and no matter how hard he tried he could not remember what he looked like. What he could remember was his smell... a mix of sweat and fish guts and cologne. Sometimes, over the years, when his mother was working, Tommy would open the small door and bring a piece of clothing up to his nostrils. Instantly he would be transported back to a time when he was so very young and his father had not yet gone off to war. As he held the clothes to his nose he could almost feel his father's warm arms around him, protecting him from the chilly bay air. Tommy never told his mother

137

how very glad he was she kept them.

Tommy was then struck by a wave of regret, as he realized giving the Anglins these clothes would sever the only physical connection he had to his father. He hesitated, for a moment, as he brought the clothes to his nostrils and breathed in the memories for a last time. Then, to his surprise, he felt another wave of emotion, an odd sense of justice that his father's clothes might keep the Anglin brothers safe from Tony Marianetti, the man who had promised to protect him.

His eyes now caught sight of the kitchen clock. Holy cow, it was 10:30 already and there was so much more he had to do. Now that he had clothes for the Anglins, he needed to put as much food as he could carry into the duffel. He began with two containers of Spam he had slipped into the shopping cart back at the Purity. (Spam. Ugh. He and his mom never ate the stuff, how did she miss seeing it at the cash register? Must have been when he mentioned the escape to Dotty. Tommy felt very clever and smiled to himself.) Okay, back to the duffel. Let's see what else to bring... two cans of beans. Check. Two cans of potatoes. Check again. Two cans of fruit... wait a minute. Cans. How were the Anglins supposed to open them? With a can opener, of course, stupid. Tommy went to the utensil drawer and, afraid of making noise which could wake up his mother, very slowly extracted the can opener from a pile of utensils and placed it in the duffel.

Utensils. What a dope. How were the Anglins supposed to eat without forks? Tommy began reaching for a couple of forks, then saw his hand stop and hover over them. Should he really be giving two escaped criminals forks that could be used as weapons against him? Tommy watched, detached, as his hands instead picked up two spoons and put them into the duffel bag.

10:34 am

In the interrogation room at Alcatraz assistant warden Art Dollison stood in front of Allen West and squared his shoulders. "Where'd they go, Allen? Come on, thanks to that hole in your cell we know you were involved. Just tell us where they went and we'll go easy on you."

The prisoner remained grimly silent.

The assistant warden kneeled next to him and said, softly, "We don't want those men to die, Allen. I'm sure you don't either. Even if they did leave you behind." He looked for a reaction but, damn it, the prisoner didn't take the bait. Dollison decided to take another approach. "Allen, we need your help to save them from their own stupidity. You boys must have been crazy to think you could survive in that water. Do you know how cold it is? Do you know what hypothermia is?"

Allen West turned and smugly looked the assistant warden in the eyes. "Do you know what a raft is?"

Art Dollison and the guards standing behind the prisoner exchanged confused looks.

"A raft."

"Yea, and it was big enough for all four of us."

An escape was nothing to joke about, but none of the guards could stop themselves from smiling in disbelief. Dollison scoffed. "How the hell could you smuggle a raft in here?"

Now it was Allen West's turn to be amused. With a smile of superiority he said "we didn't smuggle nothing. We made it. Right here, in the prison. In our workshop."

The smiles disappeared. "Workshop," Dollison said, skeptically.

"Look for yourselves. It was right above the cell block, just below the roof."

139

Dollison glanced quizzically, at the guards. "Could this be true?"

"We did find a room, yes sir," Jim Albright said. "Just above the cell block and below the roof, like he said. A table was found under where the vent is located. The cover had been removed. That's how they got to the roof. But we didn't see anything else up there."

"Is that where you made the raft, Allen?" Dollison asked.

"First, what about my deal?" West replied as he sat back in his chair and folded his arms.

Dollison stood up and looked over to the guards and winked. Jimmy Albright nudged Paul with his elbow and whispered. "Watch this."

The assistant warden paced slowly in front of the prisoner. "Look, Allen, we know who the brains of the operation was. I mean, everyone in the joint knows Frank Morris was the smartest one in here –"

Allen West bolted upright in his chair. "Screw you. I'm sick and tired of hearing about how damn smart Frank Morris was," Allen West sputtered. "It was me who figured out how to use a vacuum cleaner motor for a drill. I'm the one they trusted to make the life jackets and the paddles. When there was a hitch they turned to me, not Frank Morris. You know what that asshole once said to us? Swear to God, he says 'you know what, West, when they make the movie about this escape I'm gonna be the star.' Can you believe the balls on that guy?"

Art Dollison looked at him sympathetically. "And then that bastard left you here. Allen, look at me. Where were they going?"

Allen West pursed his lips and sighed. "Angel Island. They was headed for Angel Island."

140

10:45 am

Back on his bicycle, with his duffel bag secured on the rack over his bike's rear tire, Tommy headed again down East Road towards Yellow Bluff. Being a workday there were a lot of cars on the road and he worried about other people stopping, as he did earlier, to look at all activity out on the bay. What if somebody had walked to the edge of the bluff and seen the brothers, huddled on the beach below? He pedaled even harder until he saw the turnoff for Yellow Bluff, elated not to see any cars or people. He pulled off the road and hid his bicycle behind a bush, then grabbed the duffle bag, slung it over his shoulder and headed for the cliff. One more check of the area... then he turned so he could climb backwards down the steep path to the beach.

He was about halfway down when he heard a voice, raspy but strong. He recognized it as John's. "Who's there? Tommy is that you?"

"Yes, it's me," he said as he continued his way down to the beach. He slipped a few times from the uneven weight caused by the duffel, but made his way to the bottom without falling. Tommy was greeted by a pathetic site. John was still cradling his brother in his arms, and Clarence didn't look good.

"How's he doing?" Tommy asked.

"Leg still hurts. Needs water."

Tommy reached into the duffel bag and pulled out two orange juice containers and handed one to John. "Here, this one has water in it but the other one has orange juice, I figured you should have some."

"Thanks."

Tommy watched as, once again, John made sure his brother got the first sips of water. Only when Clarence

141

weakly pushed John's hand away did his brother take a drink. From John's face Tommy could tell he really wanted that drink, which made Tommy even more impressed with his unselfishness.

"We wasn't sure you was coming back," John said, between sips.

"My mom was up. A neighbor woke her with the big news about you guys. Everyone's talking about the escape."

Both of the brothers sat up (Clarence not without wincing.) "What are they saying?" John asked.

"Most everybody seems to think you're out there," Tommy said, indicating the bay behind them.

"Like Frank," croaked Clarence.

John lowered his head, sadly. "Yea, poor bastard."

"Frank was the third man?"

John nodded. "Frank Morris."

"Don't forget West," Clarence said.

"A fourth guy," John said to Tommy. "Allen West. Was supposed to be with us but he never made it out."

Clarence suddenly winced.

"The leg again?" John asked. Clarence nodded. John looked to Tommy. "Do you got any aspirin?"

"I can bring some when I come get you later." Tommy said as he reached into the duffel bag." But I did bring some food," he said as he pulled out a can of beans and handed it to John. "Hold on, I got a can opener somewhere in here." Tommy rummaged around before feeling the handle of the opener, which he pulled out and gave to John.

"Thanks," John said as he gratefully took the can and the opener. Tommy watched as John managed to fit the wedge of the opener over the lip of the can but was unable to twist the handle more than a couple of turns.

"Here, let me," Tommy sad as he took the can and

142

opener from John and finished opening the beans, which he handed to John, who mumbled an embarrassed "thanks." Tommy reached back into the bag and pulled out the two spoons he had taken from his kitchen. "Here," he said as his handed them to John. In the back of his mind Tommy wondered if John noticed his choice of utensils. Then, quickly, "I got some dry clothes in here, too."

Tommy got startled when he saw Clarence wince again. "How bad is it?"

"It's not broken," John said as he brought a spoonful of beans to his brother's lips, which Clarence took gratefully. "No cuts, either. He must have sprained it getting onto the beach here." John saw the surprise on Tommy's face. "We didn't have doctors much growing up. There were a dozen of us and someone was always sick or getting hurt so we learned a few things."

"How long before he can walk?"

"I figure a few days. Do you think we can hide out for that long at the place you got?"

"Yea, pretty sure. I mean almost no one goes up there. It's an old, abandoned fort. There's a whole string of them from the Golden Gate up north along the coast. Most of them are empty, now. Plenty of bunkers and other places you can stay in and hide. The one I'm gonna take you to is called Battery Kirby, it's just west of here under the bridge.

"Why that one?" John asked, his mouth full.

"I can bring the skiff right up on the beach and the path to the fort itself is a short walk almost at beach level, so Clarence won't have to climb."

The monotonous drone of speeding boats was suddenly broken by the distant sound of an air horn. All three turned and looked out into the bay.

"Maybe they found Frank," Clarence said.

"Maybe," John replied. "But they ain't gonna find us." He turned to Tommy. "When can you get us out of here?"

"Tonight, after it gets dark. My mom goes to work around six. It gets dark around nine and that's when I'll come with the skiff. Meanwhile I better go to meet my friend at the marina."

"You're not gonna tell him about us, are you?"

"No. He's no snitch, but I gotta warn him what I said to my mom so he doesn't say the wrong thing to his mom," Tommy said, taking satisfaction in using the prison word 'snitch' to the brothers. Tommy picked up the now-empty duffel bag and slung it over his shoulder. "See you guys later, okay?"

"Sure. And hey, thank you," John said.

"Yea, kid, thanks," Clarence added.

"Put on those dry clothes I brought you. We'll take the wet ones with us later. And the empty cans, too. Don't want to leave any evidence you were here, right?"

John smirked. "You're a little too smart for your age, kid."

Tommy couldn't hide how much he liked hearing that. He smiled back, turned, and headed to the cliff and back to the road.

11:02 am

"They had a raft?"

Warden Blackwell shook his head so rapidly his cigarette flew from his mouth and landed on his desk. It sounded so preposterous, so out of the realm of possibility... he had to repeat what they just told him. "Our prisoners... made a raft."

"Yes, sir," the assistant warden replied. "And paddles

144

for rowing, too."

Blackwell fell back into his chair like he had been punched in the stomach. He ran his hand over the stubble he had started to grow on his vacation. Then he had a rueful thought. His next vacation might be permanent. Just as quickly, he cast off his moment of self-pity and stood up.

"Dollison," he said to the assistant warden as he put the cigarette back in his mouth, "Let's get the Coast Guard on the phone so they can give us predictions how far these three men might have gotten in a... raft. A raft. Jesus, I can't believe I'm saying it out loud. Barone, what else has this... what's his name?"

"West, sir. Allen West."

"Right. What else has he told us? Why the hell didn't he go with them? Cold feet?" Blackwell saw smirks on the faces of the guards. Even Arthur Dollison was grinning. "What? Is somebody going to let me in on the joke?"

"Sorry, Blackie," Dollison said in a breach of protocol, using the warden's nickname in public. "The dumb bastard might have been a decent raft-maker but he was too good a mason. The patch he used to keep the vent in his cell in place hardened like concrete. He couldn't loosen it so he couldn't get out of his cell into the corridor behind it."

Blackwell stifled a smile of his own. Now was not the time. "So what else can West tell us? Please tell me they weren't being met by someone in a boat?"

"No, sir. Definitely not," Dollison replied.

Paul Barone cleared his throat.

"You have something to say, Mister Barone?" Blackwell asked.

Paul looked at Dollison, who gave him a look that said 'go ahead – it's your funeral.' Barone cleared his throat again. "It's just I was thinking if one of them did

145

arrange for a boat they might not have shared that information with the others."

Blackwell shook his head. "It's tough enough planning an escape, but coordinating with someone on the outside when we read all their mail? Sorry, Barone, I just don't see how that could have slipped by us."

"Yes, sir."

"So if we assume there was no boat, does West have anything to say about where they planned on going?"

"Angel Island," Dollison said. "Which we all figured anyway since it's closest to Alcatraz."

Blackwell looked confused. "Yes, I suppose, but why go through all the trouble to get off one island so they can go to another one? And that island is a Nike missile base crawling with armed airmen." He took another drag on his cigarette. "Doesn't make any sense."

"Neither does robbing banks, but that's what they all did anyway," Dollison replied.

Blackwell sighed and nodded. "Damn fools. All right, I want to meet this Allen West. But first call the army let them know about the... God damn it... the raft..."

12 Noon

Priscilla Baker – Prissy to her friends – stood over the small propane stove in her modest kitchen, gently turning over the scrambled eggs she was cooking for her husband. The aroma of freshly brewed coffee mixed with the bacon she had prepared earlier. She smiled. Just a few more minutes and her husband would emerge from the bedroom in his crisply ironed Master Sergeant uniform.

Discipline. Attention to detail. Executing an order correctly. Prissy had always admired Gus for sticking to those principles, even as far back as high school where they first met before he shyly asked her out on that first date almost six years ago. Now she was an Air Force wife and life was an adventure, although the pace of life here on Angel Island was not quite the E-ticket she had imagined when she agreed to marry a missile man. Where they send them after the last of the Nike missiles were removed from the island later this year, well, they would be told when they needed to be told, although she made no secret of her wish for him getting an assignment in Europe.

Turning the eggs one last time, Prissy thought she caught the sight of something outside the cabin, just out of the corner of her eye. She blinked, thinking it was an errant eyelash. But it wasn't. It was a soldier in battle fatigues emerging from the woods near their cabin. Within seconds there were more soldiers in fatigues, carrying rifles, poised as if stalking prey.

"Gus, get out here, quick," she yelled to her husband.

"I'll be out in a minute," he replied from the bedroom.

"You need to get out here right now."

Gus Winters flung open the door of the bedroom. He wanted to be annoyed, but the look of fear on his wife's face quickly changed his demeanor. "Prissy," he said as he raced over to her, "what is it...?" His wife didn't answer, she just turned her head towards the window. Gus looked and saw at least a dozen soldiers, weapons in hand, spreading out around their property. "What the hell...?"

That's when there was a knock on the door. Gus smiled, which he could see confused Prissy. "It's okay, honey, burglars and Russians don't knock. I'll find out what's going on. Meanwhile," he said with a grin as he walked to the door, "I think the eggs are burning."

Prissy turned and saw a column of smoke rising from

147

the pan. She ran the stove, grabbed the flaming mess and dropped it in the sink.

"Sorry for the intrusion, sir," Prissy heard a young man saying from the other side of the door. She wanted to hear more and started inching closer to the door when the phone rang. Gus leaned back into the house and motioned for her to answer it. Reluctantly, she reversed direction and picked up the receiver.

"We've been ordered to evacuate everyone living on the island."

"An evacuation? I didn't hear about an evacuation. Someone from command center would have called if –"

"Gus?" Prissy interrupted.

Annoyed, Gus glared at his wife. "What is it?"

His wife sheepishly held up the phone. "It's Captain Lynch at the command center."

"Wait here," Gus said to the soldier, motioning for him to step inside. Prissy was struck by young he looked. He strode across the room and took the phone from his wife, who listened to his side of the conversation. "Yes, sir... Uh huh... Yes, sir, they are here now.... Really? Three of them? Do they really think they could have...? No, sir. Of course, right away, sir."

Gus hung up the phone and turned to the soldier. "That was my base commander. He's just told me why you are here."

"Gus, what's going on?" Prissy asked.

"There was an escape from Alcatraz prison last night by three men. They have intelligence that Angel Island was their destination."

"Do they really think anyone could swim here in that water?" she replied.

"Actually, ma'am, they may have been in a raft."

Gus exploded. "A raft? How the hell –"

"I don't know sir, it's what we heard from our

148

commander." Fearing he had been far too casual, the young soldier swiftly reverted back to a military posture and tone. "There's a launch at Ayala Cove on the other side of the island to take you and your family to your base, sir."

Gus smiled, paternally. "Thank you, Corporal, I know where it is."

"We can drive you –"

"Won't be necessary, we have a car."

"Copy that. They want everyone off by noon."

"Understood. Thank you."

The two men saluted each other and the soldier walked back to his unit. Gus shut the door and looked at his wife who was waving away smoke from the burnt eggs.

"Did he say they had a raft?" Prissy asked, with wide eyes.

Gus shook his head. "Nah, he must have misunderstood."

"Do you think they could have made it? They couldn't have made it? Could they? Are we in any danger?"

Gus wrapped his arms around her. "Prissy, with or without a raft even if they somehow made it here to Angel it's a sure bet they're not armed. And we are," he said as he patted the gun tucked in its holster. "Come on, let's pack a couple of duffels and get down to the Cove."

12:05 pm

"What do you mean we can't come back?"

Sharon Barone sat in one of the telephone booths at the Ferry Building, her two girls squirming on her lap as she spoke to her husband Paul back at Alcatraz.

"I'm sorry, honey, but we're on lockdown. Nobody on or off until tomorrow. It's obviously crazy here. I'm lucky to get a few minutes to take your call."

149

"What am I supposed to do with the girls? Where do we sleep tonight?"

"Do you have the number of my cousin in San Jose?"

"San Jose? But Paul –"

"I'd rather you and the girls be there than here."

Sharon looked at her girls, patiently sitting on her lap, and smiled. "I worry about you."

"I'll be fine, we're pretty sure they're dead, floating somewhere in the bay."

"Those poor men."

"That's the chance they took, Sharon. Look, I gotta go. Call Gene and he'll come and get you. Love you."

"Love you, too. Girls, say 'I love you' to your father." Their screams of "I love you" echoing loud enough to draw the attention of several people walking past the tiny phone booth.

"Are we going home now, Mommy?" Stephanie asked.

From the phone, Sharon heard her husband urgently say "You have your hands full. I'll call you at Gene's later, if I can. Gotta go."

Paul hung up, but Sharon longingly kept the receiver to her ear until she heard the dial tone return. As she returned the phone to its cradle she said, "Hey girls, who wants to have an adventure and visit Uncle Gene?"

"Uncle Gene, oh we like him," Katherine said.

Stephanie nodded and added, "Yea, he's got the hot dog puppy."

"That's right Steph, he has the dachshund. Well daddy is having a really busy day today so we're going to visit Gene and his dachshund and your cousins, too."

The girls cheered again. Sharon sighed as she dug into her pocketbook for another dime. Being married to an Alcatraz prison guard was proving to be a lot more interesting than advertised.

150

1:00 pm

Billy Winslow and three of his friends sat on the dock at the Yacht Club at Horseshoe Bay, their bare feet dangling in the water as they listened to Billy's transistor radio.

"It's one o'clock and time for the news here on KCBS, San Francisco. Topping the news at this hour officials have reported a daring escape from Alcatraz prison. KCBS news has confirmed three men were found missing this morning..."

Jeffrey Grable heard Billy laugh. "What's so funny, Winslow?"

"I dunno... it sounds funny when they say they were 'found missing.' I mean they're either found... or they're still missing, right?"

Jeffrey shook his head. "You are so weird."

"Quiet, I wanna hear this," one of the other boys interrupted.

"KCBS has learned the escape happened last night, meaning it has been at least ten hours before it was discovered by prison guards before breakfast this morning. KCBS has also learned that a detachment of soldiers has been sent to Angel Island, which is closest to Alcatraz Island and, according to prison officials, a likely landing spot for the escapees. However, our sources within the prison also tell KCBS there is little chance the men survived for any length of time in the cold waters of San Francisco Bay, however police departments all around the bay area have been placed on alert. KCBS news time is three past one o'clock. Next news at two, bulletins when they happen..."

Billy switched off the radio. "So now what do we do?"

"I thought we were going out on the boat?"

"Nah," Billy replied.

"Why, because O'Conner didn't show?"

"No, my father says I'm not allowed to go out in the bay cause of all the traffic out there."

Deflated, the boys sat glumly on the dock kicking the water.

"Okay, so maybe we can't go out on the boat, but at least we're not in school," Jeff said.

"Yea, I suppose," Billy said, although the glum looks on the other boys told a different story.

Patrick, looking thoughtful, suddenly brightened. "Oh, man, can you imagine how cool it would be if we saw one of the bodies?"

"Oh, yea. Then when the teacher asks what we did on our summer vacation we'd have the best story, ever."

They all nodded in agreement.

"Wonder what it looks like," Billy said.

"What what looks like?"

"You know, a drowned body."

"Bloated, I guess."

"Yea, all gross and stuff."

More nods of agreement before the group again descended into more bored splashing off the dock.

"Hey, I got an idea," Patrick said. "Let's get some slices at the Venice, then bring 'em to the benches near the water. We'll have the best view of what's going on at Angel Island."

Three faces brightened. The day was saved. The boys extracted their feet from the water, put on their sneakers and mounted their bicycles. This could be a pretty cool way to start vacation...

1:15 pm

Even before the police station's receptionist hung up the

152

phone Roger McGloin knew he had drawn the short straw. Ethel Mackenzie had called the Sausalito Police station and Roger was low man on the totem pole. Tony gently provided basic instructions for the rookie.

"Take her statement," Tony began. "And take it seriously. Pretend she might have actually seen something, okay? After you're done, drive around town a bit... Bridgeway, Second Street, Richardson and Main. It's good for the public to see a cruiser. If you see a store owner or anyone outside their home roll up and ask how things are going. Keep the tension low... calmly let 'em know we got everything covered."

Roger nodded and began to salute when he remembered one of the first things Tony said to him when the rookie started two months ago. "Save your salutes for weekends with the Reserves."

Now, at Ethel's, the rookie was learning first-hand what all the eye-rolling back at the station was about. "Nobody remembers but I do when they first said they was gonna turn the old military prison into a Federal joint. Oh you shoulda heard some of them old-timers squawking about spending millions so as hardened criminals can enjoy a summer resort." She cackled. "Ha, summer resort. You ever been out there, son?"

"A few weeks ago, actually, yes ma'am. As part of our training they send us out to –"

"Does it look like a resort to you?"

"Not with all those the bars on the windows, no, ma'am."

The older woman cocked her head and narrowed her eyes at the young officer. Roger winced. He did not mean to sound like a smart-ass. He was relieved to see Ethel smile.

"I like you, son. I like your boss, too. Known Tony since he was a boy and his dad was running rum back

153

during prohibition." Roger, who had been dutifully taking notes (if only to be polite) froze in place and his eyes widened. She cackled again. "You didn't know that, didja?"

"No, ma'am."

Ethel sat forward in her chair and smiled, happy to have a captive audience. "The story goes that one night Tony and his best friend Connor followed their dads to the local speak – that's Speakeasy – which was in the carriage house of the old Witsch place. Oh, that place was the most fun you could have around here back then... there were slot machines and a craps table and plenty of Canadian Club – which that night Tony learned was coming in on his father's fishing boat."

"Did Tony ever... you know, help out on the boat?"

"Nah, by the time he was old enough Prohibition ended and that was the end of the Witsch Speakeasy."

"Wow."

"Kind of ironic Capone ended up at Alcatraz."

"Why?"

"Cause he was there one night."

"Wait a minute... Capone was here in Sausalito?"

"That's the story folks around here tell. Pretty Boy Floyd and Baby Face Nelson, too."

"Holy shit." Roger, embarrassed, lowered his head. "Sorry, ma'am."

"Oh, that's okay. I heard worse. Look, son, what I'm trying to tell you is there's lots that goes on out there on the Bay no one knows about. Or folks pretend not to know about. And just 'cause some egghead says surviving a swim from Alcatraz is impossible don't mean it's so. Lots of men swam to freedom back when it was a military prison. Made it all the way to San Francisco and Angel Island alive and kicking. Did you know that?"

"I read that, sure. But since the Feds took it over and

added all the extra security we were told any man who's tried to escape has failed or died."

"So what are you doing here?" she asked, sitting back in her chair.

He smiled back. "Getting an education from you, ma'am."

3:32 pm

"What you are asking is out of the question. I've got five hundred square miles of water to search for three bodies and —"

"Bodies? So you think they're dead?"

Ron Lowendowski was in the office of the commander of Coast Guard Station Golden Gate, using his best 'it's a great way to show the public what the Coast Guard does' argument for him to ride with one of the crews searching for the Alcatraz escapees. But when he heard the word "bodies" his reporter instinct kicked in. Was this the headline he had been looking for?

The commander bristled. "Don't put words in my mouth. Especially when you're asking me for a favor." He cleared his throat, a trick he used to reset a conversation. "Our men are trained to work as a team. Having a civilian roaming around the deck —"

"With all due respect, commander, you said earlier crews were being pulled together using recent boot camp graduates —"

"All the more reason we can't have a civilian on board during the operation."

"I understand what you're saying, but I'm no stranger to the deck of a ship. I did four years in the navy."

The commander sat up. "Really?"

"I joined the service in early 1950 and was assigned

to the Worcester, a light cruiser. Great timing for me because a few months later Korea happened and the next thing I knew the Worcester was at Inchon supporting MacArthur's landing."

By the commander's relaxed posture Ron could see he had made a connection. He also knew what to say next to clinch the deal. "The Worcester was also part of the rescue of men off the Brush after it hit a landmine." Ron leaned forward and looked him in the eyes. "What I'm saying is I know all about Search and Rescue. I know how hard the job is. I won't get in the way."

A voice over the intercom on the commander's desk interrupted them. "Sir, you asked to be notified when the first patrols returned."

The commander pushed a button on his intercom. "Very good. Call Otis Blackwell at the prison. Tell him to be ready for a call after the debrief, as he requested." The commander released the button, stood up and looked the newsman in the eyes. "Tell you what, Lowendowski. I think I can allow this. But not tomorrow. Let's say Thursday, the fourteenth. I respect your Navy experience but I've still got a lot of rookies out there and I want to give them another day working a search under their belt."

Ron found it hard to hide his disappointment. "I appreciate the opportunity, commander. I guess I have to hope you don't find three bodies out there tomorrow."

The commander smiled sardonically. "Best I can do." Then, as he put on his hat and started for the door he stopped. "Tell you what, I'll let you sit in on the debrief, so long as we agree it's off-the-record only."

The newsman returned the commander's sardonic smile. "Off the record... the three words every reporter loves to hear."

"Take it or leave it," the commander said as he opened the door.

156

"No, no, I'll take it," Ron said as he followed him out of the office.

4:34 pm

Ron was glum. The debriefing from the crewmen in first wave of Coast Guard boats was a bust. What could have – should have – been a dramatic moment in the unfolding story of the Alcatraz escape was, instead, a mind-numbing parade of data on currents, wind measurements and flow analysis. But no sightings of any bodies.

He had pretty much lost hope when he saw a Warrant Officer hurriedly enter the room and hand a note to an Ensign standing behind the commander. The Ensign read the note, which he then passed to a Lieutenant standing next to him. The Lieutenant read the note, then disbelievingly looked at the Ensign and the Warrant Officer. Both of them nodded. Ron saw the Lieutenant's eyes widen. Ron sat up. Something big had happened. He saw the Lieutenant take a deep breath and tap the commander, who was still speaking, on the shoulder. Annoyed, the commander turned around and the Lieutenant handed him the note. He read it, turned back to the podium, and cleared his throat.

"Gentlemen, I have news from the warden at Alcatraz. Apparently..." he paused, looked at the note again and shook head, as if not believing what he was about to say. "They had a raft."

The coiled spring inside Ron unleashed all its energy as his reporter instincts took over. He jumped up and called out, "What can you tell us about the raft?"

The commander stiffened behind the podium. "Mr. Lowendowski, as we discussed earlier this briefing was for background, only. The Coast Guard's role is search and

157

rescue. Any statements about the raft or the tools used by
–"

"Tools? They had tools? What kind of tools did they have? How did they get them?"

The commander's back stiffened even further. "As I was saying, any statements to the press on the prisoner's method of escape will have to come from prison authorities. I'll be meeting with my executive officers now." With a terse nod the commander bolted from the podium. As he passed the Lieutenant he said a few words and was out the door.

The Lieutenant walked to the podium. "You men did a fine job today. Get some rest tonight. Be prepared to report to your boats at day's light tomorrow morning. Based on what else we learn today you will likely have new orders. Dismissed."

Once the higher ranking officers left the room exploded with excited chatter. But Ron heard none of it. He was already pushing his way through the crowd and was soon out in the hallway. He had a good old-fashioned scoop – the escapees had a raft! If he could get to a phone and call the station he'd beat everyone in town. The key was getting the report out there first. It was all about being first. He looked up and down the hall for a phone. There, in an empty office, he saw one. After a furtive look to see if anyone was coming he ducked inside and walked behind the desk. He picked up the receiver, his dialing finger in place –"

"What the hell are you doing in my office?"

Ron's hand froze over the phone. Chagrined, he looked up and saw the angry face of the Lieutenant from the briefing. He cringed. Nothing he could now do but fall on his sword. "I'm sorry, I just needed to make a quick call, I'm –"

"I know who you are and I also know everything you

heard at the briefing was supposed to be off the record."

"Yes, but a raft? Come on. Surely that's something we want the public to know –"

"A decision they will make at the prison." Holding the door open with one hand the Lieutenant peered back into the hallway and called out "Petty Officer Young."

A second later a crisply dressed young man was at the door, standing at attention. "Sir?"

The Lieutenant pointed to Ron, who laid the handset back on its cradle and, like a schoolboy caught throwing a piece of chalk, walked to the door.

"Show this man off the base," the Lieutenant said with what Ron was sure was a small smile.

"Aye aye, sir."

The Petty Officer held Ron's elbow as he guided him on a short but brisk walk down the hallway to the front entrance of the building. Before Ron knew it he was outside. "At least they don't have me clapping erasers," Ron mused. Okay, now to find a phone. Fast. He looked to his left and saw, near the docks on Horseshoe Bay, a few small buildings. The Yacht Club. There must be a phone there, he thought. Ron hurried to his car and drove to the dock where he saw, outside a small, corrugated metal building, a payphone mounted just outside the door. He parked and got out. Checking his pants for change (wouldn't empty pockets be the perfect end to the day?) he found a dime, dropped it into the slot and dialed the station.

After three anxious rings (don't they know I have a scoop?) Rae, who also served as the station's bookkeeper, picked up the phone and said, without much enthusiasm, "K-R-A-N home of the hits where you can win –"

"Rae," Ron interrupted. "It's Ron, get me the newsroom –"

"Ron, holy shit... where the hell have you been?"

159

"Working the Alcatraz story. I've got something. And it's big."

"Yea, Gene's in the newsroom going crazy."

In unison, both said "they had a raft."

There was a moment of confusion. Then, again in unison, "How did you know they had a raft?"

"I was calling to tell you about the raft," Ron said impatiently. "They just announced it here at the Coast Guard Station."

"Well, the AP wire had it ten minutes ago. Gene already went on the air with a bulletin."

A disappointed "oh," was all Ron could muster. He looked glumly out at the bay and took a deep breath, consoling himself with the boat ride on Thursday he had just been promised.

"And you got a call," Rae said.

"Yea?"

"A Lieutenant somebody at the Coast Guard station."

Ron knew he didn't have to ask, but he did anyway. "What's the message?"

"He said now that they know the escapees had a raft, the search has become more complicated and they can't let you ride one of the boats."

"Swell" Ron said as he looked glumly out into the bay.

"He said something else."

"What?"

"He said if you ever enter an office uninvited or touch government property again he'll have you arrested. He sounded pretty pissed. What the hell went on up there?"

"A reporter went looking for a scoop, is all."

"Uh huh. Sure. Oh, one more thing."

"What?"

"The Colonel says bring back his tape recorder."

7:00 pm

The setting sun cast long shadows across the crumbling concrete of abandoned Fort Spencer, high above the Golden Gate. Inside one of the long-abandoned buildings Frank Morris slept, his body slowly repairing itself from the trauma of the past day. It was Frank's fate that his mind had never been similarly restorative. Frank Morris didn't dream as much as he had flashbacks.

A woman's tear-stained face. A man, angry yet... relieved. A different woman, taking him by the hand. "We hope you'll be happy here." Then, the freedom and thrill of the street. A plan. Another voice "Halt!" Capture. Now, in a shower. A hand suddenly around his mouth. "Make a sound and I'll shiv ya." Pain. Blood. Humiliation. Escape. Then, a question. Why didn't I just let the bay take me last night?

The setting sun's light now bounced off a building across the path and splashed across Frank's closed eyes. He roused, the smell of concrete, dank and softened by sea water, insinuated his nostrils. Eyes still shut, Frank wondered... were the past twenty-two hours a dream? One in which he hadn't escaped from Alcatraz in a home-made raft and then fallen into the cold bay and somehow, miraculously, landed near the Golden Gate Bridge? It was all too fantastic to be anything but a dream. Surely he was still in cell 138 on B-Block at Alcatraz and if he opened his eyes he would see it was true.

A rat, having detected the smell of army rations, sat hunched in a corner of the room jealously eyeing the duffel bag, hunger and fear arguing within its primeval brain whether to advance. The frustrated rat had stayed put all night but now, sensing the intruder was beginning to stir, let hunger win the battle, and the rat tiptoed

161

tentatively across the concrete floor. It reached the source of the tantalizing odor but found its way blocked by canvas. Only one thing for a rat to do. It scratched at the canvas with its tiny, sharp claws. Frank's head, resting on the duffel, was mere inches away.

Frank hated rats. They seriously disgusted him. Okay, so he knew a few cons who kept field mice as pets. He made allowances for mice, as long as they kept them in their own cells. But hump-backed disease-laden rats? If he saw one it was all he could do to keep from screaming like a little girl. Still laying with his head on the duffel, Frank opened his eyes. The rat stopped what it was doing and stared back at him.

Frank screamed.

Like a little girl.

He jolted upright as the rat, even more scared than he, squealed, bared its teeth, then scurried away. Frank clutched his chest, cursed the rat, and then cursed himself for his damn phobia. He was grateful no one was around to hear him scream. As the adrenaline wore off his breathing returned to normal. That's when everything he had done yesterday to survive – rowing the raft, swimming to shore, foraging at the lighthouse and walking up hill to this abandoned fort – hit him like a medicine ball to the chest. He fell back onto the floor, breathing coming in big gulps. Everything hurt. Worse, despite the hot shower back at the lighthouse, spasms of agonizing cold still shot through his body.

He wasn't going anywhere tonight.

Aspirin. He had almost forgotten he had swiped some from the lighthouse. As he reached into his pocket he winced from this simple movement. Fumbling with the bottle Frank managed to get the top off and sprinkle three pills into his hand. Reaching around to unzip the duffel was no less agonizing, but he was able to extract the canteen with his other hand, pop the pills in his mouth and swallow them with a swig of water. He cursed. Just taking some damn aspirin exhausted him. No way he would be moving west tonight. Even worse, despite how much he hated the smell of the place and how much he really hated his rat roommate, he was sure he couldn't even make it outside of the room.

9:00 pm

It was torture for Tommy waiting for his mother to leave for work.

He sat on the deck of houseboat remembering all those comedies on TV in which the frustrated husband explodes because his wife was taking so long to get ready to go out. Obviously, adults thought it was funny because Tommy had seen it so many times on so many different shows. But he had never gotten the joke. Now he did. It still wasn't funny. He had so much to do tonight but couldn't start until his mother went to work. Finally, she emerged from below deck.

"So how come you're not listening to the Giants game?" Molly asked as she walked up to the deck.

"Huh? Oh, uh, they played this afternoon." He was only guessing. Baseball? Seriously? With everything going on today?

"Well, don't stay up too late, okay? I know it's vacation time but you still need your rest."

Tommy rolled his eyes.

"And don't roll your eyes."

What the hell? She wasn't even looking in his direction. How did she do that? "I wasn't, ma."

Molly turned and gave her son the classic mom 'not

163

much you weren't look.' Tommy smiled sheepishly.

"Have a good night, dear," she said as she kissed him on the cheek.

"You too, ma," he replied, watching her slowly step off the dock onto – wait, what's that? A pair of headlights turning into the boatyard parking lot? Who could it be at this...? Shit, it was a police cruiser. Tony's car. Deflated, Tommy watched as it rolled to a stop and the last person he wanted to see tonight emerge from the vehicle.

"Evening, Molly. Tommy," Tony said as he placed his Stetson on his head.

"Oh, hello, Tony, what are you doing here?" Molly asked. "I was just on my way to work."

"I figured you would be. Glad I got here in time. I'm here to drive you."

"Oh, you're very sweet but that's not necessary," she said.

"Look, Molly, not to frighten you but we still have three escaped prisoners out there."

Great job trying not to frighten us, Tommy thought. And what's this 'we' stuff? "Most folks are saying it's too cold out there for them to have made it," he heard himself say out loud. "And if they did, word is they were heading for Angel Island, anyway."

Tony scowled as he grabbed his gun belt and hitched it up his waist. "I think folks ought to let the police decide where they could or could not have gone, or if they did or did not make it."

Molly placed her hand gently on the policeman's arm. "Tony, my son is only saying what everyone else in town is saying. Those men couldn't possibly have –"

"When I see the bodies then I'll stop looking," he said as he guided Molly to his cruiser. "Meanwhile, it's night and I don't want you out walking alone," he said as he opened the passenger door.

164

By her slow, deliberate walk Tommy could tell she was going grudgingly, but he also saw the super-annoying grin on Tony's face as he waltzed around the cruiser. Just before he got in his car the officer looked back to Tommy and tipped his hat. Tommy scowled back.

After he watched them drive off Tommy went back inside the houseboat and grabbed the duffel bag in which he had packed more cans of food and water. He slung it over his shoulder, then hopped down to the floating dock on the boat's starboard side and walked to the skiff. The last thing Tommy wanted was for some nosy neighbor to tell his mother they had heard him going out on the water after she left for work. So, after untying the skiff from its mooring post he first rowed away from the other houseboats before starting the small, noisy engine.

Tommy shivered as the skiff accelerated and the cool, night air hit him in the face. He admired the Anglins even more for making it across the bay while in the water. At least he was above it. Tommy guided the skiff close enough to shore to keep his bearings, but not so close his engine would draw attention. He looked starboard to Sausalito and watched the places he grew up glide by... the Trade Fair (which was really nothing more than an old ferry boat dragged on shore and turned into a mall)... then past the town's only movie theater, which next to its only hardware store. He panicked, for a moment, thinking he saw someone looking out of a back window of the hardware store, then realized it was just a reflection of the moon off a window. It rattled him a bit, but he resisted the reaction to move further away from the shore. It was dark and he couldn't risk losing his bearings. Besides, Tommy was coming to a place very special to him.

Huck and Finn had their great adventures, but those were on a river with lots of people nearby. On the other hand Jack London's adventures were set on oceans and in the wilderness – places where a man was truly on his own. And there – right there – near the Boardwalk in Sausalito, that was where London actually lived and wrote Tommy's favorite book, *Sea Wolf*. Yea, sure, some people said he didn't actually write it here but Tommy's father said he did and that was good enough for him. (Why were some people so quick to deny Sausalito its place in the creation of London's greatest book?) Okay, truth be told Tommy didn't understand all the philosophy stuff at the beginning of *Sea* Wolf but the shipwrecks, cruel captain and survival on a deserted island... well, there was more than enough adventure to make up for all the 'man's place in the world' stuff.

Tommy didn't feel so cold now. Jack London made him think, again, of his father and of all the times he would take him out on the water. Sometimes, when he saw his mother was feeling down Tommy would surprise her with the clarity of the memory of his father placing Tommy's small hands on the wheel of the boat and letting go. He could remember his father's proud voice, "look at you, son, you're driving a boat" as the smell of salt water, aftershave and sweat filled the young boy's nostrils. Now, tonight, as he piloted his skiff along the shore, Tommy swore he could still his father's strong hands on his shoulders guiding him through the same waters, shrouded in darkness.

Tommy caught sight of the Boardwalk, where Bridgeway turned inland, which meant he was very near the southern end of the town. From the deck of the Valhalla restaurant laughter and the clinking of glasses wafted over the water. Afraid of being noticed he throttled down the engine and coasted for a bit. When he saw Swede's Beach he smiled because it meant he was past the danger point of being seen from shore. He revved the engine and headed south, his excitement and anxiousness

166

fully returned.

Next stop: Yellow Bluff.

10:13 pm

To the passengers and crew of Flight 55 from Washington, D.C. the balding, middle-aged man in row ten wearing the dark suit and tie was just another well-dressed businessman. Few noticed he spent the entire flight scowling over a stack of papers and maps he had pulled from a well-worn briefcase. Those who did notice figured him for just another salesman planning a trip to pitch some product.

The man in row ten was actually Fred Wilkinson, the Assistant Director of the Federal Bureau of Prisons. Fred had woken this morning on the other side of the country expecting June 12th to be just another day in his Washington, D.C. office. It was around ten o'clock and he was busy processing supply requests, prisoner transfers and piles of other paperwork needed to keep over a hundred correctional facilities around the country functioning, when his phone rang. It was the assistant warden at Alcatraz. There had been an escape.

One of the secretaries in the department would joke how, when one of those calls came in, it was like watching mild-mannered Clark Kent turn into Superman. Fred Wilkinson, the congenial bureaucrat, would quickly transform into the young Marine who had survived the battle for Iwo Jima as he authoritatively barked out orders to his regiment of paper-pushers. Within two hours Wilkinson was on a noon flight from Friendship Airport in Baltimore to San Francisco, his always-ready "go" bag (packed with clothes and toiletries) stowed below. In his

167

well-worn briefcase were the department's files on the prison and the men who had, somehow, gotten off his island. Yes, his island.

Fred Wilkinson had hoped to arrive during the day so he could get a first-hand look at the search effort, but midway through the flight the plane made an unplanned stop in St. Louis because of bad weather over the Rockies. From the airport he telephoned Warden Blackwell who, by then, had made it back from his aborted fishing trip. It would be a phone call Wilkinson would never forget.

"Fred, are you alone?" he heard Olin Blackwell ask.

"I'm in a phone booth, yes," he replied.

"Are you sitting down?"

"Olin, please just get to the –"

"They had a raft."

Silence. Then, "Olin, we must have a bad connection. Did you say they had a raft?"

"Yes."

"How in hell did they get a raft?"

"They made it. Right here in the prison."

Fred wished now he really were Superman so he could use the phone booth to change into costume and fly to San Francisco. Instead, he had to settle for a discrete conversation with the pilot before the plane took off. When, three hours late, the Boeing 707 finally rolled to a satisfying stop in San Francisco, the passengers heard the pilot's reassuring drawl. "Ladies and gentlemen, I know ya'll are anxious to get off the plane and I don't blame you. We're sure sorry for the delay. But we're gonna ask you to sit tight for just another minute as we have a passenger with an emergency who needs to get off this plane as quickly as possible. I thank you for your cooperation and for flying TWA."

As passengers throughout the plane strained for a glimpse of the man getting all this special treatment Fred

168

Wilkinson walked briskly to the front of the plane. "What the hell makes that salesman so important?" he heard one of the passengers gripe as Wilkinson walked out the plane and hurried down the stairs to a black sedan idling on the tarmac. In the back seat, Olin Blackwell took a last drag from his cigarette and crushed it into the ashtray as Fred Wilkinson opened the door and got in.

"Take us to the Ferry Building," Warden Blackwell said to the driver. "And radio the command center that Assistant Director Wilkinson is on the way. He'll want a full report from all teams once he arrives."

"Yes, sir," replied the driver as he put the sedan into gear and drove away from the plane.

Fred extended his hand to the Warden and they shook. "Sorry for the delay, Olin. Bad weather over the mountains, they told us."

"Not your fault, Fred. Sorry to drag you cross country but... well, you know what we found. Say, do you mind if I smoke?"

"Go right ahead."

"Nasty habit," he said as he lit a cigarette. "My wife says I oughta quit, but, you know..." he stopped when he saw Wilkinson's stern expression. "Sorry. Fred. We haven't found them, yet. No bodies or debris we could tie to the escape. Got a stack of sightings coming in from around the bay. Oh, and one even from Oregon and another from Washington. Those boys would had to have wings to make it that far."

Wilkinson acknowledged the joke with another nod but without a smile. "Anything worth following up?"

"Nothing yet. We lean on the local authorities. They know their towns and their people better than we do. If they think a lead is worth following up they'll ask for help."

"You sure they will? None of them going to go John

Wayne on us and try to capture these boys by themselves?"

"Hard to say. We can only control what we can. They're good men out there, most of 'em ex-military. They know how to follow orders but they also know sometimes you have to improvise, right?"

Wilkinson scowled. "To a point. All right, tell me what you can about the escapees."

Blackwell reached down to the car floor and pulled his briefcase onto his lap, the two latches making loud snaps as they unlocked. After pulling out a folder he closed the briefcase. "Frank Morris, at 36 years is the oldest. Orphaned at eleven and first arrested at thirteen, he then –"

"Blackie," Wilkinson interrupted. He used the warden's nickname – an old trick he learned when he started out in the system as a guard – which allowed him to be commanding, yet, still friendly. "I read their files on the plane. What I want to know about these men isn't on paper. The more we understand them as men helps us understand their weaknesses, and maybe figure out where they might slip up."

"You're assuming they made it to shore."

"I'm not assuming they didn't. Tell me about Morris. He's supposed to be the smart one, right?"

"Yes, he was given a standard IQ test while at Louisiana and scored over 130."

"Right. Everyone seems to be making a big deal about his intellect. So let's dive into that. Did he get along with the other prisoners?"

Blackwell mulled over the question as he took a long drag on his cigarette. "He wasn't a troublemaker, I mean he didn't go out of his way to interact with the others. From what I observed he only socialized with those who... I guess respected is the right word... yes, respected his intellect. To most of the population he was seen as aloof, you know, like he felt superior."

"Do you think Morris felt he was superior?"

Blackwell smiled. "I think I see where you're going with this, Fred. A dominating leader who doesn't see the value in the opinions of others – because he's actually been told by authorities he's smarter than most of the other prisoners – put him with team members who are prone to deferring to him..."

"Exactly. If he has complete control because no one feels qualified to question any part of the plan –" Deputy Director Wilkinson stopped as he saw a cryptic smile on Olin Blackwell's face. "What?" he asked.

"We found something in our searches of the cells today, Fred. Something huge I didn't know we had when we spoke a few hours ago, when you were stuck in St. Louis."

"Bigger than a raft?"

Blackwell smiled, with chagrin. "Naw, I guess not. But we think you're gonna like it."

"I'd like to hear something positive."

"This morning, we found another vent cover cut loose from the wall, just like in the three empty cells. But this cell was occupied. This poor bastard – name is Allen West – was supposed to be with the others but never made it out of his cell."

"Is he talking?"

Warden Blackwell smiled and took a satisfying drag on his cigarette. "Immunity is a great lubricant. He'll answer all your questions about the gang. Also... and I think you'll enjoy this... he's pissed."

"Because they left without him?"

Blackwell chuckled. "Even better. He says we're giving Frank Morris too much credit. West says he was the brains of the outfit."

171

"Can't wait to talk to this guy." and, for the first time, Fred Wilkinson allowed himself a smile. But it lasted only a second as a nagging doubt crept into his head. "Olin, you know the bay better than me. Could any of them have made it?"

"Not likely. The water is extra cold this time of year, about 54 degrees, thanks to the spring snow melt from up in the mountains. In fact, that's where I was this morning, up at Lake Berryessa when –"

"But these boys were in raft," Wilkinson said, quick to interrupt another fishing story from the warden. "So they weren't actually in the water. And unless you found some debris, or something else to indicate otherwise, we have to assume it stayed inflated long enough to get them close enough to shore, somewhere." Fred Wilkinson sat back in his seat and exhaled. He looked out of the window as the sedan turned onto Market Street, crowded as always with tourists, diners, businessmen and the usual assortment of characters found in this quirky city. He scowled again, struck by a disturbing thought. What if they had made it to shore? What if, among the thousands of people making their way through the city right now were three men who, only last night, resided in Alcatraz's prison cells.

"Blackie, I want to hear more about this raft."

11:01 pm

As Fred Wilkinson, newly arrived at Alcatraz, was being shown the workshop where the escapees constructed their raft, Tommy O'Conner was skillfully piloting his skiff towards the tiny beach at Yellow Bluff. In the glow from the rising moon he could see the outlines of John and

Clarence Anglin, huddled against the wall of the bluff. Hearing the skiff's outboard motor John got up and made his way to the water's edge. The skiff scraped over the pebbles of the beach and ground to a halt at his feet.

"You made it," John said as Tommy hopped out of the skiff and pulled it up onto the tiny beach, its bow almost touching the bottom of the bluff. John hovered over him, a torrent of questions tumbling out of his mouth. "Any trouble? Did they find our raft? What about the other guy with us? The one who fell overboard... did they find his body yet?" Tommy turned to face him and John saw how tired he looked. "Sorry, kid, I guess none of us have gotten much sleep the past day, huh?"

Tommy smiled wanly. "That's okay. I... I brought you more food and water and, oh, I got a bottle of aspirin. Figured Clarence could use it."

"I can move, if that's what you're worried about," came the surprisingly strong voice of Clarence. John and Tommy were both startled to see him standing up.

"Hey, you were supposed to wait for me," John said.

"Yea, well, you two old ladies were gabbing so much... hey Tommy."

"Hey, Clarence." Tommy said. He watched John then drape Clarence's arm around his neck and gently lower him into the skiff. "Okay, John, your turn. You get in and I'll go back and get the duffel bag."

When Tommy returned to the skiff he handed the bag to John. "I'm going to give you a push into the water. John. We'll need to turn the skiff around so I can get in the back by the motor." John nodded. "Here we go," Tommy said as he gave the skiff a shove. Thanks to its shallow draft it slid easily off the beach into the water. John reached out and grabbed Tommy's hand and the boat turned around. Tommy hopped in. It was a bit more crowded and heavier than Tommy had hoped, but they were still afloat. With a quick pull of the starter cord the small motor buzzed to life and Yellow Bluff disappeared behind them in the night.

11:55 pm

It was almost midnight on June 12, 1962, and a remarkable day around San Francisco Bay was almost at an end.

Up at Juanita's, Molly was taking an order from two well-dressed couples who joked, not so subtly, about how much fun it was to "go slumming" near the houseboats. At another table across the room an unsuspecting slob was being told by the bosom-ed proprietress to "eat it or wear it." The placed buzzed with pronouncements from bar stool detectives on the fate of the Alcatraz escapees.

On the southern end of town Police Chief Tony Marianetti stood in his favorite speed trap along Bridgeway. He was exhausted and tried, unsuccessfully, to shake off a yawn. It had been a very long and frustrating day chasing down bogus sightings of the escapees and calming nervous residents. Yet, despite – or actually, because the day had been so frenetic – Tony felt like he needed to be here. It was his way to telling the town it was safe in his hands. He even refused to carry his Colt, keeping it in the trunk of his cruiser – just as he done had since becoming Chief five years ago. Locals had taken to calling him Andy Taylor, after the popular television sheriff in a small southern town. Tony liked the comparison. Sausalito was still a small town, too. Now, with the escape, it was important to maintain that level of easy confidence. He looked out into the bay and saw Alcatraz Island ablaze in floodlights. No doubt investigators were still collecting evidence to figure out how those three men had been able to pull off the greatest prison break since Napoleon left Elba. Tony took a long, last drag on his cigarette and, after flicking it to the ground, got into his cruiser for the ride home.

As the last embers of Tony's cigarette winked out into ashes, Ron Lowendowski was tossing and turning in his Noe Valley studio apartment. He kept running through the events of the day, his mind reeling with a string of "what ifs" and "should have done" which would have gotten him on one of those Coast Guard ships tomorrow. Now he was just another schmuck with a reporter's notebook, waiting for the story to come to him, instead of being where the action was. Resigning himself to his failure, he got up and poured himself a drink and looked at the clock. Ugh. Only five hours to go until he had to be at work.

After an exhilarating day on their first mission (which had come far too soon after their exuberant night at Juanita's) Cadets Hector Gonzales and Ian Jacoby slept soundly (and gratefully) in their bunks at Coast Guard Station Golden Gate. Earlier, during mess, the commander had given a short speech. A very short speech. "The raft means we must expand our search zone. Get a good night's sleep, men, you are all back on the water at first light."

Laying on the floor in the tiny concrete room at Fort

175

Spencer, Frank Morris was fighting several losing battles. Despite swaddling himself in the blankets he had purloined from the lighthouse, the bay would not release its frozen grip, and spasms of cold still jolted his body. Every bone in his body hurt (an expression he had heard a million times but only now truly understood.) Sleep, when it came, brought only limited relief from the pain, which insinuated itself into his dreams. He would wake, sometimes gasping for air as if he were again sinking below the deflated raft into the bay. Then there was his rat nemesis, whom he was sure was planning another attack on the duffel bag. It was going to be a long night.

In the middle of San Francisco Bay, in his new cell at Alcatraz Federal Prison, inmate Allen West sobbed. Some of his tears were genuine sadness for Frank Morris and the Anglin brothers, his co-conspirators who had made it off the island but who, everyone seemed to agree, had likely drowned. Most of Allen West's tears, though, were from guilt. After the bulls discovered the vent in his cell had been loosened – just like in Morris' and the Anglin's cells – they knew he had been in on the plan and the warden, anxious to learn as much as possible as (and as quickly as possible) offered him a deal. Immunity for information. He wouldn't suffer an extension of his sentence if he just explained how they did it. West complied. And now, he cried.

Prisons are notoriously poor places to keep a secret, and word of Allen West's cooperation with authorities had spread to all corners of Alcatraz. Every inmate had an opinion, but none were stronger than prisoner AZ-1428, a bank robber from Boston who resided in Block C, Cell 314.

176

He had heard of Allen West's cooperation with authorities, how he was telling the bulls everything he knew, including details of how Morris and the others had constructed a raft big enough for four men. Some of the inmates were willing to forgive Allen West for singing. After all, the other three were already gone and nothing he could say would be of much help to the authorities, anyway. But prisoner AZ-1428 was not so forgiving. Disgusted at how quickly Allen West had flipped, Whitey Bulger kept repeating "What a fucking rat."

It was now precisely midnight, and at this late hour no one saw or heard the skiff with three people putt-putted its way west towards the Golden Gate Bridge. How surprised the world would be to learn a thirteen year-old boy held the day's biggest secret; how two of the escapees had survived a harrowing trip across the bay and were now in his care.

How surprised the boy and the two men would be to learn the third escapee was still alive.

June 13, 1962

2:00 am

Frank Morris had had enough. Angry at the unrelenting cold, angry at his aching body and, mostly, angry at his rat roommate, Frank vowed to make himself walk. He had to. The sooner he could walk the sooner he could make his way to freedom.

Easier said than done.

The effort just to roll over and get onto his knees left him gasping for air. It also made him angrier and more determined to walk. But first, he had to stand.

Again, easier said than done.

"Jesus," Frank swore as he straightened his upper body and brought his right foot out to rest flat on the ground. He pushed in front of him with the palms of his hands and slowly, agonizingly, straightened his left leg. Heavy breathing echoed through the room as he wobbled onto his two aching legs. "That was the hard part," Frank said out loud to the rat as he walked stiff-legged, like Frankenstein's monster, to the opening of the room. He stopped and leaned against the door jam, waiting for his breathing to slow. After about a minute he stepped outside onto the dirt path, pleased he was able to stand without holding onto anything. The moon cast a somber light on the battlement. He grimaced at the prospect of walking up the hill.

He had only taken one step when he remembered the duffel bag back in the room and the jealous rat no doubt waiting for an opportunity to attack it. Frank thought about going back but admitted to himself he hadn't the strength to carry – or even drag – the duffel with him. His best defense was to make this as quick a walk as possible.

Frank aimed his body towards the battlement, pushing himself forward, grunting with each step. It was torture and he was beginning to regret the effort, but when he got to the top of the hill and saw the view he was glad he had tried. Brilliantly bathed by floodlights the north tower of the Golden Gate Bridge seemed so close he felt he could almost touch it. Below, through the legs of the tower, flowed a steady stream of car lights. Frank thought jealously of the people behind those lights. Free people who could afford those cars and drive them anywhere, anytime they wanted, even at this early hour. Through the open windows of those cars Frank swore he could hear laughter and music. He imagined the cars heading north were couples going home to their children after a night in San Francisco, and the ones moving swiftly south were going clubbing in the city. No wonder they all seemed to be in a rush, with so much to live for.

Across the water, beyond the bridge, San Francisco sparkled like a young bride. Frank sighed, sadly. He had never been there and probably never would. He needed to get as far away from here as possible. An escapee can never stop running, can he? Damn, he could use a cigarette. He lamented not looking for some smokes back at the lighthouse, just as a breeze from the bay climbed up to the battlement and sent a shiver through his body. Time to go back to his hovel he thought, grudgingly, and agonizingly made his way back down the path.

If Frank had stayed up on the battlement for a while longer he might have heard it... a different sound mixing with all those rushing cars and music and laughter – the whine of a small motor propelling a skiff being skillfully piloted through the Gate by a thirteen year-old boy. On that skiff were the two men on whom he had sworn revenge.

They would soon land at Kirby Cove just a few hundred feet from where Frank was standing at that moment...

As the skiff glided under the Golden Gate Bridge, Clarence Anglin looked up, in awe, at the towers piercing the night sky. He thought about the night the Martians attacked.

"Hey John."

His brother, sitting in the front of the small craft, looked back. "Yea?"

"Look up. Do you remember?"

John looked, but just shrugged his shoulders. "Remember what?"

"Halloween back in '38. We were in Donalsonville before heading down to Florida for the winter harvest. And Pa had gotten that used radio and we was listening when they said the Martians was attacking?

John brightened. "Oh, yea, sure. I remember. It turned out it was just a play but some folks thought it was real."

"How that old Barney Entwistle? He come running and pounding on our door telling us we were all gonna get eaten by Martians." Clarence and John laughed.

"What are you two talking about?" Tommy, sitting

behind them, his hand steady on the tiller, asked.

"You're too young," Clarence said. "This was before TV. Before the war. Everyone had a radio."

"Yea, it may have been used but even we had one," John said. "See how tall the tower is and how it's all lit up? There was this part where the Martians was about to attack New York and the announcer is looking across the river and he says, 'they're as tall as the skyscrapers,' but in all the towns we had been at I don't think we'd ever seen a building taller'n four stories."

"But we'd seen pictures of New York and knew them Martians had to be pretty tall."

"I heard old Barney slept with his rifle by his bed after that."

"His wife said it was better company, anyways."

The brothers laughed at the shared memory. It got very quiet for a while as the skiff putted from under the bridge and plied its way west. Clarence, his leg still throbbing, closed his eyes. John had been watching the shore and was riveted by the daunting height of the rock face vaulting from the water.

"Hey kid, you said there was a beach."

Tommy lifted his arm and motioned in front of them to a small, inviting stretch of sand glowing in reflected moonlight. "Kirby Cove," he said.

John smiled and nodded, gratefully. "Almost there, brother."

Tommy's brow furrowed with worry. "Are you sure he can walk?"

Clarence was quick to answer. "I'll be okay." Tommy sensed he was annoyed by the attention.

"Yea, he'll be fine," John added.

Even though the brothers were in front, facing away from him, Tommy still nodded. "Okay, get ready," he said loudly, pushing the rudder to one side to point so the skiff

182

was precisely perpendicular to the shore.

"Get ready for what?" John asked just as Tommy gunned the engine to full throttle. John's eyes grew wider, his back arched as the beach grew larger and wider by the second. Then he realized the kid was not going to stop until –

The skiff slid onto the sand Tommy and cut the engine. They quickly skidded to a satisfying stop on the beach. "We're here," he said proudly. John breathing heavily, turned around and Tommy was surprised how angry he looked.

"Jesus Christ, kid. You coulda warned us."

Tommy looked crestfallen. "I'm sorry, John. Because of Clarence's leg I thought you'd want to be as far up on the beach..."

"John, what are you doing?" came Clarence's stern voice. "Give the kid a break, he was just doing what we asked."

Now it was John's turn to feel bad. He quickly raised his hands. "I'm sorry kid. You got us here just like you said. I just... aw shit, I'm sorry."

Tommy nodded understandingly. Maybe this was what it was like to have a brother (Not your run-of-the-mill brother, but a brother who had escaped from prison only 24 hours ago.) "It's okay, John, Look, we're real close, see?" he said as he pointed to a dirt path which curved behind a small brush-covered hill. "The fort is just on the other side."

John nodded and smiled, letting Tommy know everything was okay between them. "Come on, let's get Clarence out of the boat," John said.

"I'm way head of –" they heard Clarence start to say as he tried to lift himself out of the skiff. "Shit," he said, wincing as he slid back into the boat. He looked up and saw creases of worry on John's face. "It's okay, my leg is just a bit stiff from the boat ride. Just help me get to my feet."

"Hey kid, a little help?"

Tommy hurried to John's side and they brought Clarence first to a sitting position then, with John supporting him under his armpits, got him standing in the skiff.

"Okay, let's have you step out of the boat, now," John said as he wrapped an arm around Clarence's waist. "That's it... just lean on me. There you go. Tommy, get the duffel bag while we start walking up that path." Tommy nodded and hoisted the bag over his small shoulders. He saw Clarence limping as he used John as a crutch, but overall he thought he was moving at a pretty good pace considering what they had been through. They reached the top of the path and waited for Tommy to catch up.

They were all now about ten feet above the beach. To their left were two, connected, single-story curved concrete structures built into the ground, their roof overgrown with weeds and beach grass merging seamlessly into the hill which rose above the beach.

"Above... that's where the guns were," Tommy said, pointing as he moved in front of them and led them down a short flight of stairs. "Over there, see?" he said, pointing an opening where a door had once hung. "That's an old bunker. You can stay in there until Clarence's leg is better. Almost no one ever comes up here and if someone does you can say you're just a couple of hikers enjoying the view, right?"

John looked impressed. "You really figured it all out, didn't you?"

Tommy, embarrassed, smiled. "I gotta get going now. It'll be sunrise soon and I gotta get back before my mom comes home from work. But I'll be back tomorrow night."

"With more of that great food from your mom's place, I hope," Clarence said.

"You bet."

"Listen if you can get us a couple of razors we could both use a shave for when we finally head out.," John said as he helped Clarence limp to the door-sized opening in the structure.

"Yea, sure. My mom has some. I can bring them tomorrow night."

"Here that Clarence? A girl's razor just for your tender skin," John said with a grin. Clarence responded with the appropriate finger. "Thanks," John said to Tommy as he guided Clarence inside the bunker. "See you tomorrow night, kid."

Only when Tommy saw them completely disappear into the dark of the bunker did he turn and walk back to the beach, get in his skiff, and ride home.

3:03 am

At Juanita's, the escape continued to be all people could talk about. And everyone seemed to be an expert.

"No way they survived. The water's too cold."

"But they were in a raft."

"Ah, you've only been out fishing during the day. I've been out there at night and let me tell you it's pretty damn cold even on the deck of a boat."

"I dunno, I heard back in the thirties some women made the swim from Alcatraz to the ferry building in San Francisco."

"Really?"

"Oh, don't listen to him, those girls were on a swim team. They were trained athletes."

"Exactly. No way prisoners can prepare for something like that."

"I heard they were heading for Angel Island."

"Ha! Good luck, then. The place is crawling with soldiers. Let 'em try something."

Dressed in her bright, flower-patterned, flowing muumuu Juanita floated between tables putting the brakes on any conversation she felt was getting too heated. "Honey, I say anything is possible," was her standard response to anyone who asked her opinion. Juanita's watchful eye (backed in no small measure by her imposing physical presence) worked because Molly couldn't remember a quieter night. The last table of customers (still arguing the finer points of currents and navigation) had left the restaurant a half-hour ago and Molly was grateful to be done for the night. She was slipping on her sweater and heading for the door when Juanita's bellowed from across the restaurant.

"Hey, where do you think you're going?"

"Did you need something, Juanita?"

"Are you going home?"

Molly nodded. Juanita scowled. "Well, yer not walking. Ernesto will drive you home." Molly started to speak but Juanita stopped her with a wave of her arm. "Don't argue with me."

"Is this about the escape? Why, you don't really think they survived, do you? Or that they made it all the way here to Sausalito?"

"Honey, I wasn't just slinging hash back there. When I say anything is possible I mean anything is possible."

Molly had worked for Juanita long enough to know when not to argue.

"Thank you," she said, appreciatively.

After a few minutes, the cook emerged from the kitchen and they walked to his car.

As they began the short ride to her houseboat, Molly asked "you're from around here, right?"

Ernesto nodded. "Born and raised. You are from Kansas, no?"

Molly nodded. "You've fished out there, right?"

"Si. My dad first took me out when I was two. At least that's what my mother says."

"My husband used to take our son out." Molly smiled at the memory. "So, what do you think?"

The cook just shook his head. "*Imposible*," he replied, in Spanish. "My dad, he says the same thing."

She nodded, surprised at how comforted his response made her feel. The car pulled up to the gate and she got out and shut the door, then poked her head through the open passenger window. "Gracias, Ernesto. See you tomorrow night."

"De nada," he replied.

Gravel spewed from beneath the wheels as the car surged forward. Was he in a rush to get home to his wife and child, Molly wondered. Maybe he was more concerned about the escapees than he wished to admit. Nah, it was crazy to think those men were still alive. She walked down the ramp along the walkway to her houseboat and stepped onto the deck and stretched, looking out at the slowly setting moon. She happily slipped off her shoes and walked down into the houseboat's kitchen area. There, Molly took a small wad of bills from her pocketbook and smiled. Not a bad night for tips, she thought. All that talk about the escape seemed to make people thirsty.

She sat down at the small kitchen table and allowed herself a moment to just to sit and do nothing. Molly reveled in the reliable rocking of the boat and heard the soft sloshing of water on the hull... a seagull cawing... wind rustling through hung laundry... sounds which

187

brought comfort and... to her horror she realized one sound was missing.

Tommy. Breathing as he slept.

Molly raced to the door of her son's room and flung it open. To her horror, she saw an empty bed. "Tommy?" she said, tentatively, at first, as if he were pulling some Hallowe'en prank. But Tommy didn't pop out of his closet or from a pile of clothes yelling "boo." Fear rising, she rushed over to his closet, desperately flinging pieces of clothing aside in the futile hope he was hiding there. She stopped and exhaled. Tommy was not in his room. Then, a hopeful idea – maybe he had a bad dream and went into her bed? She raced through the kitchen and looked into her bedroom. Her shoulders slumped with disappointment. He wasn't there, either. The chalk board! Maybe one of his friends was in trouble and he left her a note. Molly raced back to the kitchen, her heart sinking when she saw a blank chalk board.

Molly felt panic rising and she brought her hands to her chest as her breathing increased. She forced herself to think... where else could he be? Then she had a terrifying thought. She raced to the deck and looked over the port side and, to her horror, saw Tommy's skiff was missing.

She was furious. Tommy had broken the house rule not to go out after she went to work.

Okay, now to figure out... what to do first... whom should she call? Tommy's friend, Billy. Yes. They were supposed to be together yesterday but Tommy had said something happened with Billy's family so they had to cancel. Maybe Billy knew where Tommy was. She hurried back to the kitchen area and looked at the clock. It was almost 3:30 in the morning. Molly hesitated – just for a moment – then picked up the phone and dialed.

Up in the Marin Hills, high above Sausalito in a spectacular home impossible not to envy, Cynthia and

Brad Winslow's sound sleep was shattered by the urgent ringing of the telephone. (Funny how a telephone's ring can be described as 'urgent' when it happens after midnight.) Cynthia fumbled valiantly for the receiver through two more rings before she finally got the handset off its cradle and to her ear.

"Hrftdf?" was the best she could offer.

"Cynthia, I am so sorry to call so late."

"Mho is fridf?"

"It's Molly O'Conner. Is Tommy with you?"

A question no parent wants to hear. Cynthia was awake, now. "What? No. I mean, I don't think so. He's not in his bed?"

Molly curbed her natural impulse for sarcasm (like, why would I be calling if he was) answering simply, "No. Could you check if he's there with your son?"

"Of course. Hold on," she said as she swung her legs off the bed and stood up.

From the comfort of the other side of their bed her husband stirred. "Cynth? Zat you? What's going on?"

"It's Molly from the houseboats. Her son isn't home."

"How is that our problem?" he asked without moving.

"Shhh, she can hear you," Cynthia replied as she headed for the door. "Just keep quiet. I'll be right back"

"Mmmph"

Cynthia returned after a few minutes and picked up the receiver. "Molly?"

"Yes?"

"I'm sorry, he's not here. I woke William and asked if he knew anything but he said the last time he heard from Tommy was yesterday when he called to say you and he had something to do."

"Wait. What? He told me Billy had canceled because your family had something to do."

Cynthia was now fully awake. "Did you try Raymond's or Freddie's?"

"You really didn't have something for Billy to do?'

"No. Sorry."

"Thank you. Sorry again for waking you."

"Let me know when you find him."

"I will," Molly replied.

Cynthia held onto the receiver before slowly returning it to its cradle.

The lump stirred again. "Cynth? What did she say?"

"She said Tommy told her our Billy canceled their boat trip because we had something to do."

From under the lump of blanket her husband emerged and sat up. "But... we didn't."

"No."

Her husband shook his head and sighed, sympathetically. "Well, you know, the sort of people who live down on the houseboats."

"Oh, Brad, don't start that again."

"I'm sure some of them are nice enough, but ... "

"Brad. A little sympathy. Her son is missing. Honestly," Cynthia said as she flounced into bed and pulled up the covers.

Her husband rolled over and placed his arm around her. "I just meant some kids are brought up with fewer rules, that's all. I'm sure he's fine. We'll call in a few hours and you'll see. He'll be there."

Down the hill in her houseboat, far from the spectacular views offered to those who lived up in the Marin Hills, Molly was beside herself. Her frantic calls to the parents of Tommy's other friends had been fruitless. With each call she imagined news of her unfitness as a mother was fast spreading around town. ("Doesn't she know where her own son is?") Molly sighed. All her life she wanted solve her own problems. But now she had to face facts. It was time to call the police. Damn it. Molly hated the idea of this becoming an official police matter. Maybe she should call Tony directly? Christ, and give him a reason to believe she was a helpless female unable to take care of her son? Molly exhaled. "You aren't in high school, damn it," she said out loud to the empty houseboat. She dialed Tony's home number.

Tony Marianetti took a Marine's pride in being able to quickly snap awake and be ready for action. It wasn't a skill they could teach in Boot Camp or one which could be taught to others – one either had it or didn't. Somewhere, in a drawer someplace, was a medal which bore the testimony of a squad of men on the Palau islands who are alive today because, even in a deep sleep, Tony reacted to the snap of a twig from an approaching enemy soldier. So, when the phone in his apartment rang at 4:30 in the morning – only a few hours after he had gotten to bed – Tony was as alert as if he had been reached in the middle of the day. Within five minutes he was dressed and in his squad car. Five minutes later he was pulling up to Molly's houseboat.

She was waiting for him on deck. "I am so sorry to wake you, but I've called all of Tommy's friends' homes and his skiff is gone and I didn't know what else to do."

Even Tony knew this was no time for swagger as he walked onto the deck and put his arms on Molly's shoulders. "It's going to be okay. Let me look around to see if I can find something that could give us a clue as to where he might have gone. If I can't find anything I'll call the state police for help."

The state police? Molly grimaced. Great. Even more

191

people getting involved in her business.

"He was supposed to be at Horseshoe Bay helping a friend with a new boat," she said as Tony walked around her son's bedroom, examining his books, pieces of clothing and papers inside the desk drawers.

"You said he went shopping with you yesterday morning. Was that something he usually did?"

"Oh, boys, you know. Who wants to go shopping with his mother?"

Tony stopped his search to look Molly in the eyes. "But he did yesterday."

"Do you think that means something?"

"Depends. Did he ask to buy anything out of the ordinary?"

"Not that I recall, no. It was a typical shop, you know, milk eggs, juice... cans of food to have around just in case."

"Uh huh."

Molly crossed the room to Tony. "What?"

The officer shook his head. "Nothing, I was just thinking, is all. Are you sure you –" Tony stopped, interrupted by a strange look which suddenly appeared on Molly's face. "What is it?"

She didn't answer, instead she bolted out of the bedroom. Tony followed her into the kitchen. She was at the bottom of the stairs to the deck. "Kill the lights," she commanded as she walked up to the deck.

"What?"

"The switch is over there," she said, leaning back down and pointed to a bank of light switches on the wall. Tony flipped all the switches down and the houseboat was plunged into darkness. He heard her footsteps heading to the stern of the boat and he followed. When he got to the back of the boat he saw her leaning on the railing, looking into the dark.

"Molly, what –"

192

"Shhh," she scowled back. Tony could see her straining to hear... to hear what? After a minute or so, without looking at him, Molly said "I could have sworn I heard a small engine."

"Like the one on –"

"Yes, the skiff."

Tommy had been pushing the outboard motor hard since leaving the Anglins at Kirby Cove. He knew he was running the risk of overheating the small outboard motor but it was vital he beat his mother home. He cut the engine as he approached the houseboat (in case a nosy neighbor was awake.) As he maneuvered the rudder and brought the skiff silently towards the stern of the houseboat he felt elated. No lights were on. His mother had not gotten home yet.

But he was wrong. As he coasted to the edge of the dock he saw her, arms folded, disappointment etched on her weary face.

In those few seconds Tommy frantically constructed a tale of an engine running out of gas, of a frenzied row to Horseshoe Bay and a desperate, almost heroic search for gasoline. As he tied up the skiff he was sure his mother would be so happy to see him she would forgive him breaking her number one rule... not to go out at night. Then, when he stepped onto the deck, he saw Tony, thumbs thrust firmly behind his gun belt in that 'I'm the law' stance Tommy always hated.

"Well?" was all his mother said.

The heroic tale stuck in his throat, Tommy could only, meekly, squeak, "does he have to be here?"

"He... for your information, is here because I had to call him in a panic at four this morning because my son was missing. Anything you have to say to me you will say

193

in front of Officer Marianetti."

Tommy's eyes were locked on his mother but, in his peripheral vision, saw Tony hitch up his gun belt.

"Well? We're waiting."

He was desperate. The lie was out of his mouth before he could think it through. "I was clamming. With Billy... and... the skiff ran out of gas so we had to row to the marina. There wasn't a phone booth and you were working, and we looked for gas but couldn't find any, and... I'm sorry." Tommy lowered his head to emphasize the sorry, then glanced up to see Tony and his mother shaking their heads.

"Tommy?" He raised his head to look at his mother. "I called Billy's house. It was the first thing I did when I got home and found out you weren't here. Do you know what his mother said? She said Billy was home asleep."

Tommy's mind raced to produce a patch for the growing leak of lies. "Well, sure, of course. After we found gas for the skiff – did I mention we found a can near the Yacht Club? Anyway afterwards I dropped him off at Swede's Beach and he walked home."

Now it was Tony's turn. "So you're telling your mother that your friend walked almost a mile uphill to the highlands to get home, crossing the 101 in the process? And you're telling your mother your friend got home on foot faster than you did on your skiff?"

"Well?" his mother said firmly. "Answer Officer Marianetti."

Tommy felt like one of those rats in a maze looking for the piece of cheese but instead faces an empty dead end. But at least the rat could turn around and go back. Tommy couldn't. It would just lead to more questions which might lead to the two men he had been protecting. Maybe... maybe after the Anglins were safely away he could tell his mother everything. No, of course he couldn't. What was he thinking? He could never tell anyone. Not even his own mother. He remained silent.

Molly sighed. She turned to Tony. "Maybe it's best if you go. I'm sorry he's so stubborn about lying. Thank you for coming so quickly, Tony."

"Of course. You know, anytime..."

She nodded gratefully. "I do. It's late. Or early. I don't know anymore. Maybe he'll be more cooperative tomorrow after some sleep."

Tony nodded and tipped his hat. Then, after a quick glare at Tommy, he walked to his patrol car. Molly watched him drive away and then, without turning around, in a voice now devoid of emotion, "Go to bed, Tommy."

He sullenly slunk into his room and flopped miserably onto his bed, too tired to take off his clothes. Off in the distance the sun, just rising, was peeking under the Bay Bridge and shining through the prism on his windowsill. Tommy watched a stretched-out rainbow began to form on the wall. He mused how this is how it usually was when he woke up... how he would watch the rainbow move across his ceiling and down the far wall, and how dramatically his life changed two days ago when he stopped at Yellow Bluff and saw something move on the beach below. He fell, guiltily, into a deep sleep.

11:00 am

Thank you, God, for creating coffee.

Ron Lowendowski had needed five cups to get through his morning news shift, every hour repeating the same story every other station in town had; the Alcatraz escapees were still at large and a prison informant revealed they had a raft. He winced every time he read about the raft. If he hadn't been so stupid at the Coast Guard station yesterday he'd be on one of those boats today reporting first-hand on the search for the escapees. Now, after delivering his last newscast of the morning, Ron leaned back in the newsroom's lone, broken-down office chair and closed his eyes. The caffeine had served its purpose. It had gotten him through the morning. Now it was an unwelcome guest, his body practically vibrating from all the stimulant in his system.

"Jesus, you look like crap."

Ron poked open one eye and saw Nick leaning heavily on the door frame. "Look who's talking," he replied.

Nick snorted a self-deprecating laugh. "You wanna grab some lunch before you head home? Marichal beat the Reds last night. I won ten bucks so lunch is on me."

"Naw," Ron said, both eyes now closed, again. "I just need to –" The staccato of four bells from the teletype machine interrupted him.

"You gonna check on that?" Nick asked.

His eyes still closed, Ron lazily responded "four bells, probably some city councilor announcing a plan to clean up the parks."

"Yea," the disc-jockey grunted. "Well, I'm gonna get some lunch. Last chance." Ron remained inert. Nick was about to leave when he glanced over to the teletype machine, quiet after pounding out the bulletin. Shrugging his shoulders, he ambled over to the printout and read:

Alcatraz Escapees Charged
June 13, 1962
San Francisco (AP) An authorized complaint was filed today before the United States Circuit Court charging the Alcatraz escapees Frank Morris, John Anglin, and Clarence Anglin with a violation

196

of title 18, section 751, U.S. Code. This code makes it a federal crime to escape a federal prison.

Federal Warrants were issued for their arrest and these were lodged with United States Marshal Woelflen who recommended bond of $50,000 each. that on or about June 11, 1962, at Alcatraz, San Francisco County, Northern District of California, they did escape from an institution; to wit, United States Penitentiary, Alcatraz, California, in which they had been confined by direction of the Attorney General of the United States. The warrant concludes that "the subjects, still at large, are all convicted bank robbers and should be considered extremely dangerous."

Anyone with information of the whereabouts of Morris or the Anglins is to call NATIONAL 8-7117.

Nick blinked hard to be sure he was reading the bulletin correctly. Those three men... the ones who had been convicted of bank robbery? The ones who planned a daring escape from an island prison? They better hope they got away, because now they had officially committed the crime of... escaping from prison. Nick started to chuckle at the irony. Soon he was laughing hysterically.

"What the hell, Nick?" Ron spat.

Still laughing, Nick ripped the bulletin off the wire and handed it to the newsman.

Ron did not see the humor.

12 Noon

From his post on the mess hall catwalk Paul Barone could

sense a change in the prisoners. The dreary, mind-numbing routine of Alcatraz had been disrupted by the shocking discovery, only yesterday, of the incredible achievement of three prisoners. Everybody from the warden down to the cooks and the gardener had heard about the fake heads, the dislodged vents and – most embarrassing to the guards – the homemade raft three men had constructed in a hidden workshop just above the cell block.

The mess hall buzzed with talk of their triumph, one for which many claimed a supporting role. Prisoners proudly regaled listeners how they collected scrap wood for paddles or raincoats for the raft. Occasionally an inmate would look up to the catwalk and sneer smugly at the patrolling guards.

As ordered, the guards remained impassive. Warden Blackwell's instructions at the morning meeting were clear. "Let them have their fun," he had said. "We still have a prison to run. Restoring routine is the order of the day. I promise you within a few days Alcatraz will be back to normal."

Paul wasn't sure he would ever feel normal, and he gripped his baton tighter. He was beginning to wonder if his wife Sharon was right. Maybe they should have stayed in Virginia.

"Hey, Barone."

He turned and saw Jim Albright standing next to him. He nodded, somberly. With a knowing smile the older guard said, "You're thinking about Robert Williams, aren't you?"

At the mention of the prisoner's name, Paul gripped his baton even tighter. This was one secret that somehow they had managed to keep from the public and the prisoners – that there were two more cons in on the plan. Both had dropped out months before the escape. One was

198

a burglar named Stephens. He was no big deal. But it was this sixth man, Williams, whose participation sent chills down Barone's spine. "And why the hell not," he said to Albright. "Those others... Morris, the Anglins, Allen West... they were just thieves and burglars. Not choir boys, for sure, but Williams was a murderer. Can you imagine the panic if he had escaped with the others? My wife and children are out there, for Christ's sake."

Albright chuckled.

"You think that's funny?"

"No, of course not. But I couldn't help notice you just said 'were.'"

"Huh?"

"You just said 'they were thieves and burglars'. Not 'are' but 'were.' Come on, Paul, you know they don't have a chance in hell out there."

"Even with a raft?"

Jim Albright smiled back. "Trust me, Paul," he said with a fatherly tone. "Not even with a raft."

1:03 pm

Molly had given up trying to sleep an hour ago. Angrily throwing back the covers she had gone to the kitchen where she made a pot of coffee, lit a cigarette, and stewed... fighting the urge to wake Tommy (how dare he be able to sleep after what he had done) and demand the truth.

Tommy emerged from his room as she was pouring herself another cup of coffee. She searched his face vainly for a hint of contrition. There was none. She watched, bitterly, as he entered the galley, made himself a bowl of cereal and sat down at the table across from her. Just as if it were a typical morning and he had not been caught in the biggest lie of his life. She watched him eat and sighed. Loudly.

"Yea?" he said.

"I didn't say anything."

"Oh."

"I was hoping you would be ready to talk."

"There's nothing to talk about," he said as he stood up and put his bowl in the sink.

Molly fumed. "You were out all night. You show up at the break of dawn and lie about who you're with. I think there's plenty to talk about."

Tommy whirled around. "Look, I'm sorry I got you worried," he said. "I was just out... you know, on the skiff."

"With Billy."

"Yea."

"I told you I talked to his parents last night. They said he never left the house." Tommy shrugged his shoulders and shook his head. "So they didn't know their son was gone?"

"Well, neither did I." She glared at him, then sighed. "Don't you trust me? If there's something wrong, Tommy, if someone is threatening you –"

"No, that's not it," he said, looking down at the floor.

"Then what is it?" she asked, softly. "You know you can tell me anything."

He stopped himself from rolling his eyes. Yea. Right. This was way more than just anything. Damn it, why hadn't he told Billy to tell his parents they were together? Because Billy couldn't keep a secret, that's why. And there was no secret bigger than this one.

"Tommy, are you listening to me?"

"Uh, yea, sure."

She gave him the we-both-know-you-weren't look before saying "I was saying that I would prefer not to be out tonight, but unfortunately, Juanita is short-handed and I have work. But you are grounded, Tommy. You are not to leave this house."

Wait. What? His mother wouldn't be home tonight? This was great news. He could still make his run to Kirby Cove. He'd just have to be sure to get back in time so –"

"And don't look for your skiff, either, because it's gone."

Wait. What? "Gone? Where... where is it?"

"It's not here is all you need to know," she said, her tone decidedly chilly. Then, just a swiftly, mother's instinct took over as she said, softly, "I brought home dinner from Juanita's. As I always do. You can have that for dinner. Listen to the ballgame if you like. But –"

"I know, I know. Stay home," he replied. Then, just loud enough for her to hear, "Not like I can go anywhere now, anyway."

Molly's head whipped around with a withering glare which caused Tommy to fearfully fall back. "Excuse me?" He wisely dropped his head. "That's what I thought. Now go to your room."

He couldn't show it, but Tommy wanted to cry. He felt terrible about lying to his mother. As he stood in his bedroom and looked out at the bay he could hear the whine of engines – Coast Guard boats, he reckoned – out on the water scouring for three bodies. But he knew they would only find one, that of the third man who the Anglins said had fallen out of their raft. It was a strange feeling to be thirteen and know something the rest of the world does not. It made him smile... just a bit.

So did the fact that his mother had forgotten about his bicycle. After she left for work he would use it to return to Kirby Cove.

9:00 pm

As Frank Morris slept, he dreamed of home.

Home? How ironic. What was home to someone whose life was a string of foster homes which only served as temporary way-stations between incarcerations? Yet, somehow, his mind had conjured the false memory of a cozy, comfortable bed in a room filled with books and trophies and a closet full of new clothes... sunlight filtering through lace curtains... robins and bluebirds on the limbs of a dogwood tree just outside his window joyfully chirping the beginning of a new day... and the smell of sizzling bacon and warm flapjacks from the kitchen downstairs wafting into his nostrils. He smiled and opened his eyes.

Blackness muscled aside the sunshine and ripped the lace curtains off the window and the aroma of bacon and flapjacks were brutally replaced with the musty smell of the abandoned concrete bunker. The robins and bluebirds were gone, too, their gentle chirping replaced by his own breathing, labored and disappointed.

He sighed sadly. Those flapjacks sure smelled good. Okay, tough guy, back to reality. Frank raised his head and – hey, this was a good sign – it didn't feel as if it were going to fall off. Maybe tonight he could finally get moving. Unsure if his legs agreed, Frank moved them slowly inward towards his body and stood up. To his surprise they actually felt pretty good. Better than good, he decided, as he tentatively stepped around the bunker. They still ached but the debilitating twinges were gone. Frank smiled. Grabbing the map he had taken from the lighthouse he walked outside (the fresh air sure smelled good) and plotted his course along the shore to the next fort.

Frank stepped back inside the bunker, walked to the duffel bag, and took out another package of C-rations. He grunted. Any gratitude when he first found the trove of old army food had disappeared a dozen bites ago. This may be survival but it wasn't living. Soon enough, though, if he had any luck he'd have some real food. He grunted again. The universe owed him some luck, for once.

Back at the houseboat Tommy had been feigning sleep as his mother prepared for her shift at Juanita's. It wasn't about sparing her feelings, it was because the last thing he wanted was another argument which would delay her departure. He had calculated how much time he would need tonight; an hour to bike to Kirby Cove, an hour to get back and half an hour – tops – to deliver the food his mother brought from Juanita's last night. Even on his bike he calculated he could complete his mission long before she returned.

"Good night Tommy, I'm leaving now. I love you," his mother called out, plaintively.

He froze. Should he respond? No, better not. Don't have the time to risk another scene. He heard the crunch of gravel under her feet as she climbed into the cab of the cook's truck. Tommy walked to the deck of the boat and saw her glance, sadly, back at the houseboat as they drove off. He wondered if she knew he was 'playing possum?' But he had no time for guilt. He had his mission. When he saw the truck's taillights disappear onto Bridgeway, he headed for his bicycle. From nearby boats he heard televisions blaring Russ Hodges' play-by-play of tonight's Giants game against Cincinnati. Thank you, Willie Mays, for distracting the neighbors. With a furtive glance around the dock, Tommy hopped onto his bicycle and began his ride south, down Bridgeway to Kirby Cove.

Sitting in his patrol car tucked neatly between two buildings on the southern end of Bridgeway, Tony Marianetti took a grateful sip of black coffee from his thermos. He smiled at every local who honked as they drove by because he knew they would spread the word he was in his regular place, which meant the escape wasn't worth worrying about. Everything would be back to normal before –

Whoosh. A boy in a bicycle flew past him, heading south. Tony recognized him immediately.

Tommy. What the hell was he doing now? Tony threw the rest of his coffee out of the open window, put the cruiser in gear and pulled out onto Bridgeway. He picked up the microphone of the police radio to report he was in motion but decided, for Molly's sake, not to explain why. Better see where this kid was going, first. At the end of Bridgeway, where it curved and became Richardson Street, Tony saw his headlights throwing bright light in front of his cruiser. Damn it. He didn't want the boy to know there was someone behind him. He turned off his headlights. Then he prayed no one was driving in the opposite direction...

Ahead, in the dark, Tommy pedaled slowly and cautiously down narrow East Road. He wanted to go faster but, last summer, on this same road, he had drifted onto the unpaved shoulder and, as he later described it, "the wheels of my bike went one way and I went another." He still had the scars on his elbows and knees. Unaware of Tony's car trailing stealthily behind him, Tommy coasted past the Coast Guard Station and then around Horseshoe Bay until he saw the narrow road which ran under the

Golden Gate Bridge towards Kirby Cove. He figured to be with the Anglins in about fifteen minutes, which meant he was on schedule to make it back home before his mother. Tommy looked to his left at Alcatraz Island, urgently lit by searchlights in the middle of the dark bay.

He felt a surge of emotions and feelings. Power. Control. "I could end it with a phone call," he mused. But he knew he wouldn't. At least, he had no reason to. Not yet, anyway.

Tony saw Tommy veer onto the small road which ran under the approach to the Golden Gate Bridge. He knew the road – it was a winding affair walkers and bicyclers used to meander around the Marin headlands. What the hell would the kid be doing up here at night? A thought popped in his head... could he be meeting a girl? He smirked. Ha. Didn't think the kid had it in him. Can't wait to see how Molly would react to that. Tony was still smirking when he saw Tommy veer off, again, onto a dirt path which, damn it, was too narrow for the cruiser. Tony stopped and got out in time to see Tommy's bicycle disappear under the bridge, into the night. He knew the path from his own exploration of the area when he was younger. It ended not too far from here, at Kirby Beach. Tony reached into the cruiser and opened the glove compartment. He was about to retrieve his flashlight when the two-way radio came to life.

"Car One this is dispatch. Come in Tony."

He picked up the microphone. "This is One. What's up?"

"Disturbance at Juanita's."

"What's happening?"

The dispatcher didn't try to hide her amusement as she said, "A customer didn't believe it when Juanita said he would have to 'eat it or wear it'."

"Let me guess. He ended up wearing it."

"10-4."

Tony sighed. "Okay, I'll head over."

"Have fun, Chief."

"Thank you, dispatch." Tony put down the microphone, took one last look under the bridge and reluctantly drove back to town.

Frank Morris looked at his map and saw a path running along a ridge. Taking the path would be easier, sure, and it was unlikely anyone would be out at night. But his instincts, honed from years of evading capture, told him to avoid taking even the smallest of chances, so he hoisted the duffel bag on his shoulders and began to walk downhill, through the woods. Going downhill was quickly proving to be a challenge after the grueling treatment his body had received over the past two days. By the time he reached the bottom of the hill he was exhausted. He dropped his bag and sat down.

The map showed another abandoned fort at the top of the upcoming hill. He didn't relish the thought of another night in another concrete cell. But what choice did he have? His legs – hell, his whole body – were screaming for more time to recuperate. He grudgingly stood up and hoisted the duffel bag over his shoulders and, grunting with every step, slowly made his way up to the crest of the hill. Before him was another abandoned concrete gun emplacement, a bit smaller than the one he had just left. He sighed and, like a weary traveling salesman pulling into another cheap motel, looked around at his home for the night.

A set of stairs led down to several small concrete structures so thickly covered in vines and vegetation it looked as if the buildings themselves had grown out of the ground. Frank was soon standing at the opening of a small concrete room which looked – and smelled – just like the one he had just left. Damn it. If only his legs didn't hurt so much. Okay, it's just for the night, he assured himself as he limped into the darkness. He couldn't see his entrance had scared the bunker's current occupant.

Four little feet scampered across his.

A rat.

Frank's scream was long and loud.

Tommy O'Conner was close to Kirby Cove when he heard the scream and jammed on his brakes. He was confused. He had left the Anglins at Kirby Battery, which was in front of him but the scream had come from the woods on the left. Was it one of the Anglins? Did they have to leave Kirby? Had someone spotted them? Should he go and investigate? Tommy looked frantically at his watch. No, there wasn't time, not if he was sure to be back home before his mother. He had no choice. Continue to Kirby Cove and hope the Anglins were still there. As for the scream, well, he knew the area well enough to know how sounds bounced around the hills. Maybe he just thought it came from there. He certainly hoped so.

When he reached Kirby Battery he was relieved to see John and Clarence sitting outside their bunker. They seemed calm, so they must not have heard the scream. Tommy decided not to bring it up. Instead, he held up the bag of leftover food. "I brought you this," he said. John took the bag, opened it, and sniffed gratefully.

"Know what, Clarence, we gotta make it to this..." John said as he looked at Tommy.

"Juanita's."

"Yea, Juanita's. We should go there someday," John

207

said. Tommy watched, enviously, as John evenly distributed the food between himself and his brother.

"Ha, might be fun to actually sit down and be served a meal instead of standing in line like in the joint," Clarence added through a mouthful of hamburger.

Tommy imagined the sight of his mother serving the Anglin brothers as if they were any two men who had come to Juanita's for dinner. His mother, who must be thinking so many troubling things about her son. A wave of sadness came over him, so complete John was taken aback.

"Hey kid, you okay?"

Tommy, embarrassed, quickly threw on a smile. "Yea, I just... my mom may be getting out of work early so I better be in bed before she comes home."

"Same time tomorrow night?"

"Yea, should be no problem."

"Try to come earlier tomorrow so we can talk."

"Talk?"

"Yea, John's leg is still hurting but we need to talk to you about some people we need to get in touch with."

"People? Who?"

"The less you know the better. Let's just say we didn't bust out without a plan of our own," John said.

"Yea, Frank didn't know everything about us."

John could see Tommy was not sure how to process what he and his brother were saying. "It's okay, Tommy, you got us this far. When you bring the food tomorrow if you could bring us a map it would help us a lot."

"Yea, sure. I can find one for you. But I gotta get going. My mom and all..."

"See you tomorrow, then."

"Thanks again," Clarence said, his mouth full.

Tommy climbed the steps from the bunker, got on his bike and headed back to the main road near the marina. As he passed under a streetlight he glanced at his watch. He should beat his mother home, although his confidence was tempered by the lingering shock, from last night, of seeing her waiting for him on deck. When he got to the parking lot he hopped off his bicycle and walked it slowly to the houseboat. He saw the lights were off – that was good thing – but, then, they were off last night when he returned on his skiff. Tommy tentatively walked onto the houseboat, exhaling relief when he confirmed his mother was not home. Before long he was in bed listening to the sound of water lapping against the hull of the houseboat. He sighed. Tonight, it brought him little comfort.

All he could think of was the huge tear in his relationship with his mother. Whatever childhood transgressions he had committed before this week, they had always been able to patch things up. This time... well this would be the biggest patch job yet. Tommy convinced himself that once the brothers were gone he could make it happen. He and his mother... they were inseparable, after all. It was them against the world, right? Had been for all these years. Yea, sure, everything would work out.

Within five minutes he was asleep, blissfully unaware Tony had been tailing him or of the dispatcher's call which had sent him to Juanita's.

His tracking of Tommy interrupted by the police call, Tony was already in a foul mood as he pulled his cruiser outside Juanita's. He stepped out of the car, drawing himself up to his full height. He placed one hand firmly on the handle of his nightstick, strode authoritatively into the restaurant and heard... laughter.

At the bar he saw two men, neither of whom he recognized, standing next to Juanita. One of them was covered in what Tony presumed were the remnants of the night's special. Juanita's infectious cackle filled the room and everyone, including the man wearing the dinner, seemed to be in on the joke.

But Tony was pissed. For this they called the police? "Hey? What's this about a fight?" he bellowed.

As if a switch had been thrown, the laughter stopped. Every head in the restaurant whipped around to see Tony at the restaurant's entrance.

Juanita broke the silence. "Yer too late, Chief," she said, pointing her thumb at the man with clumps of food clinging to his hair. "We're all out of the special." With that, the room exploded again into laughter.

Molly walked over to Tony, apology written all over her face. "I'm sorry, Tony. I'm the one who called. Usually I'm sure Juanita can handle a customer but I don't know these two men and, what with everything happening the past few days... Anyway I hope I didn't pull you from anything important."

Tony took a deep breath, gently touched her elbow, and guided her to the front door. "We need to talk."

June 14, 1962

7:00 am

For two days Ian Jacoby and Hector Gonzales had faithfully manned their posts on the deck of their TRS, searching for what prison officials confidently predicted would be the bodies of the three escaped prisoners. Yet, for two days, they had returned to Golden Gate Station with nothing to report except monotonous stretches of water.

"With no reliable reports from anywhere around the bay, we will continue to employ the grid system to search the waters for the missing prisoners," the Commander was saying at this morning's briefing.

Ian saw a hand shoot up in the air. His own. All eyes turned towards him. "Sir, how much longer will we continue to search?" he asked.

Hector, standing next to him, was struck how the Commander could look both annoyed and understanding at the same time. "Cadet," he said in fatherly repose, "there are upwards of a million people living around the bay. Many are scared not knowing where three escaped prisoners might be at this very moment. We keep looking until we either find those men, their bodies, or evidence to prove they are dead." Then, with a stern look, he said "not every mission is the Pendleton, son."

The Pendleton.

A reverential hush filled the room at the mention of one of the greatest rescues in Coast Guard history. It was only a few years ago when the crew of a TRS pulled 32 survivors off the tanker Pendleton, which had split in half during a vicious Nor'easter. Every Coastie knew the name of coxswain Bernie Webber who risked his life to save the men on that tanker. Like so many cadets who heard the story, Hector had wondered if he could match Webber's bravery. He guessed every young man who joined the service wondered the same thing.

"I expect you..." he started to say directly at Ian then, after a pause, to the whole room, "I expect everyone to perform as you have been trained. Semper Paratus."

In unison, as they had all through training, they stood up and responded. "Semper Paratus."

A few hours later, on the deck of the TRS as it plowed the water near Angel Island, Cadet Ian Jacoby looked jealously around the deck at the other men. They all seemed very much at home on deck, even after two long, tedious days on the bay. Ian, who had been so excited for this first assignment, was now feeling burdened by a growing tedium which – wait a second...

"Bobby," he yelled to the other cadet stationed on his side of the boat. "Do you see that? Over there," Ian pointed.

His crew-mate nodded and both men grabbed the whistles hanging around their necks and blew them loudly, to get the captain's attention. As they were trained, neither took their eyes off the object as the captain cut the engine and the boat quickly coasted to a stop.

"What do you have?" the captain yelled from the cockpit.

Ian and Bobby both pointed to the object, now astern of the boat. The captain nodded and reversed the boat until both cadets waved for him to stop. By now both Hector and the other crewman had crossed to Ian's side of the boat. For a few seconds nobody said a word. They just looked at the object gently floating before them.

It was a paddle.

"Okay, let's bring it on board," the captain said. "Bobby, hand Ian the boat hook."

Finally. Something to do. Ian gripped the railing with one hand and took hold of the six foot-long hook with the other. Without too much effort he was able to reach the paddle and pull it towards him until it gently bumped against the side of the boat. He nodded to the other crewman, who reached down and pulled it into the boat. It was quickly surrounded by the crew.

Calling it a paddle was being generous. It was nothing more than a two by four, about three feet long, with a flat, square piece of wood (Ian estimated about eight inches on all sides) nailed to one end. But it was clear what it was supposed to be.

Ian broke the silence. "How the hell did they build this in a prison without anyone knowing?"

"That's for someone else to figure out," the captain said. He pointed at Ian. "You. Stow that thing securely." Then, to the rest of his crew, "I'm going to radio this in. Until I get orders to the contrary everyone back to their watch positions. Keep your eyes open. Let's see what else is out here."

The excitement on the boat was palpable. After two and a half days they were the first ones to find a clue to the fate of the escapees. As the boat's engines revved back up the men – cadets and veterans like – exchanged satisfied smiles across the deck. Okay, this isn't the Pendleton but, shit, it was exciting.

Back at his post on the railing Ian felt the adrenaline quickly ebb from his body. Tedium returned. He thought about an expression he once heard about war being long periods of boredom punctuated by moments of sheer terror. Not that finding the paddle was in any way terrifying but everything in between was sure boring. He once again looked across the deck at his friend Hector, whose smile seemed even bigger than before. It made Ian feel a little sad.

"Am I in the wrong line of work?" he wondered.

11:10 am

Tommy emerged from his bedroom and the first thing he noticed was the pile of cigarette butts in the ashtray. This was not a good sign for the morning to come.

"Sit down," his mother said as she took a drag from her (sixth? seventh?) cigarette.

Tommy reluctantly lowered himself across from her at the table and waited. (Another mom trick to raise the tension, not unlike the one Tony had learned from his Marine sergeant.) It was so quiet he could hear crackling from the burning cigarette as she inhaled. His mind raced, dread increasing – her intention, of course – until he could stand it no longer. "Mom, please, what's wrong?"

She crushed her cigarette roughly into the ashtray, dislodging spent butts and ash onto the table. "Where were you last night?" From the way she asked the question Tommy knew that she knew he wasn't home. But did she know where he had gone?

"Tommy, are you listening? I'm talking to you."

214

He snapped to attention. "Yes."

"Officer Marianetti saw you on your bicycle going south on Bridgeway last night."

Of course. Tony, that son of a –

"He followed you."

Followed me! Shit, that meant he knew –

"Unfortunately, he only got as far as the bridge before dispatch called him about a fight at Juanita's."

"There was a fight? Are you okay?"

"What? No. I mean yes. We thought there was a fight but it was nothing. That's not the point, Tommy. He told me what you were doing."

Tommy's mind raced. If Tony didn't know where he had gone after losing him at the bridge then his mother didn't know, either.

"Tommy, be honest with me. Is it a girl?"

He turned beet red. "What? A girl? No, mom, it's not a girl."

"All right, then, if it's not a girl then are you and your friends meeting someplace to drink?"

"Drink? Like beer and stuff? No, mom, you know I don't do that."

"Honestly, I don't know what kind of stuff you do or don't do, anymore."

Tommy bit his lower lip. What else could he do or say? He and the Anglins had dodged a bullet, thanks to the fight (which his mother said wasn't a fight) at Juanita's. But Tony had seen him biking towards the headlands and told his mom.

"Nothing to say?" Molly emphatically extracted another cigarette from the pack. She was about to place it in her mouth when she stopped and looked mournfully at her son. "Do you know how much it hurts that I can't trust you?"

He squirmed.

215

"You're coming to work with me tonight."

"What? Wait, I –"

"I can't trust you but I can't afford to take a night off, either. So you're coming with me. Juanita says she has a place behind the kitchen where you can sleep."

"But –"

Molly jabbed her finger at Tommy. "Really, are you seriously going to argue with me?"

"For how long?"

"What?"

"I mean for how many nights do I hafta –"

Molly stood up and banged her fist onto the table. "You will hafta until I say you don't hafta. And don't bother looking for your bicycle."

"My bike...?" he stammered as he began to stand up.

With a laser-like glare from her dark eyes, Molly cut off Tommy mid-whine. He shrank into his seat. "You are not leaving this boat until it is time for me to go to work, do you understand?"

Tommy nodded numbly.

"And tomorrow afternoon you will come with me to the Artist's Center. I have a commission I need to finish and I'm not letting you out of my sight. Now eat your breakfast." She whirled around and strode angrily into her bedroom.

Only after the door to his mother's bedroom closed did he exhale. He had felt awful about lying to her the past two days. Yet it wasn't guilt which now weighed on his shoulders.

What were John and Clarence going to think when he didn't show up tonight?

1:13 pm

216

As he pointed to the objects laid out on the conference room table, flakes of ash fell from Olin Blackwell's cigarette. "A wooden paddle, found near Angel Island by the Coast Guard. A life jacket, made of the same material as our guard's raincoats. This was found only 50 yards off Angel. Finally we have these papers found on the southern end of Angel Island, wrapped and waterproofed in the same rubber as prison raincoats. They are filled with names, addresses and photos of relatives of the Anglin brothers." He looked up. "Clearly, they had plans if they reached the mainland. But we still have no credible reports of unusual activity from anywhere around the bay. Which leads me to think they are dead." He paused as he pulled another cigarette from the pack. "How about it, Fred? Do you agree?"

Fred Wilkinson had been staring at a map of the bay area taped to a wall. Four pins, each indicating where an item related to the escape had been found, were stuck on the map. Without turning around, he said "Sorry, Olin, I don't. We don't know if these items are from before or after they landed somewhere."

"You've got to be kidding me," Blackwell said as he strode over the to the map. "Look at the distribution of the items we found... just off Alcatraz and Angel island. Nothing has washed up anywhere else."

"Doesn't prove their raft didn't get them to dry land. Then they did the smart thing. Leave it in the water. It floats away. Made of raincoats it eventually bursts into dozens of pieces. Hard to spot. You've said yourself, the bay is filled with currents and tides..."

"What about the package of letters we found near Angel? No way the Anglins leave them behind."

"I didn't say they left them. Maybe they fell out of the raft. The water's cold. They're not going to jump in to retrieve them. They didn't want to but they had to move on."

Blackwell took another drag on his cigarette and shook his head. "Maybe. Maybe. But let's talk about the letters... what does the FBI have to say?"

From across the table, a young man with a Bureau-approved crew haircut, replied. "Agents from the Southeast Bureau interviewed the Anglins on the twelfth, the day of the escape. They claimed to know nothing about John and Clarence's plans. We've got surveillance on their house just in case..."

"Don't they have another son in prison?" Dickinson asked.

The agent flipped pages in his notebook. "Yes, Alfred. He's serving time in Alabama in a state facility. They've shown our field agents the letters Alfred received over the past few months. Nothing to indicate he – or any family member – had any clue what they were going to do."

Blackwell released a cloud of smoke over the table. "If somehow, someway these boys did make it to land, what then? I'll say it again. We don't have a single credible report – and I emphasize credible – of any thefts, robberies or burglaries we can tie to the Anglins or to Frank Morris. Fred, I'll bet you a week's pay these boys never got within sight of land."

"Then where are the bodies, Olin? Where are the bodies?"

Blackwell took another puff. As a half-inch of ash fell to floor he pointed to the map. "Floating somewhere out there somewhere. You'll see. Any day now we'll get a call that someone saw a body."

Wilkinson took a deep breath, looked back again to the map, and shook his head.

"I want to believe you're right, Olin. I really do..."

218

6:00 pm

Ron Lowendowski sat at the bar in Juanita's Galley nursing a scotch. He had lost track of how long he had been sitting with the one drink, but it must have been a while since the bartender was eyeing Ron skeptically. Ron didn't care. He was too exhausted after spending all day searching, in vain, for an angle to the Alcatraz story. He had corralled store owners along Bridgeway, then cruised dozens of residential streets interviewing homeowners with questions like "Do you feel safe?" and "Are you now worried about the prison after the escape?" Then he headed down the docks buttonholing fishermen for their opinions. "Do you think they could have made it?" he asked, and "Does the news they had a raft make you think they could have made it to land?"

But, at the end of the day, all he had was same old, boring "man on the street" stuff any intern could have recorded. And a glass of warm scotch.

Perched precariously on a shelf hanging over the bar sat a small television set. Flickering images of the evening newscast, now in progress, reflected in his glass. Ron scowled at the well-dressed, perfectly coiffed anchormen on the TV. "We'll be back with more news after this," he heard him say. Ron took another sip of warm scotch. From above the bar he heard a different voice. "Hi everybody, this is Russ Hodges, join me tonight for Giants baseball as we take on the Reds in Cincinnati."

"Hodges, I can still hear him screaming 'the Giants win the pennant... the Giants win the pennant'"

Ron turned and saw a man in a rumpled coat with an equally rumpled head of hair. "Doncha remember?" the man asked. He didn't wait for Ron to answer. "Da tree game playoff against da Dodgers, doze bums. In fifty-one.

219

Bobby Thomson's home run. I was in New Yawk back den. Course, so was da Jints. Greatest day ever was when dey said dey was moving here."

Ron gripped his glass and held back a grimace. Oh, yea, he knew all about the day the Giants announced they were moving from New York to San Francisco. Ron had reported they were not coming because the mayor of New York had offered owner Horace Stoneham a new stadium in midtown Manhattan. The tip had come from a friend Ron's. A former friend, now. Because it turned out the jerk had used Ron to spread the false story about New York to put pressure on San Francisco's mayor to improve the city's offer to the Giants. Which he did.

The rumpled man saw Ron's dour face. "S'matter? Not a baseball fan?"

"Me? No. I mean yea, sure. But I was in the service in fifty-one. I didn't hear Hodges' call," Ron replied, trying to find a tone that was polite but not encouraging enough for more conversation. With no one else at the bar, he was out of luck.

"Korea?"

Ron nodded. "Navy."

The man's eyes lit up. "No shit? Me too, I went in in fifty-two —"

Ron didn't hear him. Something on the screen caught his attention. He waved to the bartender. "Would you mind turning up the sound?" he said, pointing frantically at the TV.

The bartender scowled. "While I get you another, right?"

"Huh? Oh, yea, sure," Ron said without thinking. "But first, could you..." he motioned again to the TV.

Scowling, the bartender turned a knob on the television set.

"...it is a major break in the search for the men who

220

escaped from Alcatraz prison three days ago. KCBS has exclusive footage of Alcatraz warden Olin Blackwell, seen here, examining a makeshift paddle found today floating just off Angel Island. Our own Michael Coleman was on the scene."

On the screen Ron saw another crisply-coiffed young man standing on the beach at Angel island. "The discovery of the paddle was made early this afternoon by a Coast Guard cutter searching for the escaped convicts. Warden Blackwell, in an exclusive interview with KCBS-TV news, said the paddle confirms what authorities were told by a source within the prison, that the prisoners had built paddles for a raft they had constructed for the escape."

Ron gripped his glass.

On the TV he saw Warden Blackwell holding the crudely made paddle and saying to the reporter, "This confirms our belief that Angel Island was the destination of the three men. Coast Guard boats and helicopters continue to scour near the island for their bodies."

"Bodies? So you believe the men are dead?" Ron heard the reporter ask.

Blackwell nodded. "As everyone in the Bay area knows, bay water is cold. It is highly unlikely those men could have survived for any length of time."

"But they had a raft."

Warden Blackwell smiled into the camera. "You've heard the expression 'up the creek without a paddle?' A raft is no good in that bay without one of these, either," he said, holding up the makeshift paddle.

"Thank you, warden Blackwell. As the search for Frank Morris, John Anglin and Clarence Anglin continues law enforcement around the bay reminds everyone to remain alert for any thefts of food, clothing or even, perhaps, a car. KCBS will –"

Ron had heard enough. He bolted up from his stool,

thrust a hand into his pocket and pulled out a dollar bill which he threw on the bar. "Keep the change," he said as he stomped away.

The bartender picked up the bill, quickly and dramatically pulling twice on the ends as he held it up to a light. He furtively looked around. The only person remaining at the bar was the rumpled Giants fan, whose attention was on the television. The bartender stuffed the dollar bill in his shirt pocket.

7:00 pm

As Ron drove south on Bridgeway he thought about the many skills he had learned in his eight years as a radio reporter. How to get past a police barricade to a crime scene... how to develop sources at City Hall... how to edit interviews for broadcast. But now, as he turned his car into the parking lot of the Coast Guard Station at Golden Gate, Ron knew would have to employ a very special skill if he were to salvage his escape story.

He was going to have to kiss someone's ass.

That someone being the Coast Guard Commander, in whose office Ron now sat. "Mister Lowendowski," the commander said as he leaned back in his chair, "as a Navy veteran you understand that just like every other branch of the military the Coast Guard has rules and regulations."

"Yes sir."

"A breach of the rules must have consequences or else there cannot be order."

"You sound like the captain of the Worcester. He would say the same thing."

"So you understand that when I give you permission to attend a briefing that by all convention is for Coast

Guard personnel only, and then you interrupt that meeting to turn it into a press conference –"

"I know sir, and I wanted to come back and sincerely apologize for my behavior. I –"

"Then there is the matter of entering the office of one of my subordinates to use their phone without permission –"

Ron shifted uncomfortably. "I know, sir, and I have to fall on my sword about that, as well. Call it a reporter's reaction. I just wanted to get the story out as soon as possible."

The commander cleared his throat and leaned forward over his desk. "Yes, well, Colonel Bailey called me today."

Ron suppressed the urge to roll his eyes at the word 'colonel,' instead forcing his mouth into an appreciative smile. "Oh, he did?"

"Yes. The Colonel is a good man who supports his people. Even when they behave like a horse's ass."

"Yes, sir." (Now a practiced look of chagrin... that's it, Ron, nicely done.)

"He explained your... enthusiasm can sometimes get the better of you, and he asked that I give you another chance. I was going to have one of my men call you tomorrow but since you are here tonight I can personally authorize you to ride on one of our boats in the morning."

Ron jumped up out of his chair, beaming, extending his hand to the commander. "Thank you, sir. Thank you very much."

"Thank your boss, Mr. Lowendowski. He's a good man and an asset to the bay area. When you arrive tomorrow morning you'll be assigned a boat." His eyes narrowed. "Once you step on that boat you are to obey any and all commands from the captain, do you understand?"

Ron looked solemnly back at the commander. "Yes,

223

sir."

"All right then," he said as he leaned back again into his chair and waved his hand. "Dismissed."

Instinctively, Ron saw his hand rise up in a salute. "Thank you, sir."

The commander couldn't resist a smile. "Old habits, eh, Lowendowski?"

Ron smiled and walked out of the office, already dreaming of recording the moment the crew would see the body of one of the escapees floating beside their boat. "Channel 2, here I come..." he said to himself...

10:00 pm

The kitchen at Juanita's was a noisy, frantic place. The chef was a whirlwind, bouncing between boiling pots, sizzling pans, and smoking ovens. Every few minutes Molly swept in, placing heaping plates of food on her tray and racing back out to the dining room.

Off in a corner of the kitchen Tommy sat inert and glum at a small table. In front of him a pile of french fries sat, untouched. How could he eat? All he could think about were the two men he had promised to help who were, by now, probably thinking he had abandoned them.

What Tommy could not know was that he was about to become the least of the Anglin's worries.

Frank Morris woke up in the bunker at Battery Wagner and slowly opened his eyes. Unlike the previous few nights on the run there was no panic... no strange dream to shake off. He smiled proudly, though no one could see him in the dark of the abandoned bunker. Three days on the run and he had finally captured a tempo, a regimen he felt confident would propel him far away from here. He tentatively stretched his legs and, to his surprise, they felt good. It was time to eat and move on.

After a "breakfast" of C-rations, Frank hoisted the duffel bag over his shoulder, stepped out of the bunker and began walking west, keeping the lights of San Francisco in his rear as his guide. He still hadn't decided on his next stop. Dank as they were, these abandoned forts were perfect places to stay during the day. As he walked he looked at his map and saw the next-closest one, Battery Kirby, was only a thousand feet away. He smiled, smugly. Why waste a whole night to go such a short distance when his legs were feeling so good?

Frank, still staying off any existing paths to avoid being seen, struggled through the thick brush. Every few steps a low-hanging branch would slap him in the face. Annoyed, he would push it away, then continue walking. Several more steps and then he would glance back down at the map. Slap. Another branch would hit him in the head. "Damn it." (That's it, Frank. Get angry at a branch, you idiot.) He trudged forward and, after a few steps, looked down once more at the map. There! A place called Muir Beach, where there could be car he could boost. It was only seven miles away and –"

What the hell? Frank, his eyes focused on the map, felt his legs come to a halt, even though he hadn't intended to stop. Then... a foreboding chill came over him, like his legs knew something the rest of his body didn't.

Frank slowly raised his eyes over the map and saw... nothing. No trees, no grass, no anything. He looked down at his feet. Mere inches from tips of his toes the world just... ended. He stumbled backwards into the brush and fell onto his back, clutching his chest and gasping for air, overwhelmed by the terrifying realization he had almost walked off a cliff to his death.

Slowly, his breathing returned to normal. He was in no rush to get up. Almost dying will change a man's priorities. In the past three days he had poked the Grim Reaper in the eye several times. So Frank just lay there, looking up into the night sky, listening to the water lapping onto the rocks below. Then... another sound, rising and falling in volume with the shifting and swirling of the wind. It sounded like... talking? He lifted his head to hear better and... yes, it was voices. Hey, maybe they drove out here. A car. Yea, with a car he could go anywhere.

Frank picked himself up and shouldered the duffel bag. But, before he walked away, he turned to look back at what, with one more step, would have been certain death. He shivered, as if from the cold. He headed for the voices.

A chilly wind from the bay blew over Battery Kirby. Clarence Anglin shivered. "Boy, I wish we could make a fire or something," he said.

His brother John nodded sympathetically. "Yea, me too. But we can't take a chance –"

"I know, I know. We can't chance that some boater will see it and report it to the cops."

"How's the leg tonight?" John asked. He cared, of course, but also felt Clarence needed a distraction from the cold. "Maybe if you got up and walked around. Tested it out, you know? Might warm you up."

"Good idea. Help me up." Clarence extended his arm to his brother. John grabbed his hand and slowly pulled him to his feet. Clarence walked tentatively around the perimeter of the sunken concrete structure where they had been staying for the past two nights. "Hey, not bad," he said before wincing. "Damn, spoke too soon." He limped over to John and held onto his shoulder as he eased himself back down to the ground. "I'm sorry, John. It's close."

"Don't apologize," he replied, as Clarence lowered himself to the ground.

"Are you hungry?" John asked.

"When am I not?"

John laughed. "Kid should be here soon enough."

They sat quietly together, listening to the wind.

"You suppose they've talked to Ma?" Clarence asked. John did not have to ask who his brother meant by 'they.'

"You can be sure of it. Alfred, too. That's why we couldn't even hint to the kid what we're gonna do."

"Do you think we'll ever see her again?"

John placed his arm on Clarence's shoulder. "I don't know. I don't know."

"I just want her to know we're not dead, you know? That's the worst part. Ma thinkin' we drowned out there, like Frank did."

"Maybe someday we can get a message to her. But we gotta be, you know, far away from here before we can."

Clarence nodded, sadly. A swirl of air caused both brothers to shiver. John was about to say something, when –

"You sons of bitches!"

Both men whipped their heads around to see a man carrying a large bag over his shoulder, striding purposely towards them from out of the brush.

Clarence was the first to recognize the intruder. "Holy shit, John, look, it's Frank. How the hell –" Before he could finish, he saw an arm swing around from out of the dark and a fist land squarely on his brother jaw, knocking John to the ground.

Stunned and confused, John looked up at his attacker. "Frank? Is that really you? We thought you was

_"

"Dead, yea. Well, surprise, assholes," Frank screamed. He dropped his duffel bag and jumped on top of John, angry fists flying. From the ground John blocked the punches as best he could, only occasionally hitting Frank back as the two men rolled on the ground.

"Frank, what the hell are you doing? Stop it," Clarence yelled. Either Frank didn't hear... or didn't care. Grimacing, Clarence got onto his feet and began hobbling over to the rolling pile.

"You didn't even try..." Frank yelled as he continued his assault.

"Frank, for God's sake we didn't know you was alive," Clarence pleaded.

"Bullshit," Frank screamed as he reared his arm back for another blow. John saw his chance. He rolled forward and pushed against Frank's chest, causing his attacker to fall backwards onto the ground.

Clarence had, by now, made it over to the two men. He stood over Frank with both hands balled tightly into fists, ready to defend his brother – the pain in his leg be damned. But he quickly saw that neither of the two gasping men on the ground had the energy to continue.

"You left... me... to die..." Frank wheezed.

John turned his head to look at his attacker. "Jesus, Frank. Do you really think if we had known you was alive..." he began before taking another greedy gulp of air.

"But you didn't even try," Frank said.

"He was busy saving me," Clarence said. "When you went over you hit me in the head with your foot and I got knocked into the water. Next thing I knew John was bringing me back to the surface. We looked for you but you was gone."

"You must have surfaced after we swam away," John, still gasping for sir, said.

228

"It's the truth, we wouldn't have left if we thought you was still alive. You gotta believe us" Clarence repeated.

Frank held up his hand, signaling him to stop talking. His breathing began to slow as he looked at the Anglins. Then he shook his head. "Just my luck. Look who I'm stuck with. Shit. I guess I got no choice but to believe you two. What you're saying makes as much as sense as anything."

"Thanks, Frank."

"Yea, thanks."

More silence. Then...

"So, Frank, what's in the bag?" asked Clarence hopefully, pointing to the duffel Frank had been carrying.

"Oh. I landed near the bridge and there was a lighthouse nearby. I got lucky. There weren't any people but there was a shower, clean clothes, and a bunch of food."

"Oh boy, food," Clarence said, licking his lips.

Frank smirked. "Yea, go ahead, but I'll warn you it's army surplus rations, mostly."

"That's okay, thanks," Clarence said as he rummaged through the duffel bag.

"So what about you guys? Where have you been for three days? What have you been eating? Where did you get those clothes?"

Clarence and John looked furtively at each other, wordlessly agreeing not to say anything about Tommy. John ignored Frank's actual question and replied, "we've been waiting here for John's leg to get better."

"Yea, I scraped it on some rocks when we landed on the beach."

Frank nodded, remembering his own close call earlier. "Yea, I seen the rocks."

They were quiet for a while as Clarence chewed on an

army ration chocolate bar. "Hey, what do you think they're doing to West?" he said.

""Probably grilling him for where we were going," Frank replied. Then, he smiled.

"What is it?" John said.

"West is gonna tell them we were going to Angel Island," Frank replied. "Could buy us an extra day or two. That's on top of the ten-hour jump we already got by leaving those fake heads."

"I'd love to see their faces when they find the workshop, too." Clarence smiled.

John and Frank laughed appreciatively.

"So what's your plan, now, Frank?" asked Clarence.

"I was gonna head west along the coast but..." he hesitated "...I'm thinking of heading north to Sausalito and boosting a car up there."

John leaned forward. "That's a good idea, Frank, maybe we –"

A noise from the bunker interrupted him. Instinctively, three pairs of hands balled into fists. John, Clarence, and Frank turned to the bunker entrance and saw a large rat emerge from the darkness. Frank screamed and jumped back, almost falling over. The rat, frightened, scampered back into the bunker.

John laughed. "Jesus, Frank, take it easy, it's just a rat."

"Disgusting, disease-laden animals," Frank said, breathing hard, as he clutched his chest.

"It's okay, it's gone now," John said, smiling as he looked at Clarence.

"Geez, Frank, you scream like that they'll hear you all the way on the Rock," Clarence said.

Frank managed a self-conscious laugh. "Yea, sorry."

They sat silently for a while. Clarence looked at his brother and saw an idea forming.

230

"Hey Frank," John began...

"Yea?"

"What if we go together? Boosting one car instead of two makes sense, right?"

"Maybe," Frank said. "Yea, sure. That's actually a good idea. Draw less attention. How soon could you leave?"

John looked to his brother, who gingerly flexed his leg. "Tomorrow night, for sure," Clarence said.

"Is that okay with you, Frank?" John asked.

"Yea. Guess I could use another day, too. Meantime how about we light a fire? It's chilly as hell out here."

"We was gonna but, you know, someone out on the bay might see it."

Frank pointed to the wall by the bunker. "Not if we build it over there. It'll block the view from the water fine."

John looked to Clarence. "What do you think?"

"I wouldn't mind getting warmer."

"Okay then," Frank said. "I got some matches from the lighthouse. I'll get some wood from the trail." He got up and walked to the brush behind the fort.

Clarence waited for him to get a distance away before turning to John with a worried look. "What do we do when Tommy shows up?"

"I don't know."

"Should we even tell him about the kid?"

"I don't know."

"Jesus, John, that's a lot of I don't knows."

John shook his head. "It just doesn't seem like something we should tell him. Not until we have to."

"Tell me what?" Frank was back, his arms full of wood.

Clarence opened his mouth to speak. John quickly said, "we was talking about how Clarence's leg was feeling."

231

"Yea?" Frank replied, suspiciously, as he dropped the wood on the ground and began arranging it for the fire.

"I'm gonna be okay by tomorrow, for sure, Frank," Clarence said.

"Good. Good." The wood piled to his satisfaction, Frank reached into his duffel and took out a small box of matches. Before long they were soaking in the warmth of the fire. In the glow of the burning branches Frank saw furtive glances between John and Clarence and how they would occasionally glance at the hill behind the fort, as if expecting someone. He decided not to to say anything, for now. Frank was a good poker player and he had his own cards to play, if need be.

The fire was making everyone feel better. Frank was right about the depressed concrete wall preventing the fire from being seen from the water. But none of them, not even Frank Morris – the smartest guy in the joint – considered an unwelcome visitor might come at them from the hill behind them.

Unaware of Tommy's incarceration in Juanita's kitchen, Tony planned to stake out the Bridgeway tonight. When the kid rode past him – which Tony was sure he would do – he would follow him again, only this time all the way to his destination. But the day's discovery of the escapees' paddle dropped a lit match on a pool of gasoline and, by the dozens, the people of Sausalito – convinced they had seen or heard the escaped prisoners – had been calling the station all day and night. It wasn't until after ten he could get free. Now, driving south on Bridgeway, he scowled. Not knowing Tommy was a hostage in Juanita's kitchen, he assumed the kid had long passed the speed trap on his way back to the path under the bridge.

It was time to do some recon. Tony continued driving

south until he reached the spot where he last saw Tommy the night before – on the dirt path to Kirby Cove. He glanced at the two-way radio, half-expecting the dispatcher to call him to return to town (a chief is never really off duty.) It remained silent. Tony took out his flashlight from the glove compartment and slipped it into his belt. He left his gun in the trunk. No sense in scaring Tommy (and whomever he was with) half to death. These were just kids. Besides, the walk down the path was tough enough without the extra weight of his Colt. Andy Taylor lives.

Tony began walking along the path along the headlands. He had only been walking a few minutes when something near the water caught his eye. He veered off the path and into the woods, fighting his way through branches and brush until he saw, through a clump of trees, the glow of a campfire. That's probably where Tommy is, he thought. He gingerly moved past the tree line into the clearing just above the concrete bowl of the battery and saw three figures huddled around the orange glow of a fire. They were talking, but he was too far away to hear what they were saying. "Damn kids are going to burn down the forest," he said to himself.

The fire's comforting warmth was making John, Clarence and Frank feel pretty good. They were beginning to talk about what, just a few days ago, seemed impossible. Life after Alcatraz.

"John and me got lots of experience farming," Clarence was saying. "We was thinking we should grow tomatoes. Like the kind they got in Ruskin."

"What's Ruskin?" Frank asked.

"Best tomatoes you ever tasted," Clarence said.

"Pa settled us there and we had a house and

everything," John added.

Clarence faced turned glum. "Course, we can't go back there, now."

John nodded, as he gave his brother a comforting pat on the shoulder. He looked at Frank and said, "You got any kin?" Frank was about to answer when a snap from just above the concrete froze all three men.

"Damn it, Marine," Tony cursed as the branch broke under his foot. He saw three heads turn in his direction. "Well, they know I'm here now... might as well get this over with." He stepped down onto the concrete floor and walked towards them. They slowly stood up and Tony saw they weren't kids at all. They were grown men. Three of them. Three. Holy shit. Could they be... nah, it was impossible. The prison bureau's bulletin said a paddle and life jackets were found up at Angel Island, miles north of here. He went through the possibilities. Could they have swum here from Angel to throw us off track? Impossible, not in that cold water. Did they actually land here and not Angel like the Coast Guard said? Possible, sure, but if they landed here, why stick around? Then, he kicked himself with the most difficult question of all; Andy Taylor be damned, why did he leave his gun in the trunk of the cruiser?

"Evening officer," he heard one of the men say.

Tony took a deep breath. He could see none of them had a weapon. To make them believe he did, Tony put his hands onto his gun belt, over his flashlight. Maybe it would be enough to fool them. "You boys know there's a law against vagrancy, right?"

Clarence looked anxiously at John, who was about to speak when he heard Frank laugh and say "We're not vagrants, officer. But I'm sure our wives would disagree, right guys?"

John and Clarence caught on and provided a chorus of "ha, that's right" and "boy would they ever."

"How long you been out here?" Tony asked as he slowly edged closer to the men, his hand still hovering menacingly over what only he knew was just a flashlight.

"Oh, a couple of nights."

Tony saw the duffel bag and pointed to it with his free hand. "You didn't bring a lot of gear, did you?"

Even in the night's chilly air Frank felt himself starting to sweat. "Oh, well, uh..."

John quickly said, "our stuff is back there," indicating the opening to the bunker.

Tony nodded and smiled as he circled around them.

"Our wives..." Clarence started to say, then stopped.

"He means our wives are coming to pick us up tomorrow," Frank said hastily.

"Yea, that's right," Clarence said, looking a bit sheepish.

Tony now had his back to the bunker. "Uh huh," he said. He turned to look inside. John and Clarence watched in horror as Frank lunged at the officer.

In the seconds it took for John to yell "You idiot, he has a gun," Frank had knocked Tony down and was grappling on the concrete floor for his –

"It's not a gun, it's not a gun, it's a fucking flashlight" Frank screamed. "Help me."

Convict instinct took over. John jumped, headfirst, into Tony's mid-section. As Tony gasped for breath, Frank grabbed the flashlight. He and John and rolled away and scrambled to their feet.

"I told you he didn't have a gun," Frank said, through heavy gasps for air.

The three men stood over Tony. He lifted his head and found enough breath to say, "They'll never stop

235

looking for you, you know that, don't you? This is the rest of your lives. Turn yourselves in now and save yourselves."

"Shut up," Frank said as he leaned down and struck Tony on the temple with the flashlight. The cop's head hit concrete floor with a thud.

"Frank, what the hell did you do that for?" John yelled as Frank ran over to the duffel bag.

"Are you stupid? He knows who we are," Frank said as he disconnected one of the bag's shoulder straps and brought it over to where Tony lay.

"What are you doing?" Clarence looked terrified as Frank bound Tony's hands behind him with the strap.

"Boy, you ask some stupid questions, you know that?"

John took a step towards Frank. "That's enough of that, Frank."

"Yea?" Frank sneered dismissively. "Well, I'm not getting caught," he said as he tightened the straps around Tony's wrists. "Help me move him inside."

"Holy shit, Frank, this is kidnapping."

Frank laughed. "You gotta be kidding me. We're on the run after escaping a Federal Prison and you're worried about a little kidnapping?"

"Of a police officer."

Tony groaned. Clarence jumped back, sputtering. "He's waking up. He's waking up. What do we do?"

"It's okay." Frank looked as annoyed as he sounded. "He's not going anywhere. Come on. Let's get him inside."

Tony heard them. "You'll never get away with it," he mumbled. "They know where I am and when I don't report in they'll come looking for me."

"He's right," John said, looking furiously at Frank.

"Well, we can't let him go," Frank said. He pointed angrily at the Anglins. "Listen you two. we're in this

236

together, now. If one rats, we all get caught. It's life for all of us. Now, God damn it, for the last time help me move him inside."

John and Clarence looked helplessly at each other. Frank was right. They were stuck with him and stuck with his plan because doing anything else would guarantee they get caught. And now, getting caught would put them behind bars for the rest of their lives.

Dumped on the cold floor of the bunker, his hands bound and his head an aching mess, Tony was grateful for one thing. They hadn't thought about his car.

June 15, 1962

7:15 am

Bored, bored, bored. And cold.

The Coast Guard cutter *Storis* had only just left Golden Gate station but Ron Lowendowski was already shivering on the deck and questioning his efforts to get on board. A Lieutenant proudly boasted of the boat's recent duty in the Arctic. Ron was so cold he wondered if the *Storis* had brought back some of that Arctic weather to San Francisco. But Ron still feigned an impressed smile, hoping it would loosen the Lieutenant's harness on him.

"I'd like to start collecting some sound, if that's okay," he said to the Lieutenant as he held up the station's tape recorder.

"That will be fine. But I have to go to the bridge before we make our first run. Please wait here for the Ensign before you approach the railing." Ron's face betrayed his frustration. "Sorry, sir, commander's orders. We're instructed to be with you at all times. It wouldn't make for a very good story if you fell overboard."

Ron was about to make a snide comment that it might be the only story to come out of this trip, but he just smiled, as if he really thought what the Lieutenant said was funny. The Lieutenant smiled back before walking away. With a few precious moments by himself, Ron edged closer to the railing. He felt the cutter make a sweeping turn north and could see, off the port side, a long bluff.

"There, that's where I saw it."

He heard one of the crewmen – a young kid – speaking to another crewman stationed along the railing. He was pointing to a spot at the bottom of the bluff. Ron craned his neck and saw what looked like a very small beach wedged behind a large rock.

"I should have said something," he heard the young man say.

"What are you gonna tell them, Hector, that you saw a ghost?"

"Ian, those prisoners had a raft."

"Yea, so?"

"So that means it's possible they could have made it to Yellow Bluff."

Yellow Bluff? Ron made a mental note of the name.

"Sure, Hector. Anything is possible. A Russian sub could have come and picked them up, too."

"Fuck you, Ian."

"Hey, man, I'm trying to stop you from killing your career before it even gets started. You got nothing substantial to report but a shadow –"

"A shadow that moved."

"A shadow you think you saw more than three days ago." Ian leaned in towards Hector. "Three days ago, man. And with the hangover you had after that night at Juanita's. How's that gonna make you look?"

Straining to hear more of the conversation, Ron was just about to step closer to the two men when a voice from behind said "Mr. Lowendowski? I'm Ensign David Gray."

Ron reluctantly turned away from the men at the railing. "Hello."

"Sir, if you'll follow me I'm instructed to take you to the bridge," the Ensign said, extending his arm to guide the reporter away from the railing. As they walked to the bow of the cutter Ron looked back at Hector and Ian, still arguing. Ron repeated the name. Yellow Bluff. Yellow Bluff...

10:12 am

Ron wasn't the only one bored this morning. Tommy's friends Billy, Jeff, and Patrick were sitting on the dock at Horseshoe Bay, looking mournfully at the water. Nervous parents, consumed by reports of rafts and paddles and life vests, had forbidden them from going out on the bay. Gosh. Summer was a week old and already ruined.

All heads turned to the squeal of bicycle brakes behind them. It was Danny. He was smiling as he dismounted his trusty steed.

"What are you so happy about?" Patrick asked.

"I just heard the best story from my older brother," Danny said as he sat cross-legged on the dock. He proceeded to repeat a story his brother had told him about older teenagers doing things only imagined by younger teenagers down at the abandoned lighthouse near the bridge. Eyes widened. Smiles returned. The lure was undeniable.

Within a few minutes four bicycles were skidding to a stop at the base of the lighthouse, their tires flinging pebbles into the air and raising a small cloud of dust. They dismounted and raced each other to the landing above. They stopped when they saw the door was open.

"Do you think anyone is in there?" Jeff whispered to Billy.

"How should I know?" he snapped.

"How can there be anybody here? There's no cars around..."

"They coulda walked."

"Yea, don't be dopey," Jeff said as he strode forward. He pushed the door open and looked inside. The other boys kept their distance and held their breath. A moment later, from inside... "What the heck." His eyes wide, Jeffrey popped breathlessly out of the door. "Guys, come here... you gotta see this."

The remaining three boys stepped, tentatively, to the door and peered inside.

It was a mess. Every locker was open, contents spilled on the floor in piles of shoes, underwear, pants, and shirts. In the cabinet kitchen doors were flung open. Little remained on the shelves. Boxes of C- and K-rations lay scattered on the counter and on the floor. Rats had begun taking advantage of the feast and had nibbled away the corners of several boxes of food to reach their treasure. A rude smell wafted from the bathroom. Frank had apparently forgotten to flush.

Danny had seen enough. He nervously backed up to the door.

"Where do you think you're going?" Billy asked.

"I think we better get out of here," Danny squeaked.

"Hey, man, coming here was your idea," Billy said.

"Billy's right, it was," Jeffrey said.

"That was before... all this," Danny said with a nervous sweep of his hand.

"I think Danny's right," Patrick chimed in. "We should get outta here."

"Who do ya think did this?" Jeffrey asked.

"Yea, maybe it your brother," Billy said to Danny

242

with a smug smile.

Danny approached Billy menacingly, his nose just inches from his. "You take that back."

"Why should I?"

"Because I'm telling you no way my brother had anything to with this. He knows if he trashes the place they put a bolt on the door and that's the end of that."

"So who could it be?"

"I don't know. Bums? Other kids? But right now if someone comes here and sees us they'll think we did it."

"He's right," Patrick said. "Let's get outta here."

The four boys started to file out when Billy put his hand on Patrick's chest, stopping him at the door.

"What?" Patrick asked with an annoyed look.

"Ain't you gonna flush?"

"Ha. Very funny. It's so important to you... you flush," he said as he pushed away Billy's hand. He walked out of the building and joined the others, who had already mounted their steeds.

11:24 am

Yellow Bluff. That was the place where the crewman on the Coast Guard boat said he might have seen a shadow which might have been a man.

Ron scowled at all those 'might haves.' He did some asking around and learned the crewman was a recent academy graduate and the search for the Alcatraz escapees was his very first mission. Worse, he had been out drinking the night before his sighting. Swell. What a great witness. But there was something in the young man's fervent defense told Ron there might be something to his story.

243

As the cutter approached the Coast Guard station Ron looked glumly at his tape recorder. He had collected lots of sound today, sure, but it was all waves. Lots of waves. Endless waves. He sighed. Now he had to go back to the radio station and try to make something dramatic from all those damn waves. As he lumbered down the gangplank he looked back to the cutter and saw the two crewmen still talking, animatedly. Damn, that boot seems so sure of what he saw. Ron repeated the location to himself, again. Yellow Bluff.

He reached the bottom of the gangplank. There, waiting for him, was Ensign David Gray.

"Mr. Lowendowski," Gray said, extending his hand. "Did you get what you needed today?"

"Well, finding a body would have been nice." Ron immediately regretted the remark. He held up his hands, surrender-style. "I'm sorry, Ensign, I meant –"

"No apology needed," Gray replied. "We are all anxious for a successful conclusion of the search so we can return to our regular mission keeping safe the boaters, sailors and others who use the bay."

The Ensign was good at his job. Also at repeating approved soundbites to the press. "Of course, just as I am," Ron said with an appreciative smile. "My compliments to the Lieutenant and your Captain."

"Thank you, sir, have a good rest of the day." Gray said before walking up the gangplank to the deck of the cutter.

Ron walked slowly to his car. He wasn't in a rush to get back to the station. He stood on the path at the edge of Horseshoe Bay, thinking. Maybe... maybe he should check out this Yellow Bluff for himself. Sure, why not? Might be more interesting than the sounds of waves. He was about to cross the road to his car when several boys on bicycles raced towards him. He stopped to let them pass.

They had been quiet during their dash away from the light house, pumping the pedals of their bikes to the point of exhaustion. As if on cue, when they reached the curved road along Horseshoe Bay, they all stopped pedaling. They coasted. And they talked.

"Who's idea was it to go to Lime Point, anyway?"

"Ah, what are you worried about? No one's gonna know we were there."

"I still can't believe that mess."

"I just don't wanna get in dutch."

"Don't be a pussy..."

Caught up in their adventure, the boys hadn't noticed the man standing on the side of the road. They kept talking.

Ron heard every word.

Lime Point. That was the old lighthouse under the Golden Gate bridge. Ron knew it well. He had done a story about it a few months ago, when the Coast Guard announced it would be soon be shut down. Lime Point. It was just like the little red lighthouse under the George Washington bridge, which also had been made obsolete by a bridge. The difference was the little red lighthouse was famous, thanks to a children's book. (Ron had once joked Lime Point needed a better agent.)

Ron watched the boys ride away. Those kids had gone to the light house and seen a mess inside the barrack. Big deal. Kids are always... He froze. An incredible thought – borne from three days of rumors, alleged sightings, and speculation – suddenly popped into his head.

Yellow Bluff. That young coast guardsman claimed he saw a "shadow," possibly a man.

Lime Point. Stocked with food and clothes. Recently

ransacked.

Reporter's instinct? Wild hunch? A grasping at straws? He couldn't say. Maybe it was a bit of all three. One thing he knew for sure. He had to see Lime Point lighthouse for himself...

11:27 am

Tommy's first thought as he woke after his night of imprisonment at Juanita's was "this must be what a hangover feels like." He was miserable. Miserable from the sad and weary looks his mother gave him every time she hustled into the kitchen to collect an order. Miserable because he imagined John and Clarence at Fort Kirby thinking he had abandoned them or, worse, that he had ratted them out. Miserable because he didn't get any sleep at Juanita's and precious little here back in his own bed. So much had gotten out of his control and so many pieces of his life were broken he wondered if –

The phone rang. He lifted himself out of bed and peered out into the kitchen. "Oh, hello, Marty, what can I – No, I didn't see him last night, I was at work... Really?... He was going where?" Tommy saw her face go white. "No, I can't tell you, I don't know – sorry." Tommy saw her hang up the phone and reach for an unopened pack of cigarettes. He sensed his mother had seen him and he waited for her to say something. But she just sat there, quiet and distant, absentmindedly opening the pack of cigarettes. Tommy crept slowly out of his room.

"Mom? Who was that?"

She looked so weary. "Marty Stafford, the dispatcher at the police station. Tony never checked out from his shift last night. Last time he was seen was by a deputy heading south on Bridgeway in his cruiser." Molly searched her son's face for some reaction. "South on Bridgeway, Tommy... that's where he saw you going the night before last, isn't it?"

Tommy squirmed.

"I think he might have been going to look for you. To find out..."

Her eyes narrowed into his. Unable to turn away Tommy started to feel dizzy. It was over. Everything he had done over the past three days... all the lies and sneaking around. It was the end of the road less traveled. He felt as if he were going to faint.

"Tommy, he could be hurt. He could be in danger. Do you want to be responsible for –"

"All right, all right, I'll tell you, I'll tell you..." he said, bursting into tears. "I should have told you before, but I couldn't."

"Should have told me what?"

"They won't hurt him, I just know they won't."

"Who won't hurt him? Is Tony in danger?"

"No. I mean, I don't think so."

"Tommy, if you don't tell me what's going on right away I'll have no choice. I'll have to call the police station and tell them what little I know and –"

Tommy jumped up and with tears pouring from his eyes wrapped his arms around her. "No, don't, please mom, don't." His arms still around her, he pulled back enough so he could look her in the eyes. "Look, mom, how about this? I'll show you, I'll show you. Ask Mrs. Kincaid to borrow her car. And I'll take you. But please don't call the police. Not yet. Not while they still have a chance."

"While who still has a chance?"

"Can you just get the car? I'll explain everything in the car."

11:31 am

Ron's car gasped and wheezed before sputtering gratefully to a stop outside Lime Point lighthouse. The car door opened with a noisy, rusty protest. He stepped out, shielding his eyes from the bright sun. In the stiff bay breeze flakes of paint peeled from the old building. Flung skyward, they swirled and fell around him like snowflakes, crunching under his feet as he walked the concrete stairs to the landing and then to the building. Ron opened the door and peered inside.

"Holy shit."

Somebody was here and made a helluva mess. Could this be the work of the 'shadow' the Coast Guard cadet had seen at Yellow Bluff? The shadow who, perhaps, planned all along to come here and forage for supplies. Sure, why not? These men built a God-damned raft in a maximum security prison, they must have known what they would do once they made landfall.

It was a good theory. Now to find proof.

The newsman surveyed the quarters, trying to put himself in the escapee's shoes. What would he have looked for first? Dry clothes, maybe. But if I had just been out on that cold bay at night, Ron said to himself, the first thing I would want is a good, hot shower. As he walked to the bathroom the rude smell (noted earlier by the boys) got stronger. Ron scowled. He took a deep breath and held it as he stepped inside and flushed the toilet. He exhaled and tentatively took a small breath. Ugh. Better but, wow, what do they feed those prisoners?

He looked around. More clues... someone had rifled through the medicine cabinet. Probably looking for aspirin and other medicine. Doesn't prove it was an escapee, though. Ron exited the bathroom and surveyed

248

the room. No discarded prisoner-issued clothes anywhere. If this was an escapee he did a pretty good job covering up his tracks. Grudging admiration was building. The admiration grew into a wild thought – he had been thinking of only one escapee. Could it have been two? Or was it possible all three landed at Yellow Bluff and then, as part of their master plan, come here to the lighthouse for clothes, medicine and food?

As he pondered the permutations his eye caught sight of a map hanging next to the bathroom door. The bottom of the map – everything south of Sausalito – was missing... torn off. Why would someone tear off only the bottom of the map? Then he remembered a small fact about Alcatraz. Maps were not allowed.

But why take only the southern part of the map? What was so important – wait a minute – now he remembered. The forts. Every Bay area native knew about the string of old forts lining the Marin foothills. Some had been around since the Spanish American War. Ron had even been to one, as a kid, when he and some friends went to see the new guns the army was installing along the ridge during the war. It was quite an adventure they had after an MP saw them and gave chase all the way down to Horseshoe Bay.

The forts. They were abandoned now – twelve inch mortars were no match for Soviet ICBMs – but they were the perfect places to hide. Now it was all making sense. The raft. Yellow Bluff. The Lighthouse for supplies. Head west – away from the bay. Use the forts for shelter. Then... freedom.

Okay, Ron, steady now. Think. It was now almost noon on the fifteenth, and the escape was on the night of the eleventh. The cadet had seen the Yellow Bluff shadow on the morning of the twelfth. The time fit. A trip across the bay would take several hours. The escapees would have had to wait until the night of the twelfth before they could make their way south, here, to the lighthouse. They would discard their wet prison uniforms (he'd come back later to find out where) then collect food, water, medicine – and the map – before taking off for the nearest fort. Now it would have been the thirteenth when they got to the first fort, where they would sleep for a day before heading west.

How far had they gone? Even in a raft, the trip across the bay must have been grueling, especially for prisoners who don't get much exercise. Further, he reasoned, what if one of them had gotten hurt during the crossing or landing and needed time to recuperate? Assuming some degree of loyalty (was there honor among thieves?) they would be slowed down... but for how long? Maybe a day or two, right? So there was a slim possibility they were still in the area.

The final proof was at one of those forts in the foothills. And Ron had something he was sure the escapees didn't – a car. He headed for the door with a smile. Perhaps today was not going to be a bust, after all.

11:41 am

Tony woke slowly, hoping last night had been a bad dream. A stabbing pain in his head shoved him into full consciousness. He regretfully opened his eyes. Nope, it wasn't a dream. He was prone on a concrete floor, and his hands and feet were bound.

"John, he's awake." A voice from behind. "Hey... are you okay? You got hit pretty hard and we was worried –"

"I'm fine," Tony heard himself say. He remembered everything now. "Where's the guy who slugged me?"

"He's outside," he heard a different voice answer.

"Is he in charge? I want to talk to whoever is in charge."

Tony heard the shuffling of feet. John crouched in front of him with a scowl. "No one's in charge of us, okay?"

"What's going on in here?" A third voice. Maybe the one who hit me? "He's awake now? Good. Get him on his feet."

Tony smirked at John as if to say, 'so, no one is in charge, eh?'

John's scowl deepened. "That ain't how it is, mister."

"Anglin, get him to his feet," Frank said.

As he started to help the officer to his feet, John whispered, "just do as Frank says and we'll be on our way."

Tony had difficulty standing. He blinked hard, trying clear his head. The events of the previous night were coming back to him now. John. Clarence. The Anglins. And Frank Morris. He had found the Alcatraz escapees. No, that's wrong. They had found him. Determined not to show weakness, he forced himself to stand upright and look his captor in the eyes. "You'll never get away with this," he said, glaring at Frank.

"That the best you can do, quote some bad western?" Frank sneered.

Tony stared back, grimly... silently. Always the Marine, he looked around the concrete bowl of the old fort, assessing his options against the three. He couldn't see any, for now. But Tony had faith. There was one constant he had seen in all criminals. Men like this eventually get careless. He could wait.

12:41 pm

Tommy sat sullenly in the front seat of the car Molly had borrowed from a neighbor. They drove south, silently passing the school, the movie theater... all the places which made up home to Tommy O'Conner. A home he was about to shatter with a simple declaration to his mother.

"I've been helping two of the men who escaped from Alcatraz."

It was such an impossible thing for her son to say — so completely unexpected — that there was simply no way for Molly to process what her son had just said and still be able to drive. She veered the car to the side of the road and gasped for air. As Tommy watched, helplessly, his mother opened her door and bolted from the car to the side of the road where she bent over, clutching her stomach.

Tommy opened his door and ran to her. "Mom!"

"This isn't... it couldn't be..." she managed in between gasps for air. Molly lifted her head and looked into Tommy's eyes. "How? When?"

"Tuesday morning. I was going to Horseshoe Bay to meet Billy and I saw these two men on the beach at Yellow Bluff."

"And even though you knew there were escaped prisoners you still approached them?"

"I... I didn't know until later. They said they had fallen off a freighter."

"And you believed them?"

"For about a minute, yea."

"But after you found out... you still helped them?"

"Mom, if you only had seen them. They were cold and tired and anyone could tell they weren't dangerous."

Molly fell back onto the ground, shaking her head in

disbelief as she gently rocked back and forth. "Do you understand what kind of men get sent there? Do you know what kind of men they are?"

Tommy sat down in front of his mother and placed his hands on her shoulders to stop her from rocking. Then he looked directly into her eyes. "I do, mom, because of you."

"Me? What... what are you talking about?"

"All my life you've talked about what it's like being an underdog. Your parents dying and you being left an orphan. How you came here from Kansas to work at the shipyard and how badly the men treated you and the other women welders because you were girls. How you all had to be so much better than them because you weren't men."

"I still don't —"

"Then you told me about the Negro welders who had it even worse than you. How you stood by them when they couldn't join a segregated union and then got fired because they wanted the same benefits as the white welders. How angry even some of the other white girls got at you because you wanted the Negroes to be treated fairly."

"There's a difference between underdogs and criminals —"

"What about Grandpa? You told me the stories from when dad was a boy and he and Tony found out paw-paw Tommy and Grandpa Ben were running rum to the man who ran a speakeasy."

"Tommy, that's different. There was a Depression. They were just doing what they had to do to do for their families —" She stopped and looked at her son and understood. No, helping those men was not what she would have done, but that wasn't important now. Because now it was time for her to be a mom, and join her son on his road less traveled.

"Are we sure Tony is safe with these men?"

"John and Clarence —"

"You know their names."

"Yea. Ma, they're not bad men. They did some bad things but if Tony did find them they'd never hurt him. That's not who they are."

Molly exhaled sharply. She grabbed her son's hand so he could pull her up to a standing position. "I can't believe I'm going to do this."

Tommy smiled gratefully and gave her a hug. They got back in the car and Molly drove south towards the bridge. She stopped the car at the fork in the road near the north tower. "Up there?" she asked, pointing to the narrow road which ran under the bridge. Tommy nodded. Molly put the car in gear and drove up the hill. After a few minutes on the winding road they saw it.

Tony's patrol car.

"Maybe he's asleep inside," Molly said. As soon as she stopped her car Tommy bolted for the cruiser. He cupped his hands over his eyes to block the sun as he looked through the windows. "There's no one inside."

She nodded. "Somehow I knew that would be too easy. Which way now?"

Tommy was already heading downhill towards the water. "This way," he called back to her.

Molly took a deep breath. In for a penny...

1:45 pm

It had been three days since the escape and phone calls to the Sausalito Police Department had slowed to a trickle. The discovery off Angel Island of the paddle and the package of the Anglin's letters convinced a lot of people

254

the men were gone. Drowned in the bay. But now the Sausalito Police had another mystery.

Where the hell was the Chief?

Someone suggested after several long days on duty that Tony had possibly slept late. The rookie, Roger McGloin, got the dubious honor of going to Tony's apartment. He was almost relieved Tony was not there. Roger didn't want to be the one wake up his boss from badly needed slumber. But the mystery remained. Roger decided it was a good time to see his new, favorite source of information, someone who seemed to know everything that was going on in Sausalito.

"You lost him?" Ethel Mackenzie cackled.

Roger laughed at what he hoped was a joke. "Not exactly, Miss Mackenzie. We just haven't heard from him today and —"

"You ever serve, son?"

"Of course. Two years in the army."

"Were you ever in the shit?"

Roger blushed. "No, I was too young for Korea. They sent me to —"

"That man was at the front in two wars. Saw his best friend die in the second one." Her tone softened. The cackle was gone. "No one cares more for this town than Tony. If he's decided he needs some time away, I think we should let him be."

Roger left, feeling better. Ethel was right. The Chief would call in soon. Nothing to worry about...

2:05 pm

Ron drove the winding road along the headlands until he

255

saw Fort Spencer in the distance, up a hill. The dirt path to the fort was too narrow for his car, which sputtered comically to a stop. Shouldering the heavy tape recorder he walked to the aging bunkers. Peering inside the first building he saw two empty C-ration boxes. Nearby, two rats were having their way with the remnants of an army candy bar. He smiled. His theory about the escapees using the forts for shelter was possible. The crunch of crumbling concrete and paint flakes under his feet echoed as he searched for evidence it was the escapees and not some vagrants or teenagers. He found nothing.

Exiting the bunker he looked at the map he had found in his glove compartment. Battery Wagner was the next fort along the water. He slung the tape recorder over his shoulder and walked west.

3:30 pm

It was Clarence Anglin's turn to keep watch in front of the bunker. He heard it first. A familiar voice coming from behind the fort.

"Clarence! Hey Clarence." He saw Tommy emerge from the woods. "Oh, boy, am I glad you're okay," Tommy yelled. "Where's John, is he all right?"

Inside the bunker, both Tony and Frank had the same reaction. This kid knows the Anglins?

"Who the hell is that?" Frank yelled to Clarence. Tony grimaced. Frank looked very nervous. Nervous criminals do stupid things.

"Tommy, is that your father's shirt?" A woman's voice. Tony's jaw actually dropped. That was Molly. What was she doing here?

Outside, Tommy was flustered by his mother's

question. "Uh... I'll explain later," he said as he raced to Clarence. "I'm sorry I couldn't get here last night. How's your leg?" Tommy stopped, suddenly aware of the grim expression on Clarence's face. "Aren't you happy to see me?"

"Who's this?" Clarence asked, pointing to Molly.

"This is my mom."

Clarence fell back a step, as if punched in the gut. "Your... what the hell, kid? Your ma? Why did you bring her here?"

"I had no choice, she –"

Molly pushed Tommy out of the way and locked eyes with Clarence. "Where's Tony?" Taken aback by her bravado, he could only stammer "he's... he's okay." Then, to Tommy, "kid... you have to trust me when I tell you things have changed. You can't be here and she sure as hell can't."

"What do you mean? What's changed?" Tommy asked.

From behind Clarence came a voice Tommy did not recognize. "What the hell's taking you so damn long out there?" A strange man stood at the bunker opening.

"Who is that?" Molly said to Tommy. He helplessly shrugged his shoulders.

Clarence turned to the man at the bunker entrance. "Nothing, it's just some hikers. They needed some directions," Clarence said.

"Don't bullshit me, Clarence. That kid knows your name."

"We don't want any trouble," Molly said, loudly "We were looking for a friend of ours, His name is Tony and–"

"Tony? We don't know any Tony," Frank replied.

Inside the bunker Tony heard everything. Tommy knows the Anglin brothers? Sweet Jesus, that meant the kid had known where the Alcatraz escapees have been all along. But... Clarence didn't know Molly, which meant Molly didn't know what Tommy had been up to. So the kid has been acting on his own? Why? And, just as important, how? Okay, there would be time to sort this out later. Right now Tony knew his job was to regain control of the situation. He raised his head and saw Frank step away from the bunker towards Molly, Clarence, and Tommy. Far enough away to give him an opportunity...

"John," he said softly.

"What?" John replied, his eyes trained on Frank and other others outside.

"I don't know how, but I know the kid out there is mixed up with you three."

John turned his head and looked at Tony. "No, not Frank. Just me and Clarence. Frank showed up last night and just –"

"Took over?" Tony interrupted. He was sure he detected a hint of regret in John's face. "John, if Frank would slug a cop do you think he'd hesitate to hurt a civilian? Or a woman? Think about Tommy. Think about his mother."

Outside, they heard Frank's agitated voice. "If you know what's good for him you're going to have to trust me that the cop is okay and leave us alone."

Then, Molly's voice. Defiant. "A minute ago you said he wasn't here."

Inside the bunker, Tony looked intently at John. "Does that sound like a man who is going to be reasonable?" Then, softly, though no less urgently, "John, you and I know too many guys like Frank. Guys who think they're smarter than everyone else. I've seen dozens of guys like that. They have short fuses. John... we only have a minute, at most, before something neither of us wants will happen to those two people out there."

John exhaled and his body went limp. "Shit." He

258

reached behind the policeman's back and began untying the straps. Even before he was finished Tony was wrestling them off and, with his now-free hands, untying his ankles. Within seconds he was on his feet at the entrance to the bunker.

Molly saw him emerge, her eyes immediately drawn to the large black-and-blue mark on his forehead. She had seen her share of bar fights at Juanita's, but Tony's wound caused her to scream. Frank turned around, to see the cop racing towards him. With only a second to react, he wheeled around behind Tommy and thrust his arm around the boy's neck.

"That's far enough," Frank yelled.

"Tommy," Molly cried as she started to run towards her son.

"Stay where you are, Molly," Tony said, extending his arm out to hold her back. "Let the boy go, Frank."

"After you take me to your cruiser."

The shock on John and Clarence's faces was almost comical. "Frank, what the fuck?" John said. "A car? How long have you known?"

He smirked. "A little while. I was searching his pockets for some dough and found these." He held up a set of keys. "I should have known the cop didn't walk here all the way from town."

Clarence glared at Frank. "You know what, John? I don't think he was gonna tell us about the car. He was gonna blow and leave us here with the cop."

Frank sneered at Clarence. "You're not so stupid after all."

John took a step towards Frank. "I've already told you, Frank, cut that shit out."

Frank tightened his grip on Tommy's neck. "I was doing fine by myself. But after meeting you two I've had nothing but trouble." The boy's eyes widened in fear.

259

Molly let out a whimper. Only Tony's outstretched arm kept her from advancing on Frank.

John saw all of Frank's attention was on Tony and Molly, and he got an idea. It was time for the brothers to put their special bond to work. With a slight movement of his elbow he nudged his brother. Clarence turned his head and saw John thrust his two front teeth over his lower lip and move his jaw rapidly up and down. Like a rat. Clarence acknowledged with a slight nod. All John needed to do now was get Tommy's attention. "Hey kid, you okay?"

Tommy, his head held in place by Frank's arm, said "Yea, I can still breathe, if that's what you mean."

"What the hell Frank, do you really think we'd ever rat on you?" John said as he winked at Tommy. Clarence was ready as John yelled "A rat!" and pointed to the ground near Frank.

Frank screamed. "Where?"

"Now Tommy," yelled John. Tommy stomped down – hard – on Frank's foot.

"Son of a bitch," Frank said as he released his grip on Tommy's neck. As Tommy pushed himself away from Frank, Tony lunged and they both fell to the ground. The two men began exchanging punches as they rolled around the concrete floor. It was Marine training versus prison experience and, so far, it was a draw. John, Clarence, Molly, and Tommy looked on helplessly as Frank somehow managed to wriggle away from Tony and launch himself to a standing position. Tony reached out to grab Frank's leg.

"No you don't," Tony said just as Frank swung his other foot and kicked the policeman in the head. Tony went rolling backwards, blood pouring from his forehead.

"Tony," Molly cried, as she ran over him.

"I won't forget this you sons-of-bitches," Frank spat

at John and Clarence. "You better hope we don't cross paths again." Frank took an extra moment to catch his breath and glare at Tommy. "You, too, you little bastard." He turned and ran toward the woods.

Tony, blood flowing from his forehead, lifted himself off the ground. "Stay here. If he doubles back..."

"We'll be ready," John said.

"Tony, no, you're bleeding," Molly cried.

Tony brushed her aside. "Not now." He turned to the Anglins. "You two... stay right where you are." Racing in a half-limp to the far end of the battery he climbed up the concrete stairs and disappeared into the woods.

"Morris," Tony yelled to the woods in front of him.

Ahead by a dozen steps, Frank scowled. Shit. The cop was right behind him. Ignoring the pain his legs Frank tried to run faster through the thickening woods, swiping away some branches but missing many others, which slapped him sharply in his face.

"It's no use running Frank. I know you're out here and soon everyone else will," came the voice from behind. Damn it, the cop was getting closer. Desperate to put distance between them Frank put on a burst of speed, nearly tripping over a downed tree trunk. As he stumbled, Frank turned his head to see how far behind him the cop was when –

His legs were still making a running motion but... something was missing. Where was the sound of his feet hitting the ground? Frank whipped his head forward. It took a second for his mind to grasp that what was wrong.

The earth was gone.

For the second time in as many days Frank Morris had found the edge of a cliff. Only this time it was too late to stop. Too late to turn back. Not even enough time to scream. The last sound he heard, just before his body shattered on the rocks below, was a voice from above yelling his name.

The leather strap of the heavy tape recorder dug deep into Ron Lowendowski's shoulder as he hiked briskly along the ridge. He ignored the pain. Ron was too focused on getting to the next fort, Battery Wagner, along the ridge. If the escapees were there, his plan was to sneak close enough to record them talking. Then he'd go to the authorities with their location. In their gratitude (so he imagined) they would let him tag along at the arrest. Or arrests, plural.

He reached the lip of the concrete bowl of Battery Wagner. Sunlight reflecting off the concrete wall on the opposite side allowed him to see inside both bunkers. They appeared empty. Disappointed, Ron trundled gingerly down into the bowl and peered inside the first bunker. Yep, save for a family of happy rats, busy nibbling away at a leftover box of rations scattered on the ground, it was empty.

Well, as long as he was here with a tape recorder... "This is Ron Lowendowski reporting from high above the San Francisco gate," he said dramatically into the microphone. "The bay area has been in the grip of fear for three days now, ever since the escape of three dangerous prisoners from Alcatraz. Authorities have repeatedly stated their belief that the escapees did not survive the trip in the cold waters of San Francisco bay, despite the fact they were in a homemade raft. But this intrepid reporter has discovered the truth, here in the string of abandoned battery emplacements along the Marin highlands. The truth is they not only survived but are on the loose."

Now to add some extra drama... courtesy of the echo inside the bunker. He stepped through the doorway and walked to the middle of the room. He could feel his heart pounding as he pressed the RECORD button.

"I'm now speaking to you from inside the bunker at Battery Spencer. Here lies proof at least one of the escapees used this place to hide, waiting for night to take over the bay area when he – or they – would be free to move west to freedom. I am looking at boxes of C-rations which have been stolen from the Lime Point lighthouse barracks by one or more of the escapees. He – or they – have left behind not just these clues but the smell of sweat and desperation. How much further they can go... nobody knows. But this reporter will continue the search for the answer to the great mystery of our time, where are the Alcatraz escapees? From Battery Spencer, this is Ron Lowendowski."

He chuckled as he turned off the machine. "That's right, Colonel. I said Lowendowski. Once I find those men you'll have to run the story and run it my way." He swung the strap of the tape recorder back over his shoulder and pulled the map from his pocket. Just under a quarter of a mile away was his next stop, Battery Kirby.

Ron walked westward, whistling, thinking about where in his new Nob Hill apartment he would display the Pulitzer undoubtedly in his future.

Back at Kirby Battery Molly's arms were wrapped protectively around her son as she gently rocked back and forth. "It's okay, mom, I'm okay," Tommy kept repeating, but Molly would not release her grip. Both Anglin brothers, drawn to the sight, had the same, sad thought. They would never see their own mother, Rachel, again. To protect her they had to keep their survival a secret.

263

There was so much John wanted to say to Molly. How loyal her son had been to them. How brave he had been over the past three days. And how grateful they would always be. He was conjuring up the words when, from the other side of the battery, Tony emerged, stumbling and limping, from the woods.

"Tony," Molly cried out. She raced to him, placing his arm over her shoulders as she walked him back to the fire.

"Where's Frank?" John asked.

"Water," was all Tony said as he held out his hand.

Clarence pulled a canteen out of the duffel bag and handed it to him. Tony took several gulps of water, followed by several equally large gulps of air, then drank some more.

"Well," John said again, impatiently, "where is he?"

Tony heaved out one last breath. Then, in a voice devoid of emotion, "he's gone."

"Gone? What do you mean? Where?"

Tony pointed over the battery towards the cove. "Out there. In the water."

"He jumped?" Clarence asked, incredulously.

Tony shook his head.

"Fell?"

Tony shook his head. "No, he... just ran right off the cliff..."

"Holy shit."

"Dead?"

"I'm sure of it, yea," Tony replied.

"Are you okay?" Molly asked as she examined the gash on his head.

"Yea. I swear it was like nothing I'd ever seen before. One second he was right in front of me – I mean I had almost caught up to him and the next second he was... flying." He allowed himself a sardonic chuckle. "Not very well, of course. I might've gone over, too, if I didn't run myself into a tree."

Tommy watched as Molly put her arms around Tony and hug him. "Thank God you're okay, that's all that's important," she said. Four days ago this sight would have made him angry. Now... he didn't know how to feel.

Everyone was quiet, now. One by one, Tommy looked around at everyone. John... Clarence... Tony... Molly... it felt strange to see them all together. It felt even stranger that the adventure was all over.

Not quite.

He saw John pick up Frank's duffel bag. "Grab our bag, Clarence," he said. "Time for us to go."

Tony broke away from Molly. "The hell you are." Bringing himself to full Marine height he looked John squarely in the eyes. "You think you two can just walk away?"

"Tony," Clarence began... The officer was taken aback hearing the inmate say his name for the first time. "You did us all a favor. Well, Frank did. Once they see his body floating out there it will all be over."

"They won't stop because of one body."

"Yes they will. That's all they need. Just one and they can say 'see, we told you no one can escape from Alcatraz.'"

"I can't just let you go."

"You think you're just gonna march us down Main Street with our hands up?" John pointed to his belt. "Look at you. You got no gun, no handcuffs..."

"And there's two of us," Clarence added.

"I don't need a gun." Tony took a menacing step towards John.

John's smile took Tony by surprise. "How are you gonna explain how you missed three escaped prisoners in your own backyard?"

Now it was Tony's turn to smile. "I didn't miss them.

Two of them are right here in front of me. And I found them before the FBI, the Bureau of Prisons or any other cop did. They'll give me a medal."

"Sure they will. And then Tommy will get a record for helping us."

"Yea, I can just see the headlines," Clarence added. "'Authorities outwitted by thirteen year-old boy.'"

Tommy was crestfallen. "John.. Clarence... I don't understand... you would do this to me?"

"Don't worry, Tommy, the officer here ain't gonna do nothin'." Then, mockingly, to Tony, "Are you?"

"Tony..." Molly began, her eyes filling with tears.

Tony's shoulders sagged. "Molly, all I've ever wanted to do is protect you and Tommy. Ever since..."

Molly gently touched Tony's arm. "I've never blamed you for what happened to Connor and I've never asked for anything from you. But now I'm asking... I'm begging... if you won't do this for me... if you won't do it for Tommy... do it for Connor."

"Molly, what do you think will happen when they get caught?

"We won't"

Tony looked at John, smugly. "Frank didn't think he was going to die."

"Just proves Frank wasn't a smart as everyone said he was."

"But you are?"

Clarence was smiling. "Frank had nobody on the outside."

"Clarence!" yelled John. The staccato burst of anger took Tommy by surprise. He had never seen John yell at his brother. But now he knew for certain what he had already guessed. The brothers had a plan.

John turned back to Tony. "This is the only way. We save the kid... and his ma doesn't hate you for the rest of her life."

Tony's shoulders slumped. He looked at Molly, then at Tommy, then back to John. He nodded, numbly.

John nodded back, then walked over to Molly. "We're sorry for the trouble we caused you, Mrs. Tommy. Your son... he saved our lives. We'll never forget that."

"Yea, me and my brother woulda died without his help," Clarence added.

"And now, thanks to him, we get a fresh start," John said. Then, looking deeply into Molly's eyes, "I promise, Mrs. Tommy, we'll make good use of our second chance."

Molly smiled. "Somehow – I don't know why – I know you will. Good luck."

John now stood in front of Tommy, who couldn't bring himself to make eye contact. He said, softly, "Tommy, after everything you did for us do you really think we was gonna let you take the rap?"

Tommy raised his head and glared at John. "You couldn't know what Tony was gonna do," he replied.

"But I did," John said with a broad smile. He then leaned forward and whispered into Tommy's ear, "I knew by the way he's been looking at your mom ever since you got here."

Tommy pulled his head back quickly and looked at John, confusion in the eyes. "But how..."

The older Anglin laughed. "We wasn't always in prison, Tommy. There was plenty of girls in Ruskin. You're thirteen. You'll learn soon enough."

The sun was hurtling towards twilight. The soft chirping of crickets from the woods mixed with the sound of water lapping on the beach below. Grudging acceptance slowly grew on the boy's face and John smiled. Tommy reached out and hugged him.

"Good luck, John." Then, turning to his brother, "and you, too, Clarence."

"Thanks, Tommy. And don't worry, we'll never rat."

John, Clarence, and Tommy laughed. The brothers started to walk away. John stopped and looked back at Tony. With a reluctant nod from the officer, the brothers walked into the woods.

"Tony, I," Molly began...

"Don't..." Tony said, holding up his hand. "There's nothing left for you to say."

"But there's something I need to say," Tommy said. "I owe you an apology."

"Look, kid, what's done is done. I'll probably never understand why you helped those two men –"

"No, not about that," the boy interrupted. "About the way I've been acting towards you all these years."

"You don't have to do this."

"Let him." Molly said. "Go head, Tommy."

"I've been blaming you for my dad dying and that was wrong. And I've been kind of a jerk to you because when I've seen you with my mom, well, I thought... you know..."

Molly knelt down in front of her son and looked him in the eyes. "Honey, Tony and I have known each other since I got to Sausalito during the war. Which means we've been friends for almost twenty years. But that's it. We're just friends. Nothing more." She turned and looked up at Tony.

"Yea, sure. Friends..." he said, smiling bravely. "Look, let's clean this place up and get back to town. It's been a long week. I'm glad it's over."

But Tony was wrong. It wasn't over. Not yet.

Ron Lowendowski had followed the trail of C-ration boxes and aspirin bottles from Lime Point lighthouse to Battery Spencer to Battery Wagner. Almost near the bottom of the steep hill to Battery Kirby, he could now hear voices. He

268

moved his hand to the tape recorder, ready to record what he was sure would be a conversation between the Alcatraz escapees.

Wait, was that a woman's voice? What the hell was a woman doing there? Distracted, he didn't see the fallen tree in front of him.

"Shit!"

Ron pitched forward, instinctively sticking his arms out to stop his fall. But he fell anyway. The heavy tape machine rotated forward up and over his head.

Outside the bunker at Fort Kirby Tony, Molly, and Tommy were almost done cleaning the escapees camp when they saw Ron tumble down the grassy hill and land with a thud on the concrete floor. One second later a metal box smashed into the ground. What looked like a small hubcap rolled away from the box, trailing a thin, brown line behind it. They heard the body groan.

Ron opened his eyes to see a policeman, a woman and a boy staring down at him.

"Are you okay?" he heard the woman ask.

"Who the hell are you and what are you doing here?" the cop asked.

The boy said nothing. He just stared at him.

Ron stared back at them. "My name is Ron Lowendowski. I'm a reporter for KRAN radio. Now would someone help me, please?"

"Hold on," Tony said. "Let's first make sure you didn't break anything."

"Other than that thing you were carrying," Tommy added.

"My tape recorder," Ron said, his eyes wide with panic. Bolting to his feet, he twisted his body frantically in all directions until he saw the machine lying on the ground, behind him. He dropped to his knees and breathed a sigh of relief... the cover had broken off but otherwise the machine looked fine. Except... where was the tape on which he had been recording all his reports? Then he heard the boy's voice again.

"Hey mister, is that what you're looking for?"

Ron looked up. The boy was pointing at the reel of tape which, at that moment, was still unrolling itself on the concrete floor. Wind from the gate was picking up the unrolled tape, which danced haphazardly in the air.

"All right, mister, what's this all about?" Tony demanded as Ron, on his hands and knees, attempted to collect the flying ribbon. "Well?"

Ron rolled from his knees into a sitting position and, gripping the tape, looked up at Tony. "Have you fielded any reports of strange men in the area?"

"Mister, ever since the escape that's all I've been doing."

"And...?"

Tony shook his head. "Trash cans and stray cats."

"Yea? Well I have evidence the prisoners who escaped from Alcatraz made it here, to land, and are now heading west along the Marin headlands."

Tony squatted down next to Ron, pointing to the ribbon of tape dancing in the wind. "Is that your evidence?"

Ron nodded glumly. "No, it's a tape I was making for my broadcast."

Tony looked up at Molly and Tommy. And winked. "So... what is your evidence?"

Molly and Tommy edged closer. Ron took a steadying breath. "I was on a Coast Guard cutter today and heard a crewman say that he saw something on the beach at Yellow Bluff the morning of the escape."

At the words "Yellow Bluff" Tommy let out a small

whimper. Molly smoothly placed her arm around her son's shoulders and squeezed. She could feel his body trembling.

Ron continued. "When I got off the cutter I then heard some boys saying the Lime Point lighthouse had been ransacked. So I went down there to investigate. They were right. I just put two and two together. It's obvious the prisoners landed at Yellow Bluff then went to the lighthouse for food and clothes. They grabbed a map which showed all the forts which line the foothills. I followed the trail and ended up here. They must have been here and already gone west."

Tony looked at Molly and Tommy with a reassuring smile. He winked again just before turning to face Ron. "Well, Ron, I've got some good news and some bad news for you."

Ron stood up angrily. "Look, officer, I don't have time for –"

"I'll start with the bad news," Tony said, his eyes narrowing into a glare. "Withholding information on an active Federal investigation is a serious offense. If you really did have evidence on the whereabouts of the escaped prisoners you should have called it in. Feds come down hard on people who get in their way."

Ron rolled his eyes. "Look, you can't charge me with that crap. I'm just following a few hunches –"

"Let me finish with even worse news. You haven't been tracking escaped prisoners."

"Come on, officer. Yellow Bluff? The ransacked lighthouse? The trail of empty boxes of food at those forts back there? There's no other explanation."

"Actually, there is. Ron. Did you think to ask what the three of us are doing here?"

The reporter shook his head. "I don't know. You took your family out on a hike?"

271

Tony grimaced, ever so slightly. "No, this isn't my family. This is my friend, Molly, and that is her son Tommy. Just as you showed up he was confessing to what he did three days ago. There's your culprit who ransacked the lighthouse and left those ration boxes in the forts."

Ron looked disbelievingly at Tommy. "You?"

Out of the corner of his eye Tommy saw his mother nod slightly. He dropped his head dramatically. "Yes, sir."

"Oh, come on... why?"

"Mister, you ever been thirteen?" Tony said.

"Of course," Ron answered.

"This kid lost his father when he was only three."

"Look, I'm sorry about that but –"

"My son lashes out sometimes," Molly interrupted, looking sternly at Tommy. "Never anything this bad, though."

"There are no excuses for what he did," Tony said as his stuck his thumbs into his police belt. (A display of authority Tommy had always hated... until now.) "But believe me, he's not getting away without being punished. His mother is going to make sure this summer won't be much of a vacation."

"You can be sure of it," she added, putting on her best 'mommy-is-mad' face.

Tommy dropped his head and made sure he looked appropriately guilty. As exciting as the last three days had been helping out the Anglins, now adults were giving him a starring role in the unraveling of the reporter's story? Well, this was an extra thrill. The question now was... would it work? They all held their breath as Ron mulled the competing narratives.

The first story... of a miracle crossing of the bay by three Alcatraz prisoners and their escape to freedom with the help of a thirteen year-old boy. As Ron said those words to himself, he realized how preposterous it

272

sounded. How ridiculous he would sound if he said them on the air.

The second story... of a thirteen year-old boy with too much free time on his hands and a little too much James Dean in him. And here was a cop and the boy's angry mother to make it all sound so logical.

Tommy, Molly and Tony saw Ron's shoulders slump. They watched him kneel down and tear the end of the tape from the reel. Released and caught by the breeze it whirled lazily away into the night. Ron picked up the machine and walked solemnly, silently into the woods.

Tommy, Molly and Tony stood there for a while. Then...

"Come on, let's go home," Tony said. They walked up the hill to the cruiser and headed for Sausalito, their world, changed forever.

June 22, 1962

9:46 am

Heavy clouds were making for a gray day in Sausalito. But in Molly's workshop, through the tinted glass of their welding helmets, she and Tommy saw a blazing sun.

They had been here for a week. Soon after returning from their adventure at Fort Kirby, Molly had been seized by an idea for a sculpture. She had been working on it with a fervor during her off-hours from Juanita's. Tommy was there because his mother had no intention of letting him out of her sight. He was smart enough not to argue, yet there was still a summer outside and he was thirteen and upset not be able to partake in it. For the first few days of his incarceration he would sit, glumly, in a corner of the studio. A few days into the project, out boredom, Tommy deigned to raise his head to look at what she was creating.

What he saw almost brought him to tears.

"Is that...?" he began, unable to finish the sentence.

Molly nodded.

"It's... it's amazing, mom."

There was a summer outside but, from that moment,

Tommy wanted to be no place else as he watched, in awe, his mother craft a graceful sculpture from disparate pieces of scrap metal. Over the next few days they talked. They shared memories of Connor and the aching emptiness neither could shake. She spoke of Kansas and the void in her heart after losing one, then both of her parents. They talked about war, of Molly's pride watching ships she helped build slide into the bay, ready for duty. He spoke of the helplessness of his generation waiting for death to fall silently from the other side of the planet. Meanwhile, the sculpture grew, the whole greater than its individual pieces.

Molly turned off the generator after affixing another a piece to the now six foot-tall sculpture. She and Tommy lifted the visors to their helmets. She turned to her son. "Well?"

He smiled and nodded.

"Hey, are you hungry? How about some lunch?" she asked as she pulled off her weathered leather gloves.

"Yea, sure."

Molly reached into her pocket and handed him a dollar bill. "Here, go to the Kettle deli and get us a couple of sandwiches and drinks. There should be enough for some fries, too, if you want them."

"French fries? Sure, thanks," he said as he stuffed the bill in his pocket. As he grabbed the doorknob he realized this was the first time in a week his mother was letting him out on his own. Tommy turned and saw her smiling an unspoken "I trust you." He smiled back his own, unspoken, "thank you" and exited the studio.

Tommy had taken only a few steps outside when he heard "Hey, O'Conner, is that you?" He turned and saw Billy, Raymond, Johnny and Patrick on their bikes.

"Hey guys," Tommy said.

Four heads turned. Four bikes skidded to a stop.

Four boys barraged him with questions. "Where you been?" "Yea, we haven't seen you in, like, over a week." "We had to start summer without you!" "What have you been doing?"

Tommy smiled. He pointed to the building behind them. "Been helping my mom with a new sculpture."

"Really? On your summer vacation?" "Since when are you an artist?"

"Yea, that sounds kinda dopey."

Tommy wasn't sure how to answer. He wasn't even sure he wanted to try. He just shrugged and everyone fell silent for a few moments. Until Patrick spoke up. "Oh, hey, Tommy, didja hear what they found yesterday?"

"No, like I said I've been with ma for the past week –"

"Well this is big news, Tommy."

"They found a piece of the prisoner's raft."

"Under the bridge, near Kirby Cove."

"Everyone is saying this proves they musta drowned."

"Ah, we knew it all along."

"Yea, no way they coulda made it."

"Not without that raft."

"What do you think, Tommy?"

They leaned over the handlebars of their bikes and waited. Then...

"You know what, guys, I gotta go. I'm supposed to be getting lunch for me and ma."

"Oh, okay," Billy said, trying not to look hurt.

"I'm sorry, I just got things to do, you know?" Tommy said as he walked away.

"Hey, we gonna see you at all this summer?"

"Oh yea, for sure. We still have to work on your new boat, right?" Tommy said, over his shoulder.

"Yea, my father says it's okay to go out in the bay now

so whenever you can..."

"Okay, that will be fun, right? I'll... I'll call you, okay? Thanks for the news," Tommy said. They watched him walk away.

"Is he okay?" Johnny asked.

"Yea, he just gets like this sometimes. His dad being dead and all," Billy explained. Patrick and Raymond nodded sympathetically.

Up ahead, Tommy felt the sting of cool bay air in his nostrils. It had the smell of summer. Yet he was already looking forward to the smell of electricity from the welding arc and the company of his mother...

July 17, 1962

8:09 am

The bridge of the freighter Norefjell was busy but, save for the reassuring throb from the ship's diesel engines, quiet and businesslike. Though they had already passed under the Golden Gate Bridge and out of San Francisco's busy channel, concentration was critical. The Norefjell was still a five-thousand ton ship which could not turn on a dime, as the Americans would say.

"Kaptein!"

Captain Gustav Rodge bolted upright from his navigation charts and glared at the source of the interruption, a young man he judged no more than eighteen. "*Hva?*"

"*En kropp. I vannet!*"

"A body?" the captain grunted. Then, to his First Mate, "The boot probably saw a seal." Not making any effort to hide his impatience he nodded to the First Mate, who walked quickly to the bridge window where the young recruit was standing.

"Der! There!" he said, pointing wildly to something

in the water.

Casting a quick, knowing glance back towards the captain, First Mate Andreas Hanson approached the young sailor with a condescending smirk. What he saw erased his smirk and actually caused his jaw to drop. "*Sønn av en tispe. Kaptein, du burde se dette.* (Captain. A body! About one hundred meters off to port.)"

With the slow, reassuring walk which comes from years in command, the captain crossed to look out the window. From his years as a wartime merchant seaman he had seen the same, sad sight all too many times; the bloated body of a man who had been in the water for a while. He looked sympathetically at the visibly shaken young cadet "*Går det bra?* (Are you all right?)"

"Yes, I am... I think. *Jeg har aldri sett...* (I've just never seen a...)"

The captain placed a hand gently on the young man's shoulder. "Sail long enough, you'll see plenty."

"Are we going to pick him up?"

"No, whoever he was... is long dead. We let the Americans decide what to do." Then, turning to the bridge crew, he bellowed "Someone make a note to radio the American Coast Guard after we have cleared the harbor district and tell them there's a body in the water. Give them its coordinates."

A note was made on a little piece of paper and the Norefjell continued on its journey, leaving San Francisco Bay and the sad, lonely, bloated body behind. It got busy on the bridge. The note was forgotten.

September 5, 1962

8:32 am

Tommy O'Conner knew what teacher was going to ask his ninth grade class. After all, today was the first day of school and every teacher everywhere asks the same question on the first day of school. It must be the first thing they learn in teacher college.

"What did you do on your summer vacation?"

Tommy mused. Where to begin? Perhaps the part where he helped two Alcatraz escapees make their way to freedom? Or how he knew the reason why Police Chief Marianetti walked off the job in July? Maybe he would tell the class it was the third Alcatraz escapee and not, as described in the press, some juvenile delinquents, who trashed the Lime Point lighthouse?

A reflection off the mast of a small fishing boat in the bay caught Tommy's attention. He sighed. Why did his new classroom have to face the water? Another cruel trick by the school.

He sighed, again, as a piece of chalk silently floated through air...

October 17, 1962

3:12 pm

Petty Officer Ian Jacoby enjoyed his assignment in the communications center. His stomach was still a bit queasy after weeks spent in the fruitless search for the bodies of the Alcatraz escapees. The discovery of the paddle and waterproof wallet was exciting, but it got boring pretty quick after that. Comms... now here was a pretty cushy assignment.

From the radio came a heavily accented voice, breaking Ian's reverie. "Golden Gate Coast guard station, this is freighter Norefjell calling on channel one."

Ian bolted upright in his seat. He leaned forward. "This is Golden Gate station, we copy you Norefjell." He looked at a blackboard hung near the radio, and saw the ship was a Norwegian freighter due in today from Canada.

"We spotted a body near the bridge," Ian heard a heavily accented voice say. He keyed his microphone.

"Copy, Norefjell. Please confirm coordinates so we can send a boat for recovery."

Silence. He keyed his microphone, again. "Norefjell,

please advise coordinates of the body."

After another few seconds of silence. A different voice blared from the speaker. "This is Captain Gustav Rodge speaking."

The captain? This was unusual. "Yes, captain?"

"I beg to report we are..." He stopped. Groping for a word. Ian heard what sounded like *"Hvordan sier jeg forsinket"* – he assumed it was Norwegian – to someone nearby. "...tardy, yes, tardy in reporting the body was spotted on July 17 during our outbound trip."

July 17th? That was over three months ago. Then Ian remembered. July 17th was about a month after those three men escaped from Alcatraz. Three months since his first mission on the bay looking for bodies.

"I copy, captain. I'll pass this along to the commandant here at Golden Gate and he will advise."

"Takk skal du ha. Thank you. Norefjell out."

Ian stared at the silent speaker. This probably meant the mystery of the Alcatraz escape was solved. They had drowned, just like everyone said. And he, Ian Jacoby, was the first American to know. Pretty cool. Smiling, he picked up the phone and dialed the commander's office.

March 21, 1963

11:42 am

Alcatraz was closing today, forever.

Standing on the dock of the island, Warden Olin Blackwell braced himself against the cold, stiff wind and tried, unsuccessfully, to light another cigarette.

"Warden Blackwell?" a voice interrupted. Olin looked up. It was one of those damn reporters. A whole flock of them had crowded the dock waiting for the moment when the last prisoner would leave Alcatraz Island. Blackwell had argued with boss, Fred Wilkinson, against having so many of them milling around, upsetting what was the well-rehearsed routine of transferring a prisoner off the island. "Sorry, Olin," Wilkinson had replied, "it's what the boss wants." Blackwell sighed and kept his mouth shut. The boss was the Attorney General of the United States. He was also the president's kid brother.

The reporter, holding a battered tape machine that had clearly seen better days, thrust out a microphone in an outstretched hand as he stepped closer to the warden.

Blackwell regretfully took the cigarette out of his mouth and stuck it into his coat pocket. (No sense wasting it.) "Yes, son?" he said to the reporter.

"Some are saying the timing of the closing of Alcatraz coming so soon after the recent escapes –"

"Let me stop you there, son. The decision to close this facility was economic and not about a few escapes which made a few headlines."

"But just this past December, not six months after the escape of the three men last June, a prisoner got off this island and swam all the way to the Golden Gate Bridge –"

"I'm going to stop you again," Blackwell said, raising his hand towards the massive sandstone structure on the bluff above. "Fifty years of exposure to salt water has done a number on these buildings –"

"It was loose concrete which allowed those three men to escape last year, right?"

Blackwell saw several other reporters were listening to their conversation. "Which is exactly the point. It would cost four million dollars to repair and modernize this facility," he said loudly so they could all hear him. "Even then, you still have the problem of supplying food and fresh water not for the prisoners but staff –"

The rattling of chains interrupted his speech. Blackwell and the reporters turned to see a prisoner, his legs shackled in irons, being walked by two guards down the ramp leading to the dock. With a nod from Blackwell to several other guards, the reporters were herded away to clear path to the boat. Warden Blackwell walked up to the two guards and smiled.

"Barone. Albright," he said, using last-name formality he had always maintained with his guards. Then, to their surprise, he softened and said, with a grin, "Paul. Jim. Bet your wives and children are looking

286

forward to a drier assignment." They smiled. "All right, let's get this done." The warden stepped aside and motioned for them to continue their walk to the boat. Flashbulbs popped and reporters yelled questions to the prisoner, a gun-runner named Frank Weatherman. He had the distinction of being the last con on the island.

"Any thoughts on the closing of Alcatraz?" the reporter with the beaten-up tape recorder shouted to the prisoner.

Trained from years of incarceration to wait for permission before speaking, Frank Weatherman looked to Jim Albright, who nodded. The prisoner turned to the reporter and spoke the last words on the island by a convict.

"Alcatraz was never no good for nobody..."

August 1, 2015

5:56 pm

She was 90 years old today, the fire of her fighting spirit still burning in a now frail frame. Molly had fought the Kansas Dust Bowl and Great Depression which turned her into an orphan. She battled male welders at the shipyard who scoffed that a woman could do their job. She raised a son, alone. Later, she stood with hundreds of other Houseboat owners battling to prevent their houseboat homes from being swallowed up by developers.

Ninety years old. As many do when they reach a milestone birthday, she thought about those who weren't around to celebrate with her. Had it really been 62 years since two Marines came with news about her husband? She thought about how the letters from the friends at the shipyard arrived with less frequency, until one last letter from a daughter or granddaughter reported their passing. Molly remembered how Tony, soon after the incident at Kirby Cove, had just walked off the job and left Sausalito with no forwarding address. There were stories about him becoming a fisherman up north or a construction worker down south, but no one could ever say for certain where he had gone. Finally, she remembered her surprise when she read of the passing of Juanita. Juanita had always seemed so much older than her but, according to the papers, she was born just two years before Molly.

She had heard some say getting old is more of a curse than a blessing. To that, Molly called bullshit. As long as she could still keep an arc and weld... well, every day was a blessing and there were new memories – and sculptures – to make for herself and her customers.

"Ma?" came a voice from behind her. She smiled when she saw Tommy and his wife, Maureen, walk on deck.

"Well, it's about time," she said with a smile. "Where are my grandchildren and great-grandchildren?"

"Jennifer called me, her oldest has a soccer game this morning. They'll be here as soon as they can," Maureen said. "Daniel... well, you know he always runs late."

"Is he bringing a girlfriend, maybe?" Molly asked hopefully.

"We'll know when he shows up, Ma," Tommy said.

"Tommy, go ahead and sit with your mom," Maureen said. "I'll set up for the party."

Tommy kissed his wife appreciatively and then sat down next to his mother. He furtively turned to be sure Maureen was in the cabin. "I have something to show you," he said, softly.

"My goodness, you FBI men can sound ominous."

Tommy laughed. "Didn't you know? I got an 'A' in ominous at Quantico." His smile disappeared as he took a picture from his jacket pocket and handed it to her. Molly studied the photo. It looked to be an ordinary snapshot of two ordinary middle-age men. The only unusual thing about the picture was, in between them, a mound of dirt so tall it was almost bigger than them.

"Well?" Tommy asked, "what do you think?"

"What's that thing in the middle?

"It's a termite mound."

"I've never seen anything like that. Termites can make something that tall? Where?"

Tommy sighed, impatiently. "Brazil, ma. They're all over the rain forest. Forget the damn mound, ma, look at the men."

He watched as his mother silently studied the picture. "So they made it."

Tommy nodded. "I've been staring at this picture since it was left in my office last week and I'm sure of it.

"Where did it come from?"

"The agent in charge of the case told me it was sent a few years ago to the Anglin family by a boyhood friend of John and Clarence. The agent thinks it was mailed to them knowing the Bureau would see it."

"This doesn't make sense. Why would a friend do that to John and Clarence? ?"

"I don't know. Maybe they pissed him off and this was revenge for something. Or maybe he thought it would help John and Clarence by throwing us off their trail."

"What do you think?"

"Officially... I'm not supposed to say," Tommy replied with the boyish smirk of a once-adventuresome thirteen year-old. Then, in a serious tone, "Frankly, between us, since 9/11 the Bureau has a few other things on its plate. We say it's an open case but who knows if they're still alive after all these years..."

She nodded. They sat quietly together, now, looking out into the bay until they heard the sounds of arriving family. After one last look at the island which changed their lives Molly and Tommy got up and joined the rest of the family...

A few hours later food and drink had been consumed, birthday candles extinguished and presents opened. The children had run themselves into exhausted sleep. Grateful parents, grandparents – and one great-grandmother – sat on the deck sipping wine enjoying the cool breeze and gentle rocking of the boat. But Tommy was feeling antsy.

He excused himself from the group and walked off the boat, then several blocks to Sausalito's Town Hall. There it sat, bathed in soft floodlights. A sculpture, commissioned by the town and welded by his mother from pieces of scrap iron from when the town removed the last vestiges of the old shipyard for development. It was, without question, her best work. Lots of people said so when it was unveiled. Everyone was impressed how she made the two steel figures look as if they were moving... actually walking away. When they asked her where the name of the sculpture came from, she said it was to honor the townspeople who stuck by each other through tough years and times of conflict.

But she wasn't telling the truth. Only Molly and Tommy knew the secret of the single word which graced the base of the sculpture, of the bond two brothers vowed to keep to their dying days: **INSEPARABLE**.

The End

Notes

Inseparable is a work of fiction. However, many characters were modeled on real people who lived and worked in Sausalito between World War Two and 1962. A prime example is Molly, the mother of our protagonist, Tommy. Hundreds of women like Molly came from all over the country to Sausalito to train and work as welders at Bechtel's wartime Marinship shipyard. Molly's evolution into an artist was inspired by a real Sausalito resident who took the same journey.

The backbone of *Inseparable* is the audacious escape of three men from Alcatraz prison on June 11, 1962. Included in the novel are some of the actual people who had roles before, during and after the escape. I want to introduce to you to some of them, now.

John Anglin and his brother Clarence Anglin were two of fourteen children of Rachel and George Anglin, itinerant farm workers from Donaldsville, Georgia who eventually settled in the town of Ruskin, Florida. Along with their brother Alfred, John and Clarence began committing petty crimes as youngsters, eventually graduating to burglaries and, finally, a bank robbery. Though the bank job was committed using a toy gun, the brothers were sentenced to a state prison where they demonstrated an adept ability to leave the care of the state, albeit without permission. After several escape attempts John and Clarence were sentenced to serve at the Federal Penitentiary at Alcatraz in 1960 and 1961, respectively.

Frank Morris is the most well-known of the three escapees of our story because he had the good fortune to be played by Clint Eastwood in the 1979 movie, *Escape from Alcatraz*. The movie made a big deal about Frank's high measured IQ but crediting only Morris for the plan is not accurate, according to several of inmates who knew but did not participate in the escape for one reason or another. Not shown in the Eastwood film was the horrific childhood suffered by Frank Morris, beginning as an underfed eleven year-old abandoned at a Washington, D.C. church by his parents. He was living in a series of foster homes when he committed a theft, his first of many crimes. Thus began a life in and out of reform schools, state prisons, and federal penitentiaries. Because being "out" of prison was usually his idea (and not the authorities) Frank earned himself a trip to Alcatraz in 1960.

Allen West was the fourth active participant in the escape. His inability to loosen the vent in his cell on June 11th prevented him from being the fourth crew member on the raft. Along with the rest of the world he was left to ponder the fate of Morris, Anglin and Anglin. He gladly traded his knowledge of the planning and preparation of the escape with authorities for immunity from punishment. The FBI noted, with some amusement, the umbrage he took at their assumption of Frank Morris' dominant role in the planning.

Chain-smoking Olin Blackwell was the fourth and final warden of Alcatraz, serving from 1961 to 1963. An excellent marksman he was said to take great delight in showing up junior officers with his skills at the gun range. Along with the 1962 escape by Morris and the Anglins Alcatraz Blackwell faced the challenge of running a facility facing closure due to its decrepit condition and high operating costs. Warden Blackwell really was on a fishing trip on Lake Berryessa when the escape occurred. Contrary to the villainous way he was portrayed by Patrick McGoohan in *Escape from Alcatraz*, the real Olin Blackwell was said to be Alcatraz' least strict warden.

Juanita Musson was, without question, one of Sausalito's most colorful characters. As stated in her 2011 obituary in the Santa Rosa Press Democrat, she was "...the outrageous and muu-muued... restauranteur who 40 or 50 years ago might arrive at a table holding her pet pig or monkey and might answer a patron's complaint by tipping a heaping plate into his lap... she drank, cussed and fought like a 300-pound sailor." Just a month before the escape Juanita moved her restaurant to the *Charles Van Damme*, a decommissioned paddlewheel ferryboat. Juanita's eponymous restaurant drew ordinary Sausalito residents as well as dozens of entertainers who performed in San Francisco (Jonathon Winters, The Smothers Brothers, and Noel Coward, among others) who came for the food and the show that was Juanita herself.

Sally Stanford, (the former Mabel Busby) ran a Nob Hill bordello from 1940 until it was shut down following a 1949 raid by District Attorney Pat Brown. (In part from the fame he gained from the raid, Brown was elected the state's attorney general and, later, became its governor.) Crossing the Golden Gate in 1950 Sally resurrected a then-shuttered restaurant called the Valhalla. She refurbished the place in décor which unashamedly mirrored the source of her funding. Although beyond the chronology of *Inseparable*, it is worth noting Ms. Stanford was a pillar of the Sausalito community, funding a Little League team and later elected to a seat on the city council before becoming mayor in 1976. Her fame (or infamy) even landed her an appearance on the Tonight Show with Johnny Carson.

Several places around San Francisco Bay played prominent roles in the escape. We must begin, of course, where the drama began...

Alcatraz Island was the site of a Federal Penitentiary from 1934 to 1963. The name, which derives from the Spanish word for Pelican, was first applied to nearby Yerba Buena Island by explorer Juan Manuel de Ayala in 1775. English officer Frederick Beechey later grafted the name to the 225 acre island located just a little over a mile from San Francisco. Following the Mexican-American War when, in 1848, California became U.S. property, it was fortified for coastal defense. It also served as a military prison beginning as early as 1859. Private citizens accused of certain crimes (such as treason) were also subject to imprisonment at the prison. Over the next decades many support structures were added for the growing facility, such as the main prison block in 1909. In 1933 Alcatraz Island and everything on it were transferred to the Bureau of Prisons for use as a federal penitentiary. Despite the outcry from many residents around the bay who shuddered at the prospect of the country's most dangerous and violent criminals being housed so close by, the first 137 prisoners arrived in 1934. The list of infamous criminals housed here included Al Capone, George "Machine Gun" Kelly, Arthur "Doc" Barker, Harlem "Godfather" Bumpy Johnson, and a young bank robber from Boston named Whitey Bulger, who was there the night in 1962 when Frank Morris and the Anglins took their leave of the prison. The prison closed in 1963. It was occupied twice by Native American protesters, first briefly in 1964, the second time lasting 19 months before ending peacefully in 1971. Alcatraz is now run by the U.S. Park Service is one of the country's most visited tourist attractions. (I've been there twice. They have done a fantastic job of transporting visitors to the days when the most notorious criminals lived behind its bars.)

Angel Island was, according to Allen West, the destination

of the escapees. In 1962 the Nike missile base on the island was in the process of being decommissioned. It is now run by the Angel Island Conservatory (angelisland.org) which provides a wide range of activities for pleasure boaters and campers.

The U.S. Coast Guard Station Golden Gate began as a part of United States Life-Saving service in 1877. The Life-Saving service was merged with the U.S. Revenue Cutter Service in 1915 and renamed The United States Coast Guard. Station Golden Gate quickly evolved into one of the busiest stations on the West Coast, a distinction it still holds today, with crews executing more than 600 rescues and 300 law enforcement boardings a year.

Lime Point Lighthouse was originally a fog-bell signaling station when, in 1883, it was built on top a 100 foot-long spur of rock near the mouth of the Golden Gate. In 1900 a lantern was hung from the fog signal building and it continued as a lighthouse even after the completion of the Golden Gate Bridge in 1937. In 1961 the Coast Guard automated the lighthouse. For more details on the history of this historic lighthouse, you can visit https://www. lighthousefriends.com/light.asp?ID=146.

Battery Spencer, Battery Wagner, and Battery Kirby were conceived in 1885 by a board convened by President Grover Cleveland and chaired by his Secretary of War, William Endicott. At a time when nations such as Spain, England, Germany, and Japan were building great navies the Endicott Board was tasked with safeguarding America's vulnerable ports. Ultimately 22 concrete batteries were constructed from the Marin Headlands (on the north side of the Golden Gate Strait) and the Pacific Coast. These batteries were considered critical in the defense of the homeland following the attack on Pearl Harbor by Japan in 1941. According to the article titled *Guns and ghosts: Rambling through the ruins of early 20th century gun batteries in California's Marin County* on theroadhome.ca:

Between 1943 and 1946, the U.S. Army deactivated all coastal fortifications in the San Francisco Bay Area, including the five Endicott-era batteries in the Marin Headlands. The guns and mortars were removed and sold as scrap, and the last members of the Coast Artillery Corps left Fort Barry in the fall of 1946. The Corps was officially disestablished in 1950.

Final words from the author

Before I began writing *Inseparable,* I did a lot of research into the escape and, just as many have before me, came to my own conclusions about the still-open FBI case. I began with one basic fact: no bodies were ever recovered and positively identified as any of the three escapees.

Next is the intriguing photo, taken in Brazil in the 1970s, of two middle-aged men who bear striking resemblances to John and Clarence Anglin. Using sophisticated facial recognition software, several photo analysts have independently concluded the photo is likely of the brothers. Then, there is the body seen floating near the Golden gate Bridge five weeks after the escape. Descriptions of the body's condition and clothing (seen by crewmen of the Norwegian freighter Norjfell) make it likely it was one of the escapees.

I used these and other facts as the foundation for my fictional account of the events of June 1962. I respect that a number of people have devoted great effort to discern the truth and some will not agree with my conclusions. To them, and to anyone who will read this book, I'm quick to say I am not – nor do I claim to be – an expert on matters of tides, hypothermia, or photo analysis. I'm just a writer who came up with an idea... a fictional tale of what happened to John, Clarence, and Frank after their very real, audacious escape from Alcatraz. My goal is to entertain. I hope I have done that.

Thank you

David Kruh

Appreciations and Resources

First and foremost, thank you Daniel Willis of DX Varos Publishing. You made a dream come true.

My deepest appreciation goes to some wonderful Sausalito residents who so generously shared memories of their beloved town. Thank you Lawrence White, Virginia Rae (Windgarten), Helene Rose Rippy, Laura Roehrick, Julia Brigden, Rose DeBenedictis, and Anthony Chapman.

Thank you Coast Guard Captain Janelle Oveson (retired) for your insights into this branch of our Armed Forces whose members are *Always Prepared*. My gratitude to Seth Mayer of Mayer Construction in Lunenburg, Massachusetts (www. mayerwoodllc.com) for taking time from his busy schedule to give me the opportunity to experience stick welding.

The website of the Sausalito Historical Society (sausalitohistoricalsociety.com) features reprints of articles about the town's history from the time of its original, Native American inhabitants and was an invaluable resource to this writer. The FBI's website (fbi.gov/history/famous-cases/alcatraz-escape) is a treasure trove of pictures and details of the actual escape. The company which runs the very popular Alcatraz Cruise also has an extraordinary website (alcatrazhistory.com) with many details about life – and death – on "The Rock." The Internet Archive (archive.org) is a researcher's dream, with millions of pictures, videos, and other media—which are all for free! Information about Lime Point Lighthouse as it was in 1962 came from the Lighthouse Friends website (lighthousefriends.com).

Three excellent Arcadia publications are *Houseboats of Sausalito* (Phil Frank), *Sausalito* (Sausalito Historical

Society) and *Marinship* (Eric J. Torney). All provided details of life in this seaside town, as well as presented hundreds of photographs from early-to-mid 20th century. Also very useful was John Goodwin's *Alcatraz 1868-1963* a lively telling of life on The Rock and the many attempts at escape, including that of Morris, Anglin and Anglin.

The writing of this novel occurred during the 2020 pandemic, which prevented my travel to the bay area. Thanks to Lukáš Kutílek, an adventurous young man from the Czech Republic, I had a series of Google Map images from the batteries along the Marin headlands on which to base my narrative.

Thank you, Ron Gollobin, my friend and fellow writer. From the moment, many years ago, when Ron first heard my idea for this novel he never stopped hounding me to "write the damn book." His insights into criminals and law enforcement (garnered from years as an award-winning crime and investigative TV reporter) were invaluable, as were his readings of the novel as it evolved.

Robert Berube, Nick Sullivan, Dennis Owen and Stephanie Schorow (another writer whose many books on Boston history grace the shelves of my study) were also very generous with their time on early incarnations of *Inseparable*.

Finally, anglinbrothersmuseum.com is a terrific website built by Ken and David Widner, nephews of John, Clarence, and Alfred Anglin. The site provided me with an invaluable understanding of the brothers and their relationship, which helped guide this work.

About the Author

David is the published author of several books, notably two on Boston's erstwhile entertainment district, Scollay Square. *Always Something Doing, Boston's Infamous Scollay Square*, (Northeastern University Press, 1999) and *Scollay Square* (Arcadia Publishing, 2004). David is also the co-author, with his father Louis, of *Presidential Landmarks* (Hippocrene Press, 1992) and *Building Route 128* (Arcadia Publishing, 2003) with Yanni Tsipis.

David has been a frequent contributor to the *Boston Globe, Boston Herald*, and *History Magazine*. His work has also appeared in *Yankee Magazine, Boston Magazine* and elsewhere. A published and produced playwright, his musical about the Boston Red Sox, *The Curse of the Bambino*, premiered at Boston's Lyric Stage in 2001 and still ranks among the most successful productions in this equity theater's history. For many years David has also lectured on a variety of subjects, including the infamous escape from Alcatraz which inspired this book. For more on David, his writing, and to learn how to book a talk to your organization, visit joeandnemo.com and click on "Slide Show" in the menu.

Shawn Mackey
THIS WORLD OF LOVE AND STRIFE

Jeanne Matthews
DEVIL BY THE TAIL

C.K. McDonough
STOKING HOPE

Phillip Otts
A STORM BEFORE THE WAR
THE SOUL OF A STRANGER
THE PRICE OF BETRAYAL

Erika Rummel
THE INQUISITOR'S NIECE
THE ROAD TO GESUALDO
EVITA AND ME

Vanessa Ryan
THE TROUBLE WITH MURDER

Larry F. Sommers
PRICE OF PASSAGE (*Aug 2022*)

J. M. Stephen
NOD
INTO THE FAIRY FOREST
RISE OF THE HIDDEN PRINCE
SILENCE AND RUPTURED WATERS
THE RISE OF RUNES AND SHIELDS (*July 2022*)

305

Jessica Stilling
THE WEARY GOD OF ANCIENT TRAVELERS
BETWEEN BEFORE AND AFTER (*Nov 2022*)

Christopher Tuthill
THE OSPREY MAN (*July 2022*)

Claryn Vaile
GHOST TOUR

Felicia Watson
WHERE THE ALLEGHENY MEETS THE MONONGAHELA
WE HAVE MET THE ENEMY
SPOOKY ACTION AT A DISTANCE
THE RISKS OF DEAD RECKONING

Daniel A. Willis
IMMORTAL BETRAYAL
IMMORTAL DUPLICITY
IMMORTAL REVELATION
PROPHECY OF THE AWAKENING
FARHI AND THE CRYSTAL DOME
VICTORIA II
THE CHILDREN OF VICTORIA II

Joyce Yarrow
SANDSTORM

CPSIA information can be obtained
at www.ICGtesting.com
Printed in the USA
LVHW041317020622
720142LV00004B/26